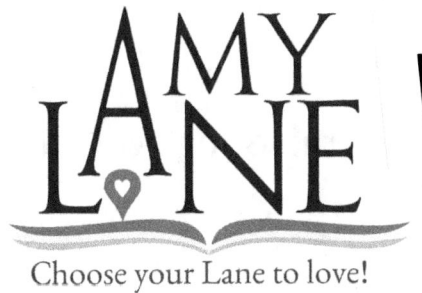

Choose your Lane to love!

Readers love the Candy Man series by AMY LANE

Candy Man

"This book broke my heart wide open, and then filled it with kittens, puppies, candy, and most importantly love!"

—Love Bytes Reviews

Bitter Taffy

"*Bitter Taffy* is a winner in my book. It's sweet and sexy and charming all wrapped up in fuzzy, warm feelings."

—Joyfully Jay

"Reading this is EXACTLY like a trip to your favorite candy store. You know you will be sad when the book/candy is over/gone but you just have to devour it as quickly as you can because it's so enjoyable!"

—The Kimi-chan Experience

Lollipop

"This book is romantic and engaging, the characters, good, good men. The love runs deep and the intimate relationship between the MCs is seriously sexy."

—Divine Magazine

More praise for AMY LANE

Immortal

"Leave it to Amy Lane to write a fairy tale that kicks my ass... Thank you Amy, for the gift of your words, for the gift of Immortal."
—MM Good Book Reviews

"A book that made me feel...made me live every emotional onslaught these men suffered! Bravo Amy Lane and thank you for giving me an unputdownable, gold star read I won't forget."
—Sinfully Gay Romance Book Reviews

"I recommend this book to fans of fantasy/fairy tales and fans of the 'Queen' herself"
—The Kimi-chan Experience

Food for Thought

"This is a SWEET Amy Lane story, and those are my favorite… I loved everything about Food for Thought…"
—My Fiction Nook

Beneath the Stain

"…this was a very enchanting book and I hope to see these characters again in the future."
—Hearts on Fire

"…though this journey has been sucking the life out of me, I wouldn't change it for the world."
—Boys in Our Books

By AMY LANE

Behind the Curtain
Beneath the Stain
Bewitched by Bella's Brother
Bolt-hole
Christmas with Danny Fit
Clear Water
Do-over
Fish Out of Water
Food for Thought
Gambling Men: The Novel
Going Up!
Grand Adventures (Dreamspinner Anthology)
Hammer & Air
If I Must
Immortal
It's Not Shakespeare
Left on St. Truth-be-Well
The Locker Room
Mourning Heaven
Phonebook
Puppy, Car, and Snow
Racing for the Sun
Raising the Stakes
Shiny!
Shirt
Sidecar
A Solid Core of Alpha
Super Sock Man
Tales of the Curious Cookbook

Published by DREAMSPINNER PRESS
www.dreamspinnerpress.com

Published by DREAMSPINNER PRESS
www.dreamspinnerpress.com

TART
and
Sweet
Amy
Lane

DREAMSPINNER
PRESS

Published by

DREAMSPINNER PRESS

5032 Capital Circle SW, Suite 2, PMB# 279, Tallahassee, FL 32305-7886 USA
www.dreamspinnerpress.com

Tart and Sweet
© 2016 Amy Lane.

Cover Art
© 2016 Paul Richmond.
http://www.paulrichmondstudio.com
Cover content is for illustrative purposes only and any person depicted on the cover is a model.

ISBN: 978-1-63477-697-4
Digital ISBN: 978-1-63477-698-1
Library of Congress Control Number: 2016909432
Published September 2016
v. 1.0

Printed in the United States of America
∞
This paper meets the requirements of
ANSI/NISO Z39.48-1992 (Permanence of Paper).

Mary: Hold my hand. It's gonna be scary.
Mate: I'm sorry for what happens next.
Kids: Sometimes doing the brave thing is simply doing your best
and hoping your intentions outweigh your flaws.

Behind Blue Eyes

ADAM'S EYES were so big, dark as the future, and Robbie felt like he could see all the possibilities in the world in them.

"So," he said, that stern, hard-boned face almost boyish as he opened up during a rare moment of privacy behind the barracks. "You and me? You promise?"

Robbie would have promised him anything—the stars, the moon, a free pass to a country with rain—if only Adam would keep moving his full-lipped mouth along the soft skin of Robbie's cock.

"Yeah," Robbie said gruffly. "You and me. We'll put in our papers. We'll be free."

ROBBIE CHAMBERS sat up abruptly and looked around his apartment, heart pounding. This was not the Middle East.

You knew that.

This was a tiny apartment out in Rocklin—*old* Rocklin, not Stanford Ranch with its zillion-dollar houses. Robbie's parents had moved to Sun City, content in their retirement, and Robbie had moved nearby when he'd left the service.

Without Adam.

"Robbie?" Ashley sighed next to him. He soothed his hand down her golden hair and wished her yawn and stretch were actually inviting.

"Getting up to pee," he murmured. "Back in five."

Five turned to ten, turned to a stolen cigarette out on the back porch in the chill of the November night.

Turned into remembering….

ADAM BLURTING out, "You didn't think I was a faggot when I was sucking your dick last month!" in front of their unit leader.

And icy silence.

Adam turned to Robbie, looking for solidarity, looking for somebody to admit that this unit was as incestuous as Deliverance *and that pretty much all of them had gone down on one another at one time or another.*

But Robbie had heard Heller talking behind the tents about how you weren't a fag if you didn't let the other guy come in your ass, and he didn't have no fucking fairies in his unit.

Robbie's father tithed money every year to a church that spent millions of dollars to fight marriage equality.

And Robbie and Adam had months left before they could leave.

He didn't even know he was going to say the word until Adam jerked back, wounded worse from the word than from shrapnel.

"Faggot."

HE DIDN'T go to bed until light edged the sky, and when he did crawl in, Ashley hit his shoulder hard because his feet were cold as ice.

"OH, BABE!" Ashley said as they pulled into Old Sac the next morning. "You look like hell. Are you sure you want to see your parents like this?"

His parents were meeting them downtown for dinner, because now that he was an adult and they were retired, spending time with their only child was suddenly a thing.

He grimaced at Ashley. "Of course. I'm sleepy. I'll go nap after you go home."

She smiled hopefully. "You know, if I give my roommates some notice, I could probably be permanent after Christmas."

Robbie tried not to grimace again. "I don't even like this apartment," he told her—which was no more than the truth. A shoe-box apartment—a solid little rectangle in shotgun formation. The thing had been built in the eighties and had all of the character of a cinder block. In fact, shoeboxes were at least designed to sell shoes.

"So?" she asked, laughing. "Are you planning on breaking up with me?"

Oh Lord. "Not today," he teased, and hated himself.

God. He'd gotten discharged, had come home, and pretty much his first act had been to go into a bar and pick up a girl just to prove he was a man.

His pecker worked—when he thought of other peckers—but he hadn't been able to put down the girl yet.

Ashley gave him a smile and rolled her eyes, but she didn't look as though breaking up was a possibility.

Damn.

The problem was, most guys in this part of the world would like her. She was fun, she liked to go to the movies, loved to go out dancing—and how could he say no to a girl who wanted to hang out on the dance floor for hours at a time?

Well, he *could* say no to her, but he felt like he shouldn't. The sex was… obligatory. And obligations were strings by their very nature.

He sighed and squinted against the late afternoon sunset as he wandered toward the parking garage. He loved this place, this little tourist trap by the river, and he loved the Tower Bridge, even when the trestle was up and traffic backed up.

Raley Field—baseball.

Adam loved baseball.

Robbie could have done without the guilt smacking him in the face, though. He parked in the structure across the street from Joe's Crab Shack, and he and Ashley trotted down the stairs and onto the boardwalk.

"Where are we eating again?" she asked breathlessly. They passed the specialty stores all tarted up for Christmas, and Robbie paused for a moment to stare at the fliers for Laughs Unlimited. He didn't recognize the names of any of the upcoming comics, but then, how would they get famous if nobody went in to see them?

Ashley couldn't see the charm in that. "C'mon, Robbie. We're going to be late, and I want them to like me!"

Robbie suppressed a wince. "Hon, this isn't a big deal. This is a 'Son, we're afraid you are too much alone' sort of thing, okay?"

"Yeah, but Candy Heaven? I'm getting diabetes just standing next to it. Can we just go?"

Robbie looked wistfully into the store as he passed, seeing the candy by the barrel and the rainbow tie-dyed banners over the top loft. And the scary clown—don't forget the scary clown! He sort of loved the place—he'd gone in on occasion as a high school student and even as an adult. Old Sacramento was one of those comfortable places his parents liked to go, and he was fine with that.

They stuck to Front Street, crossing the road with the open field to their right and the little-used park down in the middle of the block, and kept going until the storefronts started again. Right there, in the dying sunlight, a street performer was playing a mean guitar, and the most beautiful man Robbie had ever seen was dancing.

He wasn't tall—maybe five eight—and his skin was a rich, true black. His straight black blown-out hair swung down his back as he playfully shook his hips to the music.

He wore a tight, cream-colored cashmere sweater and even tighter black leather pants. As the guitar player looked up and grinned shyly, fingers bulleting over the strings, the dancer ran his fingers up through his hair, allowing it to cascade down his neck, before executing some quick, high steps forward and then whirling to swish back to the musician.

The steps were so elegant, so graceful. This guy had been dancing all his life, probably was a professional somewhere, but not here. Here, in the dying light of a dying year, he was dancing because he was beautiful, and the music moved him, and he was fabulous.

Robbie found he was staring with a sort of helpless hunger at the man's wicked white smile and almond-shaped brown eyes, yearning to be just that free.

The dancer saw him—saw *them*—standing there, and his eyes hooded, his smile turned seductive, and he extended two hands in front of him. Making eye contact with Robbie first and then Ashley, he crooked two slow fingers at them and then offered his hand.

Ashley reached first, which is why Robbie did afterward, because Robbie was a coward, dammit, and needed to know it was okay. But she did, and it was, and the man clasped Robbie's hand lightly and whirled him in, so he held both Robbie and Ashley about the waist, and started them on a slow chorus line march to the front of the boardwalk.

Just as they got near the front, he whirled them out, hands over their head, and together, the three of them did a cha-cha as the guitarist kept up the flamenco-style licks.

"Canya swing?" the dancer called, and just that quickly, the guitarist launched into a whipcrack acoustic version of a swing dance—and Robbie and Ashley were spun about in a whirlwind carnival ride.

Step kick, swing, Ashley goes, step kick, swing. The boardwalk wasn't ideal for dancing, but the stranger was wonderful at telegraphing his moves, calling out what he was going to do next, and covering for mistakes. Robbie's face ached from smiling, and he barely noticed the passersby had become a clapping, hollering audience. The dance ended when the three of them clasped hands in the center and walked the circle, shaking their fingers in rhythm. As the song wrapped up, the dancer swung them both out again and whirled them into his arms, pulling them tight at the very last beat.

The applause was deafening, and Robbie couldn't stop smiling.

For just that moment, he was free.

Of course it couldn't last. The stranger let go of them and Robbie and Ashley turned to him, laughing as they shook hands.

"You guys were awesome sports," he said, his wide, openmouthed smile hardly dimming as he spoke. "Thanks so much for dancing with me!"

He grinned and winked, sliding his hands in his back pockets as he stood, the pose making him look cocky and almost relaxed.

"Thanks for asking," Ashley said, openly flirtatious, and the dancer winked at her in kind.

"It was a pleasure." The young man—and he *was* young, now that Robbie saw him up close—bowed at the waist with a flourish. "I'm Cyril, you can call me Cy, and I will dance with either one of you any day."

"I'm Ashley, and this is my boyfriend, Robbie," Ashley said with a wink, "and I will take you up on that!"

She turned away, and as the crowd surged toward the guitarist behind them, dropping dollar bills into his case like confetti, Robbie and Cy were pushed together, chest to chest.

The world stopped, and the faint yearning Robbie had felt when watching Cy dance across the boardwalk surged up through his thighs, his groin, his chest.

He stared into those liquid brown eyes and stopped breathing entirely. Cy moved closer, close enough to breathe on his cheek, and whispered, "You and me could do some real dancing, cowboy." Questing fingers slid into the back pocket of Robbie's jeans and squeezed tight.

Robbie pulled back, almost frightened by how badly he wanted that. God, he could pull that lithe, muscular body up close and personal *right now*—he *ached* to have that heat skin to skin with his own. Cy's eyes had gone to half-mast, sultry and unapologetically aroused, particularly when Robbie licked his lips.

The world was a mad flurry of humanity around them, and they were the center of an exploding sun.

"Robbie!" Oh God, that was his father. His parents must have seen the two of them dancing and introduced themselves to Ashley while Robbie was otherwise occupied. Robbie took a step back, the icy gusts of wind off the river dousing the hot ember of desire that had sprung up between him and this beautiful stranger.

Cy winked and his lips twisted sardonically, but he didn't turn away. Robbie finally had to. Battling through the thinning throng of people who were trying to pay the guitarist, he found his parents chatting with Ashley practically in front of California Fats.

He hadn't realized how close they were.

"Nice dancing there, son." Don Chambers didn't *sound* proud of Robbie, but then, he'd herded Robbie out of theater and into football, so he probably wasn't. "Could you have gotten a little closer to that black fella? 'Cause he sure did seem to have a jones for you!" Robbie's father had this way of smiling when he was displeased. Anyone who hadn't grown up getting his ass paddled for not putting his room right or getting a B in English would assume he was a sweet, genial man in late middle age. His brown hair had long since gone salt-and-pepper, and his wide-jawed cowboy face was still strong and steely eyed, but yeah. Don Chambers was a good ol' boy who just enjoyed him some old-fashioned values—what was the matter with that?

Everything.

"We were dancing, Dad," Robbie said, trying to keep the defensiveness out of his voice. "And I see you met Ashley—"

"She's a real treat, Robbie," his mother, Hilary, said, patting Ashley's arm. "She was lovely. I guess you got separated by the crowd and she just sat and chatted with us. So nice of you to bring her to eat with us."

Robbie smiled at them both, thanking God for Ashley at the same time he hated himself for bringing her at all. "So," he said brightly, "are we ready to eat!"

As his parents filed over the boardwalk first, his mom arm in arm with Ashley, Robbie brought up the rear, feeling like the world's biggest fraud. With a sigh, he slid his hand in his back pocket, wondering if he could still feel Cyril's strong squeeze.

No—but he *did* feel a small business card.

Cyril McVeigh—Dance Teacher

Complete with e-mail and cell phone number.

Robbie stared at it for a moment, and his parents stepped inside the restaurant without him.

"Robbie!" his father snapped smartly. "You coming?"

Robbie rubbed the card with a little smile, recalling that moment of feeling absolutely free on the boardwalk.

"Yes." He looked up and gave his father an absent smile before tucking the card safely in his wallet. "Yes, in fact, I think I am."

DINNER WAS pleasant as far as those things went. Robbie caught up on his parents' illnesses and appliance disasters. His father's fasciitis was acting up, his mother's colitis had given a flare, both of them were watching their cholesterol, and his father's blood pressure was in the high range for a man his age. The car was new, the payments were high, the stove was failing but it was older than Robbie, and the refrigerator repairmen wanted thirty dollars an hour and wasn't that highway robbery.

"He was black," Robbie's mother said sincerely. "So was the man who worked on the car. They were both rude."

"Probably related," his father snorted—sadly not ironically.

"Not all black people are related," Robbie tried, knowing it was a losing battle. Never get into a political debate with your parents. *Never. Never. Never.*

"Now I know you people are taught political correctness in school," Robbie's father said with that unmistakable I'm-older-so-I-know-better tone, "but I think that's the biggest pile of garbage to ever be introduced into this country. I mean, I like black people—I *do*—but you can't deny that there's a lack of work ethic there—"

"I served with all sorts of people," Robbie snapped. "It's not political correctness to put your life in the hands of someone else and know you can trust them. Don't go into this, Dad. Not like this. Not now."

His father backed off then, because Robbie had played the served-my-country card. His father hadn't. He used to say mournfully that he'd missed Vietnam and Desert Storm by twenty years either way. Robbie's service career somehow made up for that, and it was the one thing he had done in his lifetime that his father could respect.

Robbie didn't tell him—any of them—that when he snapped at his father, he wasn't thinking of any of his Army buddies. Not even Adam, with his light brown skin and dark eyes. He was thinking of bold lips and flowing hair and a laughing smile under the darkening twilight.

"WELL, THAT was nice," Ashley said after they'd finished dinner and were making their way back across the boardwalk.

"No, it really wasn't," Robbie mumbled. God, his parents… food, clothes, church, and love. You'd think he'd be more grateful, right?

"But they seemed so—"

"Bigoted? Closed-minded? Terrifyingly ignorant?"

"Robbie Chambers, you take that back!" Ashley gasped. "They were perfectly sweet people, and I know their ideas are a little outdated, but you just cannot expect them to suddenly go all rainbow flag just because politics say we should!"

"Common sense says we should, Ashley," Robbie argued, inwardly relieved. Thank God—thank *God* they were disagreeing on this. He had a reason, an honest-to-God *reason*, to break up with her now. Political differences. Huzzah and hallelujah, he thought it could work! "People are people—black, brown, pink, green—and the easier it is to put them in a box sorted by color, the easier it is to forget that their blood is as red as ours!"

Ashley stopped on the boardwalk like she'd run into something. "Wow," she said, narrowing her eyes. "That's… that's sort of poetry, Robbie. Where did you get that?"

Oh hell. She'd had a political epiphany. He couldn't even be shitty to her now. "From watching too goddamned many people bleed," he muttered, and her look of automatic sympathy made his gut churn. God, yes. He'd seen sand and blood, and he'd lost guys from his unit, and he had some scars himself. But again and again and again, he came back to the fact that the most painful thing he'd seen in two tours was the look in Adam Macias's eyes when Robbie called the man he loved a faggot in front of their entire unit.

His painful cycle of recrimination was interrupted by the squeal of brakes and a young voice shouting, "God*dammit*!"

Robbie looked up in time to see a car round the curve onto Riverfront, speed over the cobblestones, run the stop sign, and fishtail into the traffic over the bridge.

Back on the street was a young man, gangly, slightly built, surrounded by takeout containers spilled over the road. He was struggling to get back on his feet after apparently having been knocked to the ground.

Without thinking about it, Robbie trotted across the boardwalk and down the stairs to help the kid up before the next speeding car took him out.

"You okay?" Robbie asked, offering a hand.

The kid took it awkwardly, favoring the wrist closer to Robbie. Still, he was able to put some weight on his leg, only to have it go out from under him. Robbie caught him as he was going down, muttering, "Easy, easy. Here, let me help you at least cross the street, okay?"

"Yeah," Ashley said from Robbie's elbow. "We can get you up the stairs. Where were you going?"

"Candy Heaven," the guy grunted. "I was going to bring my boyfriend his dinner, but that car just sort of sped out of nowhere."

"Oh," Ashley said, her voice not quite as warm. "You're gay?"

Robbie gasped first, and then growled, and for a minute, he and this wounded kid met eyes in the light from the streetlamp and were on the same page.

"Yes," the kid said, sarcasm dripping from his voice, "and so is my boyfriend. Does that mean you won't help me across the street now?"

Robbie laughed—he couldn't help it. "I'll help you across the street," he said dryly. "Ashley, could you pick up the takeout boxes? I hate to have that trash everywhere. It looks like crap."

Ashley made an offended little grunt, and Robbie and the kid continued across the street.

"I'm sorry," Robbie muttered, not knowing why he felt compelled to apologize for her. "She... you know. There are some conservative small towns in the area."

"Yeah," the kid grunted. "I know. I hope I wasn't too bitchy." He let out a little gasp as Robbie helped him take another step. He must have really been in pain.

"No, you were fine. She earned it." Robbie threw a glance over his shoulder and saw Ashley picking up the trash like he'd asked. "She was so close to learning how to be a tolerable human being too."

The young man laughed and then let out another whinge of pain as they got near the stairs.

"Kid—"

"Finn," he wheezed.

"Robbie," he said. "I'm going to pick you up now. Do you think your boyfriend can take you to the hospital when we get inside?"

"Aw, *man!*" Finn whined. "Yeah, but he's gonna freak out. He *hates* it when I get hurt. I bit my *tongue* in August and he called my sister and had her bring Orajel and shit—it's just so embar—"

"Finn?"

They had entered Candy Heaven now, and the employees, all of them in yellow polo shirts and green aprons, looked up and converged on Finn like they knew him. The one who'd said his name was about Robbie's age, with crystal blue eyes, dark curly hair, and a little gold cross at his throat.

"Finn, man, are you all right?" The guy ran behind the counter on the far wall and came out with a chair. "Set him down there, okay?"

Finn looked up at all the faces and grimaced. He was actually a really pretty kid—he had a vulpine face and blue eyes framed with strawberry blond hair. His mouth was wide and mobile. Robbie thought that if this kid had ever enlisted, Robbie might have taken him out behind the Humvees a time or two.

"Guys," Finn said, sounding like he was desperately trying to keep his act together, "I need you all to not look so freaked out, okay? 'Cause if Adam sees this—"

Adam? Robbie almost panicked before common sense set in. Couldn't be.

"Finn? Oh fuck—*Finn*—what in the hell, can you not even cross the fucking street?"

Robbie's stomach sank. Oh hell. Oh *fuck*. God sure had a nasty sense of humor, right? Fucking *right*?

"Yeah," Finn said, his voice sinking. The crowd of customers and employees parted. Robbie would have recognized him even if it hadn't. He was six foot four, with black hair, snapping brown eyes, and the chiseled rectangular face of a warrior angel. Robbie knew his neck tattoos, he knew his broad chest, and he knew the sound of his footsteps across the hardwood floor.

And he knew the sound of his voice, especially when he was upset or worried.

You take too many risks, Chambers. You need to come back alive.

"God, Finn, you're scaring me to death, baby. Are you okay?"

Adam Macias—the guy Robbie had betrayed in the worst way— was crouching at Finn's feet, looking at Finn with anxious eyes.

"I'm sorry, Adam," Finn said, lower lip quivering. "That guy helped me across the street, but I really can't walk so well. My hip and my knee hurt, and my wrist too, and I think he's right. I need to go to the hospital and—"

"Adam?"

A new player entered the field—a tall man with a shag haircut, a fabulously ugly shawl collared sweater, a pointed chin, and a bold nose sashayed through the store as though he owned the place. Given the way everybody deferred to him, it was possible he did.

"Yes, boss," Adam said automatically. "Finn's—"

"Yes. Here, give your keys to Ezra. You gave him a ride in today, right, boys?"

"Yes, Darrin," Adam and Finn said, almost in sync.

"Good. Ezra—"

"On it."

The really beautiful guy with the curly hair took off, and Robbie watched him go. Okay, now was the time to sneak away. He started edging for the door, hoping everybody would be so entangled with their friends that they'd never notice the stranger who had—

"Oh!" Darrin said, looking directly at Robbie. Then: "Oh—oh *hell*. You?"

"You know me?" Robbie squeaked just as Ashley came in.

"Robbie?" she said brightly. "Did we get that kid to his friend?"

"Robbie?" Adam's voice crackled, and Robbie tried hard to meet those brown eyes that had haunted him for nearly two years.

"Yeah," Finn said, voice still wobbly. "Adam, this is Robbie. He sort of helped me up and across the street."

"Yeah," Adam said, voice hard. "We know each other."

"Yeah?" Finn's wobble grew more pronounced, probably in response to Adam's anger, and Robbie was relieved when Adam tore his angry gaze away and concentrated on the boy he obviously loved.

"Yeah, baby. But don't worry. He was kind to you, and, you know, as long as someone's good to you, I'm a fan."

Finn's smile back—gah!

"I'm glad he's all right," Robbie said breathlessly. "I, uh—we, uh, have to—"

"You'll come back tomorrow," Darrin said. For a guy who had swanned in like a diva, he had the same tone of voice as Adam and Robbie's lieutenant colonel, who could *literally* make you shit faster if you got caught on the pot.

"Yes," Robbie said, looking from Adam to Darrin. He'd had this reckoning coming for a long time. "I get off work at six."

"See you at seven," Darrin told him. "Won't we, Adam?"

"But what if Finn—"

Darrin sighed and closed his eyes, and then opened them. "Yes. He'll see *me* at seven. And then he'll be back the next night."

Robbie didn't even question the order. It was like the hand of fate, put off for more than two years, had suddenly hit the timer, and Robbie's life on the karma wheel had resumed.

"Yes," he said softly, gaze not wavering from Darrin's slightly crossed brown eyes. "Yes, sir." He focused on Adam and Finn again, his heart ripping painfully in his chest as he breathed. "I'll be seeing you again," he said. "Finn, I hope you feel better."

Finn looked up at him and nodded like he was trying to be happy when he hurt really bad.

"Adam—" Robbie's voice broke, flat-out broke then, and he could no longer pretend that he didn't know this person, or that this moment didn't matter to him, or that he hadn't once loved Adam Macias with all his heart. "Adam?" he repeated, hating himself.

Adam looked at him, his brown eyes no longer limpid and needy, his mouth firm and capable, and his entire *aura* just no-bullshit. He was not the same wounded bird Robbie had nursed in the shaded bunker when they'd both been looking for some touch.

"Yeah?" And he knew it.

"Adam, I'm sorry," Robbie whispered.

He turned away then, shaking off Ashley's hand, and strode out of the store. A part of him was singing about how he should feel good about that, but the rest of him was kicking contempt all over that part. Sure, he should feel good. He should check that right off his bucket list. Because finally, after two years, he had a chance to say the thing to Adam Macias that he should have been saying all along.

Darrin—Puppy Down!

DARRIN WAS *not* happy.

Adam had taken off, Finn in the passenger's seat of the minivan, and as they'd pulled away, Ezra had called his boyfriend to come pick him up. By sheer freakin' luck, Ezra had landed an apartment in the same building as Adam and Finn's. He and Miguel had gotten permission to paint and recarpet the place before they did, because the guy who had lived there before had been a criminal. Ezra said the place reeked of gunpowder and despair—Darrin would take his word for it.

He'd known Robbie was coming—he'd seen the guy in his dreams, watched his betrayal unfolding with the Pixy Stix powder, had known it in his bones.

He had not anticipated everybody's favorite hamburger delivery boy getting hurt.

"Did you see that coming?" he asked Ezra sharply as Ezra hung up.

Ezra grimaced. "I dreamed about the containers in the street," he muttered. "I dreamed about Cy dancing with the blonde girl and Robbie. I did *not* dream about Finn getting hurt." Ezra swallowed tightly. "I wish I had."

Darrin nodded. "Have you called Rico yet? Adam's going to need him, and Finn's his friend too."

"Oh—yeah." Ezra smiled apologetically. "Thanks. Good idea."

Darrin ruffled that curly hair—soft, without product—and touched his new protégé on the nose. "Don't sound so sad, Ezra. You're still growing. You'll be fabulous like me eventually."

Ezra squinted at him. "You're not this nice to *anybody*," he said suspiciously. Then, a little panicked, "Finn's going to be okay, right?"

Normally Darrin would have rolled his eyes and said something arch, but truth be told, he was still rattled. "I'm pretty sure," he said. "I... you know. I can really only be super bitchy when my family is all healthy and happy, right?"

The look on Ezra Kellerman's face grew old and adult, and *kind*, even as Darrin watched. "He's going to be okay," Ezra said, strength in his voice. "It's a bump. You and me, we would have known if it was bigger. No, Robbie is the real pain here, and Finn is going to spend a night—" He frowned. "*Two* nights in the hospital." Again, that blue-eyed squint. "Huh. Yes. Two. And then he's going to come home and catch up with his classes and get spoiled rotten. And Joshie's gonna have—"

"Chicken pox," Darrin said in horror. "Oh God!"

They stared at each other. "The whole fucking store is going to get them," they whispered.

"Oh, no, they won't!" Darrin proclaimed. The store was nearly empty of customers at eight o'clock at night the Tuesday after Thanksgiving, but it was *very* full of employees getting the place stocked for what would be an incredibly busy morning. "People!" he called. "People—gather round!"

A lot could be said about his staff—diverse, edgy, hipster, antiauthority, young—but one thing they all had in common: when a six-foot-five man with a shag haircut, bangly earrings, and cowboy boots told them to go get their chicken pox vaccination before they came into work the next day, *not a soul* questioned the order.

Darrin didn't hire fools.

After everybody had left, Darrin waited with Ezra for Miguel to come pick him up. He felt uncharacteristically broody.

"He's going to be okay," Ezra said quietly.

Oh, this one was good. Darrin could feel it through his bones. Ezra Kellerman, New York transplant, was one of the best children he could have dreamed.

"I know he is, sweetness. Nothing can keep that boy down. No, it's not Finn. It's not even Adam, although...." That hard look in Adam's eyes—that would need to be addressed. "Adam is going to need some handling."

"Then what's wrong?"

Darrin shrugged. "Robbie. I knew Adam would need healing. Katya and the dumb yuppies—hell, *you*—you were all fixable. But Robbie—"

"What did he do?" Ezra asked with obvious reluctance. Ezra didn't like to pry, and while he could dream and guess and have the future just fly out of his mouth without any guidance of his own, he had *not* yet figured out how to look at things he wasn't shown.

Darrin had looked, and he had seen. "He did something unforgivable," Darrin said.

Ezra winced. "I did that once."

"No, dear boy." Darrin was rattled enough to put a hand on his shoulder. "You told Rico to go because you didn't want him to be hurt. Robbie turned Adam over to the dogs because he was afraid."

"But you can't say it's unforgivable!" Ezra argued. "Because—because he was a good guy. He brought Finn here, he stood up for him when his girlfriend was being sort of a bitch—"

"How did you hear that?" Darrin asked, and Ezra grinned and flushed.

"'Cause I'm getting good," he said smugly.

"Oh, my darling," Darrin said, the happiness for his young Padawan finally serving to relax him, "you're getting *great*. But you're right. Nothing is unforgivable—as long as you forgive yourself."

Ezra thought about it for a minute. "Or the person you really fucked over forgives you."

Oh, he was lovely. Darrin adored him. But he also adored the person in question, and that was going to be the problem. "I… I hope Adam can do it," he said softly. "That would be a horrible thing to live with. It could poison him and Finn forever."

Ezra's smile took him by surprise. "Don't worry," he said. "You're his employer, but I lived with the guy. You *think* you know how good he is? I know. Adam'll do us proud."

Darrin couldn't help it. He wiped his eyes with the palm of his hand. "I'm already proud," he said. God, these young people. Every time he thought the burden of caring for them got too hard, one of them did something like this. Adam had made him so proud this past year, assuming the mantle of leader, of kind patriarch, to anyone in his reach. Ezra's boyfriend, Miguel, had taken a look at Adam and had done his best to be just like him—and he'd succeeded, with a few Miguel touches.

And Ezra, who had barely been able to stock barrels by himself when he'd first shown up in Darrin's store, had become a person of importance—both in the world and in Darrin's heart.

"It's okay," Ezra said, patting him on the shoulder again. "Finn will be okay."

Darrin gave him a watery, unfettered smile. "My dear one," he said fondly, "I think that's why I'm all verklempt. It's just possible that you *all* might be okay."

"Even Robbie?"

Darrin nodded slowly. "Yes. Maybe even him."

First Steps

OH GOD. It was even worse than Robbie had imagined. Ashley's lower lip wobbled, and her eyes got red and shiny.

"But," she said, so fucking depressed he couldn't stand it, "but… why?"

Robbie sighed and ran a hand through his hair. He'd let it grow long after the service, and he could feel the layers fall as his fingers passed through.

"Honey, I… I traveled around the world to get away from people like my parents. And you're just like them. And that's not a thing against *you*"—it was, but he was trying *really* hard not to be an asshole—"that's just… it's a whole different way of looking at the world."

"But," she said again, "I can learn, Robbie. I didn't know you felt so strongly about… what is it you feel strongly about?"

Well, hell. He might as well help her out a little. Sort of like a public service. He gave a sigh and sat down on the couch, gesturing for her to sit down on the recliner. He'd tried to have this conversation in the front of his truck so she could just get in her car and go and the break could be clean.

Unfortunately, she'd had to pee, and then she'd taken off her jacket and her gloves and her scarf, and this had turned into a not-so-casual honest-to-God hurt-the-poor-kid-before-Christmas sort of breakup.

"Ashley," he said, taking her hand and hoping she didn't claw his eyes out, "the world is not all straight white Christian people."

"Well," she said, smiling a little, "I mean, other places, maybe but—"

"It's not *here* either. And I don't want it to be. You can't flirt with that guy dancing on the boardwalk one minute and then agree with my mom that all black people are lazy the next."

"What does that have to do with anything?" she asked, genuinely puzzled.

He longed for a desk to bang his head against. "It's hypocritical, Ashley."

"Well, I didn't really *mean* it when I said it!" she said, laughing. "I was just trying to, you know, keep the peace."

Robbie sighed and slumped back into the couch. "I get that too," he said sadly. "But I don't want to be that guy anymore. I want to be the guy who rocks boats for the right reason—and the man dancing on the boardwalk is one of the right reasons. Not lazy. Not a joke. A dancer." He'd been beautiful. "And the boy crossing the street. Yeah, so what, he was gay. Not the first thing we should have been worried about. He was human, and he was hurt. Making it about the gay thing—that was a low-class move, and I don't want to *be* that guy anymore."

God. He wished he had a time machine so he didn't have to be that guy *then*.

"Okay," she said like she was taking notes. "So don't make remarks about black people, or gay people, or—who else?"

He leaned forward on his elbows and rubbed his temple. "Ashley, you and I are just in very different places right now," he said, holding on to his patience. "It's not about making a list for who's in the club. It's about being the kind of human being who wants *everybody* in the club."

"I don't understand, Robbie. What club are you talking about?"

"The club of this relationship is over, and if you're lucky, someday you'll get why."

Not classy. Not even a little.

Her exit was not graceful. There was crying, stomping, some screaming, and a whole lot of throwing his few possessions around. Every minute of it was an ironclad warning about picking up his next relationship in a bar—any bar, for as long as he lived. Especially when she threw the toaster.

When it was over and she'd gone screaming down the apartment stairwell, he went back into his apartment and started clearing through the rubble, wondering what in the hell he was doing with his life.

But that wasn't *really* what he was wondering.

He was wondering about Adam.

Adam had obviously fallen in love with that beautiful kid with the great smile who didn't like to freak his boyfriend out. Adam had friends, and a job at the candy place, and people to turn to who knew him, knew his boyfriend, knew his life.

Adam was doing okay.

And Robbie, who had turned on Adam in a heartbeat, was alone in a shitty apartment after a breakup with a woman he'd barely known. Nobody in his life knew who he really was, and the only people who would care if he didn't wake up the next morning were his parents.

And they'd turn on him faster than he'd turned on Adam if he ever told them that he was gay.

Housecleaning done (save for the dent in the kitchen wall left by the toaster), he threw himself onto his beaten corduroy couch and felt a faint crinkle in the back of his jeans.

Oh yeah.

He pulled the card out and looked at it, remembering those wild, brilliant moments of dancing on the boardwalk.

He didn't even know what he was going to do until he pulled out his phone.

Cy picked it up on the first ring. "Hullo?"

"Uh, hi," Robbie said, feeling like a schmuck. Adam hadn't been his only male sex partner, but he *had* been Robbie's only relationship with a man. This talking/dating/phone thing wasn't something he'd tried before. "This is, you know, the guy—"

"Robbie!" Cy's voice rose and chimed like a bell.

"You remember?" Robbie relaxed against the couch, charmed.

"Yes, of course. Man, you were *hot*. I mean, your girlfriend was pretty hot too, but *you... mmm....*"

Robbie flushed, taking the compliment. Hell, he felt pretty shitty about himself at the moment—the compliment could be the only good thing he got for a couple of days. "Well, I'm sorry about the girlfriend. We broke up, so, not a package deal," he flirted, hoping it didn't become *any* sort of deal.

"Yeah? Why'd you break up?" Cy's voice took on a sudden panic, and he exhaled sharply, making Robbie think he might be smoking as he spoke. "Not me, right?"

That made Robbie laugh. "No, I am not declaring undying love for you after one dance," he said, thinking that if he hadn't been able to stay loyal to Adam after two years of blowjobs and leave time in hotel rooms together, one dance wasn't going to do it either.

"Oh, thank God. I mean, hot is hot, but *baby*."

"Yeah, no. She was just too much like my parents, you know? I spent eight years in the Middle East to escape them—I wasn't going to come home and marry them, right?"

Cy inhaled strongly and then let his voice go sultry and deep, seductive. "So, soldier boy, you call me looking for some strange?"

Oh God. "No," Robbie muttered, embarrassed. "Not like that. I just… I'm sorry. We just danced, and I thought you were really beautiful and…." He didn't want to talk about Adam, not to this guy, who had the illusion that Robbie was worth his time. "And I just broke up with my girlfriend, and I honestly don't have a friend here I can talk to about how I thought you were beautiful."

"Oh," Cy said, sounding surprised. "That's… that's a little honest for a flirtation."

"You're going to run away and hang up on me now," Robbie said, feeling despondent.

"No," Cy said, as though he'd been considering it. "No, not right away. Here, I'm walking home—we can talk while I go. If you bore me before then, I'll tell you straight up, it was a nice dance, but no. If it's a good convo, hey, we can have another one and then maybe meet at a club and dance some more. Deal?"

"Deal!" He'd take it! "Although that's a little bit of pressure. What if I'm not entertaining? I don't know any jokes—"

"I know one!" Cy said, his voice lighting up. "Wait—it's a good one too!"

Robbie had to laugh—he sounded like a sixth grader. "'Kay, shoot!"

"Did you hear about the chameleon who couldn't change color?"

"No…?"

"He had a reptile dysfunction!"

Robbie couldn't help it. It had been a shitty, weird night, and that was the most absurd thing he'd ever heard. He burst into laughter and countered with, "What's brown and sticky?"

"What?" Cy asked warily.

"A stick."

Cy groaned, as was only appropriate. "That's horrible. No more jokes unless you get a better phone program!"

"Deal. What else should I talk about? Remember, this is an audition, so I need to do my best."

"Okay." Cy considered a bit. "How about this. How long were you in the service?"

"Eight years," Robbie said promptly. "Two tours."

"Wow—so, you're what? Twenty-six, twenty-seven?"

"Twenty-seven. You?"

"Twenty-five. No service time, though." A pause. "So did you serve under DADT?"

Robbie sighed. "Yes and no. Part of my time was under, and part of my time wasn't. I mean, it didn't seem to change much. Guys don't suddenly put on their pink camo because someone passes a law."

"Was it hard for you?" Cy sounded genuinely interested.

Robbie wanted to groan. This was exactly the train of thought he'd been trying to get away from—but, well, this was also his idea.

"At first I didn't give a shit," Robbie said frankly. "I mean, it's not like anyone who wanted a blowjob was denied, right?"

"But?"

"But I want to talk about you!" Robbie countered, knowing he was being transparent. "How long have you been dancing?"

"Since I was five and my mom put me in dance class," Cy replied easily. "And good save. But yeah—there's a woman who teaches dance in some of the shittiest neighborhoods in the area, for a pittance. She just likes to see kids on stage having fun. And I gotta say, saved my life. I mean, my neighborhood wasn't a great place to be out—even bi—but on the dance floor, you could be as fabulous as you wanted. So I grew up and became a teacher for her and for a couple of other companies around. It's what gets me out of bed in the morning."

Robbie smiled, liking the passion in his voice. "Yeah, but what pays the bills?"

Cy's chuckle warmed him like he'd done something good. "Just got off of that job—bussing tables at a club called Gatsby's Nick. You heard of it?"

"Yeah," Robbie said. "That and Faces."

"Also a good place," Cy said smoothly. "I like Gatsby's Nick—especially because I can hop on the floor after work." He paused then, blatantly, and Robbie caught a clue for the first time in his life.

"So, like tomorrow, do you work at Nick?" he asked, heart hammering in his throat.

"Yes, yes, I do. And I get off about nine if you'd like to meet me for a drink and some dancing."

Robbie found he was grinning and pumping his fist. *Yes!* "I totally would," he said, thinking whatever he had to say to Darrin, it should be over at eight thirty. "Anything I should wear?"

"Clothes, buttercup." The open flirtation back in Cy's voice warmed him. Robbie had apparently passed the human being test by having a legitimate conversation. Damn. It was like some sort of graduation or something.

"I can wear clothes," Robbie said, smiling stupidly into the phone. "I'll be there."

"Call me if you can't make it," Cy said seriously. "I... I mean, I won't lie. Just because you don't show doesn't mean I'll spend the night alone. But it's been a nice ten minutes, soldier boy. I'd like to meet you again and see what we can do on the floor."

"Yeah." Oh God. A date. With a man who wanted to dance with him. "So would I."

"I'm home now. I'll see you tomorrow."

For the first time in a long time, Robbie felt like tomorrow was a good place to be.

"You bet your sweet ass you will," he said, and Cy ended the call.

ROBBIE WORKED at a warehouse by the railroad tracks in Roseville. Wasn't easy, wasn't hard, required a certain portion of his brain activated so he didn't get hurt but not much more than that.

He'd thought of it as an interim job when he'd taken it, and it hadn't been until he'd been there a month that he realized there were lifers here. A father and *both* his sons worked there, and so did their cousins. One of the boys was still going to college and the other had a garage band, but still.

For the first time since Robbie had gotten the job, that day, he asked himself where it was going.

Interim, right?

But what had he done in the last year and a half to make it that way? Had he applied to any colleges? Had he taken any career tests? Was there *anything* he wanted to do besides—Jesus—just date someone he wanted to and not who he was supposed to?

"So, what, Adam? We put in our papers and... just quit?"

"I want to draw." Adam—who never smiled, not then—gave a tiny, shy twist of his lips. "I'm good at it. I want to get better."

And for a moment, Robbie had seen the sweet little kid in the body of the badass soldier. His doubts—about himself, about whether he could hang on to a relationship or come out of the closet—were forgotten in an effort to hold that sweetness.

"Okay, then. Yeah, let's do it. I'll go to school too."

Well, Adam was gone—had moved on, was happy with someone else. Maybe Robbie should think about actually *figuring out* what he wanted to do with his life.

Robbie mostly worked in the silence of his own head, not engaging with his fellow workers because he'd told himself this was an interim job. Today he looked around a little more, catching people's eyes sometimes and smiling or nodding. He was starting to put stuff together. His boss, Matt Harris, for example. Robbie knew he had a degree as a youth minister, although he didn't go to church *now*. His sons had both gone to college and then had come to work for the warehouse because it was a better living than what their degrees could get them, but still. They'd gone. And watching them work, laughing, being competent and giving each other shit, was almost a treat.

Robbie thought that if he and his old man ever had to work in the same place, he'd jump under a pallet as it was being dumped just so he didn't have to do that ever again.

Matt, Micah, and Teddy weren't the only people in the warehouse who were living bigger lives than Robbie either. He knew one kid was just a few units shy of his BA in English, and another was getting his certificate in accounting. Even the receptionist, a college-aged girl with a hulking boyfriend who drove the forklift, was taking a foreign language so she and her behemoth could go to Portugal for the summer.

Adam's desire to go to school and learn to draw didn't seem any more farfetched than the aspirations and the dreams of the people around him.

What in the hell was *Robbie* doing with his life? Hiding in the hills, afraid of the horrible thing he'd done?

Well, not talking to any of the people he worked with and sleeping with a girl he barely liked didn't seem to have held *that* at bay, right?

As he was clocking out and leaving, he felt a tap on his shoulder.

"Hey, Chambers. You finally up for a beer tonight?" Micah was smiling at him. He was a handsome young man, blue eyed, brown haired, friendly and funny, and Robbie had always felt a little bit cowed by him. He seemed to have all the confidence in the world when he was in the comfort zone of his job. And he and his dad—forget about it. Matt Harris was one of the nicest—and funniest—men Robbie had ever met. He'd come to the Halloween party dressed as the guy from *Reno 911!* this year, and Robbie appreciated his originality, if not his tight little shorts.

So Robbie felt a little wrench inside to know he was finally being asked to join his peers—any peers—and he had an appointment with a long-overdue kick in the teeth.

"I'd actually love to," he said apologetically. "But I've got sort of a meeting downtown tonight. I'm going to have to hurry to get there."

"You're not looking for another job?" Matt asked at Micah's shoulder. "I mean, you're one of the most self-directed guys I've got!"

Robbie shook his head and realized he was walking out of the warehouse shoulder to shoulder with his fellow employees, which he hadn't done since he'd gotten the job. Jesus, they must think he was an asshole or something!

"No," he said, smiling automatically so Matt would believe him. "This one pays fine, thank you." And then, probably prompted by where his head had been all day, he asked, "But uh, if I decided I was going to school, could I, you know, change my schedule up?" The warehouse actually ran three shifts. He was pretty sure it could be done, but he hadn't cared enough yet to ask about company policy.

"Oh yeah," Micah said, interrupting his dad. "Yeah, that's not a problem. Hell, I got my AA in, well, nothing much, but still. I liked school—I want to go back to state college when I've saved some money. They'll totally let you adjust your schedule. Right, Dad?"

"Yes, son, that wasn't just preferential treatment," Matt Harris said—and then he winked at Robbie so Robbie would know it *wasn't* just preferential treatment.

Robbie felt a shy smile starting. "Thanks," he said. "That's good to know—and, you know. Next Friday, if you're going out for a beer, I'd love to."

Micah shook his hand cheerfully like they'd sealed the bargain, and Matt clapped him on the back.

Robbie drove to his apartment to freshen up, feeling an odd combination of joy and confusion. He wasn't sure exactly what he'd done to suddenly change his standing with the people he worked with, but for the first time since he'd arrived, he felt like maybe Ashley wasn't the only normal thing about him. Which was good, because he was pretty sure she wasn't coming back.

Maybe all he'd needed to do was look up.

And, of course, work extra hard at trying to "people" in order to put off the thought of both the good *and* the bad things he was going to have to do that night.

He dressed nicely—a green button-down shirt under a warm aran sweater, and his clean jeans, and he even remembered to wear dress shoes, not boots.

It wasn't enough to give him any confidence facing Adam's friend Darrin, but it did help to remind him there would be *dancing* afterward.

DARRIN STOOD behind the counter, smiling charmingly at customers and bidding them a sweet evening. After Robbie walked in and looked around for a moment, he caught Darrin's eye and waited for a response, expecting to be called into the back office while Darrin had someone else mind the store.

That wasn't what happened at all.

Darrin directed the line of people to the two girls on the other side of the entryway, who had the same sort of setup Darrin had. People moved without too much of a problem—the place was busy, not under water—and Darrin called him to the front of the hardwood counter.

"Ezra!" He looked around Robbie's body toward the stairs, and the young man who had first greeted Robbie the night before came swinging down, a giant bundle of bright striped canes under his arm.

Robbie squinted. No, not canes—Pixy Stix.

He smiled suddenly. "I *love* those things!" he said excitedly. "I mean… the sour? Those used to be my favorite! I used to eat all the Kool-Aid powder when I was a little kid, right? Because it was close, you know? Tart sugar?"

Darrin stared at him bemusedly. "Yes. Yes, I do know. And young man, I think you just answered a major question for me."

Robbie looked back at him nervously. "And that would be…?"

"Redemption, dear boy—isn't that what you wanted?"

Robbie swallowed nervously. "Uhm… there's no way to apologize for what I did," he said, not sure if Darrin knew what he'd done.

Darrin's look was, of all things, sympathetic. "No," he said gently. "No, there's not. But come here—you look so scared. This is a candy store, not a tribunal."

Robbie tried to force his face and his shoulders to relax, and to some small extent, he succeeded. Darrin was holding his hands out and gesturing, so Robbie, feeling like he'd stepped through the rabbit hole, moved forward and held his own hands palms out.

Darrin grasped them and turned them over so his palms were up. Gently, he rubbed Robbie's wrists with long fingers.

"See?" Darrin said, smiling. "There's no monster line here. I've got a shit-ton of confused young man and a really regrettable moment. But there's no malice here, sweetheart—"

"Do you have any idea?" Robbie choked out, remembering those horrible last few months of Adam's service time. God, Robbie had gotten up at dawn and stayed up until Adam was asleep, just fucking watching his back, because nobody else would. But he couldn't *act* like he was watching Adam's back—he had to sit on the far side of the barracks or pull duty in an adjacent part of camp. But their whole unit had stopped talking to the guy, and Robbie had just… just watched, making sure nobody stuck a knife in his back but making no effort to pull out the one he'd put in himself.

"He could have gotten killed," Robbie whispered. "Because he trusted me and—"

"And you got scared," Darrin said, rubbing the center of his palm with a thumb. "See, the problem here is, Adam knew what he was walking into, you understand? He knew what family disapproval was, and he knew he could live through it again. But you—you hadn't. You had something to lose—but you weren't sure how bad it could be."

Robbie closed his eyes and tried to snatch his hands away. "I was such a fucking coward," he whispered, just as Darrin jerked him forward, practically over the counter.

"Yes," Darrin said briskly. "Yes, you were. But don't you see? That's not the natural state of affairs for you. You helped Finn out last night without a thought. You came down here to meet a stranger without even thinking about backing out. You had a bad moment—and yes, it was a *very* bad moment. But what are you going to do about the rest of your life? Are you going to keep beating yourself with a licorice whip, or are you going to enjoy a Pixy Stix once in a while?"

Robbie gaped at him. "Don't *you* see?" he said after a moment. "It's too late—Adam, he's happy. What am I going to do? I can't... I can't *wreck* that just so I can feel better about myself, right?"

Darrin nodded. "Yes. Yes, you're right. He *has* moved on. But you don't have to *get him back* in order to, you know, have him back, right? Ezra?"

"Yes, boss?"

"Tell him what I'm talking about."

Ezra blinked truly amazing blue eyes at Darrin. "Seriously?"

"Yes. You *are* required to put your life experience in a stranger's hands. It's a horrible feeling, welcome to my life. Now speak."

Ezra made a hissing sound that had Darrin curling his upper lip like he was bristling whiskers, and then they both turned to Robbie like that moment of being cats had never happened.

"Just because it's not going to work doesn't mean you don't still want him in your heart," Ezra said baldly. He rubbed his chin like he was smoothing back fur, and unconsciously licked his lips. Robbie thought that if he didn't have a date with Cy right now, he'd totally be hitting on this guy. "The thing is," Ezra said, like his grooming pause hadn't taken place, "those times you spend with your ex, even if the relationship doesn't work, that's still a part of your life. You can pretend it didn't happen and ignore it and not have that person in your heart anymore—and trust me, that sucks—or you can acknowledge that you fucked that up."

"I fucked up," Robbie said, almost belligerently. Could they not *see* that there was nothing he could do to fix that?

"Yeah, you did." Ezra nodded in agreement. "But that one moment, that wasn't the entire relationship. Weren't there moments there *besides* you fucking up?"

Robbie closed his eyes, saw—

Adam in a hotel room when they were on leave. He was sitting at the small hotel table and looking at Robbie, who was sprawled out naked on the bed, reading. His pencil scratched with inspired speed over the paper of his ever-present sketchbook.

"Are you really drawing me?" The thought was enchanting.

"Yeah. But... it's probably not that good."

"I want to see!" Robbie stood up and ignored his nakedness as he walked over to the table. The muscles in Adam's back rippled as he drew, and Robbie smoothed his hands over them, thinking about that awesome body and how it felt moving over and inside Robbie's. Then he lowered his head, resting his chin on Adam's shoulder, and looked.

His eyes watered.

"Is that really how you see me?" Because he was beautiful. His features, which he would have described as "ordinary country boy," were delicate, ethereal almost. His eyes were big and laughing. Even his mouth took on a sensuality, a humor, that Robbie had no idea he possessed.

"Yeah," Adam said, as though he hadn't just ripped Robbie's whole person out and splayed it across the page like entrails. "You're beautiful."

"Yeah," Robbie whispered, forcing himself into the candy store with the wooden floor and the scary clowns looking out from the loft and the two nutjobs reading his life in nothing but his hands and the pain in his eyes. "Yeah—he thought I was something once." He'd kept that picture tucked in the book he'd been reading at the time. Had carried them both throughout the remainder of his tour, and then home when he'd pulled out, and then to his shitty apartment when he'd moved up to Rocklin and his family. But he hadn't *looked* at them, not once, afraid of that moment, of how happy they'd both been. Afraid that picture would show the deep well of cowardice and regret that Robbie had become.

"That... see?" Ezra said softly. "That doesn't entirely go away."

Robbie blinked away tears. God. He would give *anything* to be able to remember that moment there without the black veil of what happened less than a month afterward.

"No," he whispered.

Ezra's hand on his cheek was pure comfort, and Robbie leaned into it. "Good," Ezra said. "If you can see that, we can fix this. Not without scars, you see. But I think it's been a big gaping wound inside you. I think that's why... why you feel so empty?" He looked at Darrin as he said it, and Robbie didn't even have to look to know Darrin was nodding.

It was the truth.

Ezra kept talking. Kept stroking his cheek. "You can't have that moment back, or that feeling."

"No," he whispered again. This was truth. Adam would never love him like that again.

"But the memory of it, it shouldn't go rancid, like meat. You should still be able to keep the good memories—it's your reward for healing yourself and fixing things."

And Robbie could admit to it. The terrible desperation for fixing things, inside himself, for Adam. He gazed at this guy—this frighteningly pretty guy his age—like he was the mouth of God himself.

And this kid just nodded, like that was only right. "The thing is, if you're feeling so shitty about how things ended that you can't even *think* about the ex without wanting to cry—that's no good. How're you going to learn from that if you can't think about it? How're you going to change it? I mean, my ex, he's a good guy. We had some good times. I don't love him like I love my guy *now*, but he had some shit to teach me, you know?"

Robbie nodded. He'd learned so much from Adam—even how to love himself, his body, while he made love. Wasn't that important?

"Yeah," Robbie said. "Yeah. So… someday, I could look him in the eye again. Tell him I'm glad for him. Tell him… make sure he knows, that thing I did, it wasn't because of him. It was all me."

Ezra had been all big-eyed and serious, but now a smile broke out over his features, pure sunshine. "Darrin, this guy's easy, you think? I mean, it coulda been worse!"

Darrin flicked him in the forehead, and for a moment, Ezra glared at both of them. "What? What'd I say!"

"First lesson, junior. Other people's pain is *never* easy."

Ezra glared back. "Yeah, but it's easier to fix yourself if someone else thinks it can be done."

Darrin looked at Robbie with an air of jurisprudence. "What do you say? Did you appreciate the vote of confidence, or were you insulted by the idea that you were a cakewalk?"

Robbie thought about it. "Honestly?" he said. "He's got a great smile—for a minute there, I felt like I could fix my life. And then *you* reminded me that I'm other people, and it wasn't so exciting."

Darrin looked taken aback. "Huh. Well, okay, then, let's go with Ezra's take. You've identified the problem, now it's up to you to fix it."

He gave a wide, pointy-toothed smile and a little mock punch with his fist. "You can *do it*!"

Ezra smacked him. "Now he's afraid. Look at him—his eyes are huge. I think he's had enough of us for the night—he's got somewhere to go."

"Nnnnnn...." The sound Darrin made sounded like no and a whine, both at the same time.

"No," Ezra said, but not to Robbie. "We are not shrinks, thank God, because seriously, I don't want that job. We're not going to tell him he has to stay home and think about what he's done. Far as I can tell, he's spent a whole lot of time doing nothing *but* thinking about what he's done. So he's got somewhere to go—as long as it's not with that girl—" He stopped and looked Robbie in the eye. "It's not, right?"

Robbie shook his head, and if they hadn't effectively made him feel like a real boy for the first time in nearly two years, he would have asked them to get the fuck out of his head. "No. Uh, broke up last night. She, uh... broke my toaster. Not pretty."

Both of them regarded him, heads tilted slightly to the left, eyes wide and mouths agape in horror.

"Wow," Ezra said, and Darrin nodded in agreement.

"Honestly," Darrin said, "it's a good thing you got here when you did. Toast is sacred. You need to get rid of your internal cray-cray to get rid of the stuff on the outside too."

Robbie wanted to protest. Everything he knew said that sometimes cray-cray just sort of jumped your shit.

But then, well, in *his* case, he was right. "Well, I guess for me," he said apologetically. "Yeah. You're right. That was... I mean, picking people up in bars...."

"Not people," Ezra said, nose wrinkled. "Picking up girls when you're gay as a picnic basket. Let's keep it real here."

Yeah. "Fine. Yes. I'm gay, and that was—"

"A move of desperation," Darrin said. "Yes, we get it. You know what? Go out, get laid, come back tomorrow. I'm done. You have effectively drained the fun out of psychic encounters. I'm going to eat a Pixy Stix."

With that, he whirled on his heel, grabbed one of the plastic tubes from Ezra's armload, and flounced to the back of the store.

Robbie watched him go. "Did he mean it—*really*? I gotta come back tomorrow?"

Ezra sighed and dumped the load of candy on the counter, shaking his arm out. "Yeah. Finn is going home tomorrow, and Adam's working the night shift because they need the money for tuition next semester. So if you want to start making shit right, you should probably come by."

Robbie closed his eyes. Awesome. He opened them again and saw Ezra looking at him in sympathy. "Are you going to be there?" That's right, Robbie—beg!

"Yeah," Ezra said. "And maybe my boyfriend too, and he and Adam are tight. He used to have a crush on the guy."

Robbie let out a grunt and a sigh. "Yeah, Adam attracts that."

"You're telling me," Ezra muttered. "Anyway, go. Don't be late. Your guy—he's gonna be glad to see you."

Robbie felt a smile—unfettered, joyful, free—welling up from his chest. "Really?"

"Yeah. Swear. Go see him!"

Robbie practically ran out of the candy store, and it wasn't until he had to unlock his car to drive away that he realized Ezra had shoved three long plastic tubes filled with candy into his fist as he'd gone.

Pixy Stix.

Who knew?

Being the Rainbow

CY WASN'T *surprised* to see his soldier boy walking into Gatsby's Nick so much as he was *relieved* to see him walking in. His shift had gone long, and since nobody had shown yet to take his place, he was still running glassware to the back. His relief had shown up, though, and it was time to clock out. When Robbie came walking in, hand in his back pocket, shoving his wallet in after paying the cover, Cy felt a little shiver of anticipation ripple through him.

Soldier boy's eyes had been *so*, so pretty. Sad, yes, but sadness didn't bother Cy. Sadness just meant... a story, that was all. Everybody in his neighborhood had a story. His last lover had been a young woman who'd been out on the streets when she was fourteen. Now, at twenty-five, she had her own business, traveled extensively, and had been willing to take Cy on a cruise over the summer that Cy had enjoyed *very* much.

Still, he'd gotten off the ship and waved a happy good-bye, and both of them had known it was over.

Cy always thought he had a line on something better lurking just around the corner. Of course, he'd *thought* he'd found something better pretty much the minute he'd stepped off the ship, because he'd gotten home and his landlord's nephews had taken him out dancing, and he'd found a sweet young thing who danced like a slinky pussycat in *heat*.

He'd jonesed *hard* that first night—and every subsequent night he'd gone dancing with Ravi and Anish and their friend Ezra.

But Ezra's friend Miguel had been crushing even harder, and frankly Cy was too confident in that ineffable "something" he'd find around the corner to fight for Ezra—or even let Miguel know that he was in the running. Sometimes "something" just wasn't *your* thing, and that was okay.

Or sometimes that something walked from around the corner and into his arms, like soldier boy had the other night.

That was good too!

Cy was coming out of the busman's cubby, so he had a chance to watch his new plaything find himself a corner and take the place in. Robbie of the recently released girlfriend scanned the crowd anxiously for Cy and smiled shyly as the bartender asked him what he'd like.

A beer. Basic, domestic Miller.

Huh.

The way he'd danced on the boardwalk like a wild thing, Cy would have figured him for a Sam Adams at the very least.

Then Cy noticed the quick, almost furtive way Robbie was looking at the men dancing, holding hands, making out. Like he wasn't supposed to see them—like he wasn't supposed to be there.

Oh.

Not out.

Or not comfortable in public. Well, yeah. He *was* a soldier boy— and oh boy, that soldier had dodged the question about what it was like to serve when you liked a little male tail, hadn't he?

Well… damn.

The not-out-yet were usually sort of angsty. Self-involved. Inhibited. Not Cy's thing, really. He was up-front with his lovers—no strings, nothing too heavy, just a good time, sugar. You, me, happy bodies in the moonlight, right?

But then soldier boy had called him up, talked nicely, and then actually *showed*, which was a big deal for someone new to the scene.

The least Cy could do was dance with him.

Cy took off his apron and stashed it behind the bus stand, then hopped out onto the dance floor, taking high fives and shaking his thing with whoever wanted to shake with him. Yeah, he played around, but he knew the trick of moving quickly, and that was to just keep dancing in the direction you wanted to go. After a little be-bop, a few twirls, and a few ass-gropes, he was on the far side of the floor and soldier boy was looking up at him over his beer.

"Nicely done," Robbie said, shouting to be heard over the music. "I should probably stay off the floor—it looks like you have that covered!"

A wave of heat swept Cy. He searched Robbie's eyes for censure, wondering if his not-yet-out friend had been put off by that blatant sensuality of the dance floor or his easy familiarity with pretty much everyone in the club.

Robbie smiled back, a little shy. His eyes, big and green and still damned sad, were shiny but not accusing. He was telling the truth—Cy looked good on the dance floor, and Robbie wasn't sure if he could measure up.

"Why don't you finish your beer and come see!" Cy shouted back. "Could be we need you!"

Robbie laughed like he knew *that* was impossible, but then he tipped his beer back and put out his hand with a sort of trust. Cy seized it—it was still cool from the beer, but Robbie's grip was strong—and skipped back into the fray, his new friend dodging the crowd gamely behind him.

Oh, there you go—a pocket opening up just for them as the music slowed, turned sultry, a dirty R&B riff with a not-subtle bump and grind to it. Cy grinned then and took both of Robbie's hands and put them on Cy's hips, so he could feel the rhythm.

And then he just rocked it, baby, back and forth and side to side, and Robbie grinned wickedly at him and followed him on that ride.

Aw, *man*—something just *delicious* happened when someone clicked with your body on the dance floor. And this wasn't pounding up and down to the beat, which even dogs could do if the music was loud enough. No, this was audio-sex, and this lean soldier with the big sad eyes was giving the dance equivalent of a hand job with no hands.

Cy let the sex seep up his spine, loosen his shoulders, put the slink in his sway, and he wrapped his arms around Robbie's neck and pulled him into the mood.

Robbie went, the two of them wrapped in a cocoon of rhythm and sweat. Cy could almost hear their breathing over the blasting noise, and feel the throb of his groin pounding against his black skinny jeans as they rubbed together.

He stood on his toes then, keeping in the moment and the beat because he'd danced ballet for twenty years, dammit, and he had the toe shoes to prove it. He leaned into Robbie's space, chest to chest, and whispered, "Grab my ass, soldier," into Robbie's ear.

Robbie could follow orders like a fucking pro.

His hands slid into Cy's back pockets—and Cy approved. Not too familiar too fast, but close enough to grasp, to knead, to squeeze, and he did just that. Not too hard, not too soft, just slow, with the music, and intimate, appreciating the muscular resistance of willing flesh.

Cy groaned and pushed himself closer, groin to groin, as the music picked up tempo just enough to suggest a long, hard fuck.

Sweat dripped down Robbie's neck, probably because he was wearing a sweater in a dance club. With pushy hands and impatient fingers, Cy tugged the aran sweater over Robbie's head, not caring that he dragged up the dress shirt underneath it, just trying to get the damned thing off. Robbie ducked his head and pulled his arms out, and Cy was about to toss the thing over the crowd and into a back corner when Robbie grabbed it from him and tied it around his waist.

Cy pouted, using the knot to drag him close again.

"A present from my mother," Robbie said in his ear, and Cy actually *felt* his heart skip.

From his mother.

This man's body *screamed* sex and he was worried about a present from his mother.

Cy could blow him right there on the dance floor.

He settled for taking Robbie's face in both hands and hauling him in for a kiss, and for that bubble moment, the kiss was all there was.

Sure, their bodies moved independently, still rocking audio-sex to a trance beat, but their mouths—hot and hoppy, with an undertone of sour candy.... Cy wanted more. Robbie kissed him back like a man in the desert dying of thirst, or maybe just a man who'd needed a man and had been kissing a woman instead.

Cy didn't give a ripe shit.

He wanted more kisses, addicted with the first taste, and Robbie kept dealing. Those hands that had tucked into his pockets now *took* the liberties that they'd declined before, and Cy felt them, hot and hard, on the flesh of his bottom as he pulled their bodies into closer contact.

Cy's cock, straining against the front of his skinny jeans, pushed up hard against what felt like a decent-sized erection in Robbie's conservative 501s. Cy shuddered, so close to coming in public on the dance floor that he almost sobbed into the hollow of Robbie's shoulder to make it so.

But he had more pride than that.

He grabbed Robbie's hands, breaking away with almost physical pain, and dragged him down the hallway to the outside patio. There were couples necking, petting, a blowjob or two down that hall, and Cy didn't want to do it that way. He was heading for the back, where only the employees were allowed to go, and he knew the secret corner he used in the summer.

Robbie followed wordlessly, his breathing harsh enough for Cy to hear, and they were both running so hot that the frost in the air didn't even penetrate their wall of heat.

Cy was fully intent on shoving Robbie into a corner and sucking him down to the back of his throat when Robbie—taller, bulkier—maneuvered *Cy* into the corner—

And started up the kiss again.

Cy groaned into his mouth and shoved his hand down Robbie's pants, feeling Robbie's cock pulsing against his palm. With some maneuvering—and a big ol' suck-in-your-six-pack from Robbie—Cy managed to push the jeans down, belt and all, and get a good grip on him.

Robbie's breath hitched, and he kissed the corner of Cy's mouth on a pilgrimage to his ear. "You like that?" he whispered, nipping sharply at Cy's diamond-studded earlobe.

"Yup!"

"You wanna get me off?" Robbie whispered, hot breath in the delicate sanctum of his ear and his neck.

"God, yes!" Cy moaned, because Robbie's hands weren't still either. He'd shoved them down the back of Cy's jeans again, this time under his waistband, and then bent and grasped Cy's thighs. Cy had to let go of Robbie's cock so he could wrap his legs around Robbie's waist and they could grind together, Cy's back braced against the wooden wall. Robbie lowered his head to bite the side of Cy's neck and then scrape his teeth across his shoulder.

"I wanna fuck you," Robbie told him, biting hard.

Cy bucked against him, so close to coming Robbie's voice might do it alone. "Here?" God, rule one of grown-up life, don't drop your pants and bend over at a job you pretty much like.

"Got a better idea?" Robbie asked before running his tongue down Cy's Adam's apple. Cy tilted his head up, gave him access, and then canted sideways so he could lick, bite, and otherwise maul his other side.

"My apartment." Oh Lord, Cy was totally going off plan. He'd had *no* intention of taking Robbie to his apartment. Not tonight. Dancing, necking, having a good time. But....

Robbie dropped him carefully, making sure his feet hit the ground, and then, without fastening his belt or dragging his pants up, he dropped to a squat and pulled Cy's jeans down to his knees.

And then took Cy's cock down to the back of his throat.

Cy smacked his head back against the wall hard enough that sparks flew behind his eyes, and let that pressure build up behind his balls.

"Not in your mouth," he panted, too far gone. "I'm still in my testing window."

Robbie pulled back, and for a horrifying moment, Cy thought that might be a deal breaker, but no. He just met Cy's eyes and smiled, a lazy, evil sort of expression, then stuck his tongue out and licked the precome-slickened head of Cy's cock. And then blew on it in the cold.

Cy closed his eyes and grabbed Robbie's hair, urging him closer, closer…. God, the contrast between heat and cold was *killing him*. And he was whimpering, making terrible needy, panting grunts every time he tried to thrust down Robbie's throat again.

"Need it?" Robbie taunted.

"Yes!" Cy wasn't proud.

"Need it?"

"Please? God, please, Robbie?"

And maybe it was his name that did it—that Cy knew his name, that he used it—because he thrust his head forward and swallowed, and black washed behind Cy's closed eyes.

"Coming!" he warned, and Robbie backed away, turning sideways and pumping Cy's cock fast and hard with one hand.

Cy gasped and his orgasm ripped out of him like a cord with serrated edges, and he spasmed and came, his ejaculate landing past Robbie's shoulder on the brick-paved patio. He could have died right then, leaned back and melted into the jasmine that covered the wooden wall, but the music changed and he heard footsteps.

"Get up!" he hissed, doing up his belt as quickly as he could. Robbie had the sense to pull his pants up, and Cy looked around frantically for so much as a glass of water to throw on the ground. Robbie found a half-drunk beer on the railing of the stage next to him and used that, and when the door burst open and two men stared at them in surprise, they were merely standing cozily in the corner, sharing warmth and looking into each other's eyes.

"Fuck," one of the men muttered. "We're going to have to use my car!"

And then they turned around and left.

Robbie started to laugh, burying his face in Cy's shoulder for support, and Cy laughed with him.

"The *car*," Cy muttered. "Jesus, why didn't I think of that? You drove!"

"Yeah," Robbie said, standing up a little but not, thank heaven, removing his surprisingly wide chest or his electric-volt body heat from Cy's vicinity. "But I don't want to fuck you in my truck, if that's okay. I sorta think we've earned a bed."

Cy looked at him and nodded helplessly. Oh hells. Yeah, so he was not-out-yet. But the parts of him that *were* out were pretty smoking hot, and Cy's body still sang from his touch.

"Yeah," he whispered. "Sure. You're right. We've sorta earned a bed."

Robbie smiled at him and kissed him again. Cy was sort of expecting a letdown this time, some crucial element to be missing and Robbie's skin to be clammy or his warmth overwhelming.

Anything, anything, to make him dredge up an excuse for why Mr. Not-Out-Yet could not come over to his loft apartment over the liquor store two blocks away.

But Robbie was just as hot, and his *smell*—part beer, part Pixy Stix, part aftershave—had only gotten hotter with the sweat from the dance floor and the musk of Cy's sex.

No excuses came to mind, and Cy cupped Robbie's cheek before pulling him down for another kiss.

A night, right? Maybe two. Cy didn't do long relationships. How painful could it be to take soldier boy to his loft and fuck him silly? He'd done worse for less time and less inclination.

Cy would be fine.

The two blocks to Cy's place were magical. They stopped to make sure Robbie's truck could stay parked overnight, and Robbie paid the meter so he could get it off the street by eight, while Cy stood and blew on his hands and danced. He hadn't brought a sweater to work, and his tight red long-sleeved shirt wasn't warm enough to stand around in the thirty-degree cold. Robbie stashed his phone in his pocket and then grinned at him, tugged his sweater from around his waist, and pulled it over Cy's head.

Chivalry, unconscious and unforced. Cy stared at him with big eyes and smiled, thinking that tall, rangy pretty boy had never looked more beautiful. He thrust his arms through the sleeves, grabbed Robbie's hand, and hauled him through the Sacramento streets, desperate to have him again.

They didn't sprint but skipped, practically like children, around the club crawlers that wandered from bar to club at nine thirty on a Friday night.

Just like on the dance floor, Robbie clung to Cy's hand and kept up, and together they pelted through the frost-tinted dark, their breath pluming over their heads. Every time Cy pivoted and swerved, Robbie laughed behind him like they were playing a child's game, and Cy would cackle just to hear the sound. When he executed a sharp right toward M Street and then entered the back stairwell over the liquor store, Robbie was right at his heels, with the ultimate trust of a child with a new playmate.

Together they sprinted up the steps, and Cy started digging in his front pocket for the key before he even got to the landing.

He fumbled for the doorknob, and Robbie shoved his hands under his shirt and his thick aran sweater. Cy shrieked and shuddered, the cold of Robbie's palms and knuckles dancing along Cy's warm skin.

Robbie draped himself over Cy's back, sliding his hands across the corrugated muscle of Cy's stomach and ribs, and Cy had to work at not fumbling the key.

"Not help-ing!" he sang desperately, and Robbie put his lips on Cy's neck.

"Go faster," Robbie whispered, licking a little trail of exploding nerves from Cy's neck along the back of his shoulder.

"C'mon, c'mon, c'mon...." Cy finally got the key in the old doorknob and cracked the door open.

The two of them spilled into the room, a breathless muddle of hands and mouths and a hunger for skin to skin. Cy whirled Robbie against the door, unbuttoned his top three buttons, and hauled his dress shirt over his head. It tangled on his hands, and Cy grinned wickedly as Robbie tried to shrug the sleeves off.

"Little help?" Robbie begged, laughing.

"No," Cy murmured, pushing against his chest. He kissed Robbie's neck, feeling his arms tighten, still bound by the shirt, and then kissed his chest. He rucked up Robbie's T-shirt and kissed his nipples, sucking first one, then the other into his mouth with a hard pop and a nip on the end. Robbie's arms thrashed behind him, but Robbie was helpless to stop, well, anything as Cy sank down to a squat and paused, looking up at Robbie with mischief in his eyes.

"You'd better not," Robbie threatened, but he was laughing so hard Cy was pretty sure he wasn't serious.

"Oh I'm gonna," Cy returned, licking his lips. Robbie's belt was the solid leather kind, with a plain bronze buckle, and Cy undid it and the button fly of Robbie's jeans while Robbie was still wrestling with his shirt.

"You are *wicked*," Robbie hissed, leaning back against the door with a thump. "Wicked and...."

Cy kept his fingernails just a little long. Sometimes he liked to paint them brilliant colors to match whatever outfit he was wearing. Tonight they were unadorned, and he scraped the edge of his forefinger against Robbie's briefs from the top of his bulge, over the bell, to where the erection disappeared in the V of his jeans.

He cracked his elbow against the door in an effort to get the goddamned shirt off his hands, and Cy laughed low in his throat as he dragged Robbie's jeans and briefs down his thighs.

Robbie's cock flopped out, thicker than Cy expected, and longer than thick.

Damn.

"This," Cy breathed, letting his tongue flick out and touch the head, "is a damned fine piece of equipment."

"I enjoy it," Robbie hissed. "But don't make me come. No testing. Need a rubber."

"You *got* a rubber?" Cy asked archly, squeezing that beautiful pink appendage in a tightened fist.

"*No!*" Robbie gasped. "You?"

Cy laughed. "You bet your tight ass I do." He ran his tongue along the sides, under the crown, playing with that tight little nerve bundle where the foreskin should have been attached.

Robbie made *great* sounds—deep throated, uninhibited. Cy hadn't expected that from someone not out, but he sure did appreciate it. He wrapped his lips tightly around the bell, tasting salt and the sweetness of soft skin and hard flesh, and Robbie's groan was so earthy Cy almost forgot what happened when a man made that sound.

Then he heard the ripping of fabric and Robbie's fist caught in his hair, pulling him back.

"Easy with the blowout," Cy taunted. "I'm not paying for extensions."

Robbie's grip loosened, and he grimaced. "I'm going to come, dammit—do you want me to fuck you?"

Cy's eyes actually rolled back in his head. Oh *yes*. A considerate caveman—didn't *every* boy dream about that? The Neanderthal who wouldn't take advantage? God. Cy *had* one, and he wanted to fuck Cy into the mattress, and who was going to say no to *that*?

Cy sprang up and ran down the uncarpeted hallway, past the tiny living room/kitchen, the smaller bathroom, and into the bedroom, which was as big as all the other rooms combined. He rucked the quilt up at the foot of the bed and dove for the goodie drawer, anxious to see Robbie sprawled naked in his sheets.

Cy would bottom for that. Hell, Cy would bend over and squeal just to see Robbie, pale and muscular, helpless with orgasm on his squeaky bed.

The bed dipped and squeaked, and Robbie flopped next to Cy as he was rooting for condoms and lubricant, and suddenly that became the hardest job in the world.

Robbie's body threw off heat, and all of that marvelous warmth enveloped Cy as Robbie wrapped long arms around Cy's waist so he could unbuckle and unhook. Then he stripped Cy's jeans off while Cy lay sprawled. Shoes, socks, jeans—all gone, thrown about the room. And *then* Robbie began to explore.

Gentle gliding kisses up Cy's triceps, along the small of his back, at the indentations of his waist. Cy gave a little moan and fumbled for the box of condoms, because *that* at least was in plain sight.

"What's the matter?" he taunted when Robbie paused at his ass. "Afraid of going in?"

His response was a quick bite on the backside. "Never," Robbie admonished. "This isn't hesitation." And then he kissed Cy's right hind cheek, slowly, with the scraping of teeth and the gentle play of tongue.

Cy buried his face in his pillow and moaned. "What *would* you call it?"

Robbie ran his tongue right where the two cheeks met, and Cy did everything but pull his knees up under his chest and whimper. "Worshiping art," Robbie whispered and then licked again.

"Good answer!" Cy ripped off a condom package and reached behind his back for the handoff. Robbie took it, and the lube bottle right after, but he set them down on the bed and kept... kept *worshiping* Cy's body.

Cy could definitely handle being worshiped.

Robbie right behind him, pulling him up to his hands and knees, was just the sort of manhandling Cy loved, and then that gentle exploration again—but this time he had Cy's ass right where he wanted it.

He laved and licked Cy's pucker, down to his balls, and even down to the head of Cy's uncut cock. He played with the foreskin—proving, Cy guessed, that he did know what he was doing—and then back again.

He squirted a dollop of lubricant right on target, and Cy let out a whimper, feeling his knees collapse, and then Robbie proceeded to finger Cy's entrance for... for*ever*.

"Is that all?" Cy complained, thrusting back against Robbie's finger. "You drag me up here, make me stop dancing, and all I get is a fingerba-*ang!*"

Another finger, spreading, and Cy's thighs were shaking.

"You're not going to go for it, soldier boy? Because you got a condom, that's all you asked for—condom, lubri-*cant!*"

And the third finger, and Cy could no longer hold himself up but had to collapse on his face, ass out, as Robbie threatened to bring him to climax with his fingers alone.

Cy's taunts and self-possession deserted him. "Please," he begged. "Please, Robbie, I'll stop talking, I'll do *anything*, just put the rubber on and *fuck... me....*"

He didn't even hear the crinkle of foil before Robbie was lubed and gloved and poised right... *there*.

Cy took a deep breath and drove himself backward, taking Robbie to the root. Robbie's groan rocked Cy to the pit of his stomach, and when he started moving, the long lever of his thrust rubbing inside Cy all the way forward and then *allll* the way back, Cy pounded the bed with his fist.

"Oh. My. God! Can you *go* any slower!"

"Yes!" Robbie grunted, the excruciating pace obviously not easy for him either. "You want to see?"

Cy froze, shaking, sweating, and horrified. "*No*! Jesus, soldier, *fuck me*!"

Robbie's next thrust had the force of a fucking tank behind it, and Cy threw his hips back to meet him. Fast—oh yes, fast—but hard and powerful, and Robbie's thrusts were screaming through Cy's tautened body.

Robbie *didn't* talk like Cy did, and Cy wasn't verbal, not anymore. For a moment the only sounds in the bed were Robbie's pants as he rocketed his cock inside Cy like a battering ram and Cy's groans as Robbie hit his prostate, stretched his rim, and—oh my holy fucking God—turned him the fuck *on*.

Cy hadn't stopped shaking since Robbie had thrust in, and now he just lay there, body writhing, hands fisting the sheets. Robbie fucked him to the brink of orgasm, and then, with one quick pop on his thigh and a shouted "Come, goddammit, come!"—

Fucked him right over.

Cy came, gushing come like a fire hose, and behind him, Robbie's pounding stuttered to a halt. For a heartbeat he tried to crawl into Cy's body, cock first, right before he groaned and shouted.

And came.

Cy felt his cock pulsing and hot inside the condom, and the heat, and the knowledge that he'd pushed his lover to the edge and over, spurred an aftershock, and then another, until Robbie collapsed across his back, sweaty and cold and spent.

His own come, cool and sticky, stuck to Cy's stomach as he flattened to the sheets. Cy didn't really care.

Their breathing rattled through the small apartment until Cy reached for the tissues under the lamp and passed them behind him.

Robbie cleaned up quickly and efficiently, then handed the box of Kleenex back before looking around the bed for the trash can. Cy heard the thump of the condom, then some washing up in the small bathroom, and about the time he decided he could move again, the bed shifted and he felt the gentleness of a warm washcloth on the back of his neck.

"Mm...."

Robbie was thorough but kind, sponging away sweat and lube and, after shoving at Cy's hip a little, come. He left to rinse out the washcloth, and then he came back and rearranged the sheets, finally pulling the fleece blanket up over their shoulders. Cy rolled over to his side and peered playfully up at him.

"You're flunking One-night Stand 101," he said with a smirk.

Robbie winked. "Well, I *was* planning to take off when you fell asleep, but"—he shrugged—"I set my alarm. You'll just have to kiss me good-bye."

Cy laughed, hiding his face against his bicep and then looking back. "You surprised me—I didn't expect you to call me, and then when you did, I didn't expect you to be...."

"Worth your time?" Robbie asked dryly.

Cy grimaced. "Well—unattached, honestly!"

Robbie's turn to grimace. "Like I said," he muttered, hiding his face, "that happened right before I picked up the phone."

"Ooh—*classy!*"

Robbie sighed and hid his eyes again. "Yeah, not so much. I...."

"No, no," Cy said, fighting disappointment anyway. "You don't owe me an explanation."

"She... she was the kind of girl my parents love," Robbie said at last. "And... and I ran into an old friend that night, and... and he was with this guy—I mean, they were happy. He had a life, a community." Robbie's eyes were faraway. "Was like a wake-up. I could live the rest of my life with this girl that... that I don't think I could have lived with for another *hour*, or I could, you know. Live honest."

"And I was the first step," Cy said, thinking there were worse things to be.

Robbie's eyes focused on him, pretty gray-green eyes in a lightly tanned face. "And you were fucking *hot*," he said, laughing. "I mean, I had your number in my pocket, and *damn!*"

Cy chuckled, appreciating the compliment. "Why thank you. I do my best with what God gave me."

Robbie quirked an eyebrow and tugged gently on a strand of black hair.

Cy smirked. "Well, with a little help from Helene's House of Hair Care and Sympathy."

"Seriously?"

"Yeah—it's my mom's place! I mean, I could do it myself, but my mom's a pro."

"That's nice," he said with sort of the same earnestness Cy had felt when Robbie said his mother gave him the sweater.

"Is that it?" Cy asked, smoothing Robbie's sandy brown hair back from his eyes. "We're both mama's boys?"

Robbie grunted and looked away. "Not really. I mean, when I was younger, but, you know. You get older, Dad takes over—"

"Unless he split when you were a kid," Cy said with a shrug, because hey, old story.

"Lucky you," Robbie said with feeling. Then he winced and rolled over onto his back. "Sorry. That was… that was a shitty thing to say. My old man is not that bad."

"Yeah? What makes him not that good?" Cy could not get enough of looking at Robbie's face—high cheekbones, full lips, a triangular jaw. God, this guy was Hollywood pretty, with this sort of shyness built in to make him accessible.

Those remarkable eyes—blue, gray, green, all by turns—flickered to Cy's face.

"Because one look at us like this, he'd come after you with a shotgun," he said with a grimace. "And not listen to me tell him it was all my idea."

Cy had to think about that for a moment. "Is it the black or the gay?"

"Yes," Robbie said decisively.

"Ah."

Robbie reached out and ran a thumb along Cy's lips. "I served with a really… colorful unit," he said after a moment. "And when you're out in the desert with all these people your father thinks are trash, and you trust them with your life? You realize—just because your high school was mostly white doesn't mean the rest of the world is. And then you come home and your world is *so* much bigger. But your parents didn't go with you. They still see high school, where the schools with the mostly black football teams were 'scary' schools. They never once stop to think about what it must have been like to be that all-black football team dropped right in the middle of an all-white town, you know?"

Cy shuddered. "Yeah—fucking horrifying!"

"Yeah," Robbie said quietly. "Or, you know, being gay when your dad's making fairy jokes with all his friends. And then saying things like 'I don't got nothing against *them*, I just don't know why they can't take a joke.'"

Oh. "Not out to them?" Wasn't even a question.

"No," Robbie said, focusing on the ceiling again. "But... but this was nice. I don't want to ever have to date an Ashley again because it'll make my parents happy. Coming out is going to happen. I mean—I don't see it not. I'm a dutiful son. We have dinner a couple of times a month. Someday I'm going to bring a guy home, and I'm going to say, 'This, this is someone I love.' And that's going to be it. They can keep loving me or lose me."

Cy closed his eyes, seeing Robbie, tall and proud, beautiful, holding some man's hand and saying that. "You'd be something," he murmured softly.

"Beats being nothing," Robbie said, his voice growing drowsy. "I've been nothing for two years."

Robbie rolled closer then, wrapping arms and legs around Cy in a long-body snuggle that was surprisingly comfortable now that the sweat was dry and they were two warm bodies under a blanket. Cy reached over his head and turned the lamp off, then took the snuggle for comfort and companionship. Since all he'd signed on for was sex, he figured the last thing was a bonus.

Cy didn't look free perks in the mouth, so he didn't see the strings until later.

Skinchanging

ROBBIE HEARD his phone buzz on the rickety yellow end table next to the bed and stretched pleasantly before killing the noise.

The room was really something—gauzy silk and scraps of satin covered the walls in a sort of Harlequin patchwork that Robbie couldn't stop looking at. Cy had used some of the same brilliantly covered cloth as a top for the fleece crazy quilt that was pulled up around their waists. Between the bright, elegant fabrics, the brass-fitted king-size bed, and the thick Persian rug that covered the old hardwood, the room was like a tribute to hedonism.

Cy lay sprawled next to him, all midnight skin over elegant muscles, and as Robbie swung up to find his clothes, his breath caught.

Damn—he'd *had* him some of that.

It was like his own cachet with *himself* improved considerably just because Cy let him into this gorgeous bohemian room. Cy grumbled something as Robbie stood up, and Robbie watched his hand patting the warm spot where Robbie had just been. With a yawn and a stretch, Cy sat up in bed.

"God—seven already?" His lips were puffy and swollen.

Delicious.

Robbie grabbed his jeans and underwear, then slid over to Cy's side of the bed after he'd put them on. First he kissed—because he had to taste that lush mouth again—then he pulled back and smiled.

"My morning breath's heinous," Cy said, holding his hand in front of his mouth in a curiously vulnerable gesture.

"Yeah, well, who puts breath freshener next to the end table with the condoms?" Robbie kidded, keeping his voice down to morning levels. "I, uh—last night?"

Cy grinned impudently. "Yeah, I'm good."

"Yeah." Robbie nodded with enthusiasm. "You're great." And now he got shy, because last night had been a gift. Who asks for a second present after an unexpected first one? "Uh, I have the whole day off," he said, flushing. "I got something tonight, but—"

Cy grimaced, and for a moment Robbie's heart crashed to the floor. He expected the "this was only a night, sugar-britches" speech, but that's not what came.

"I actually teach gymnastics in North Highlands," he said. "From nine to, like, two. And then bussing tonight. I get off at nine, though…." His hopeful expression faded. "You know, I get it. You might not be able to come back tonight if I kick you out now. I don't even know where you *live*!"

"Rocklin," Robbie said. "But it's no worries coming down here—I've got to talk to someone at seven. It's sort of an appointment, you know?"

Cy grimaced. "Same person as last night?"

"Sort of. It's like a… a clearing up old business thing." Robbie kissed him again, morning breath notwithstanding, and pulled back. "I'd, uh, *really* like to see you again. Can I see you again? If I come by tonight, can we… I mean, I could try to spring for dinner or something. Like a date or—"

Cy smiled at him. "Tell you what. If you can actually darken Gatsby's Nick again tonight, we can go out for waffles tomorrow morning."

"Waffles?" Robbie wasn't big on sweets in the morning.

"It's a diner, sweetie. They make omelets too."

Robbie grinned and kissed him again. The more they kissed, the more the acidic buildup in their mouths ceased to be a thing. He pulled back, aware his car was going to get ticketed at any time, and kissed the end of Cy's nose. "It's on, then. Omelets, my treat. I'll see you tonight, okay?"

"Promise?" Cy said—and he wasn't flirting.

Robbie sobered. "That means something to you," he said, making sure. "A promise like that."

Cy shrugged. "I've heard a few broken promises, yeah."

"Then I promise I'll show up at Gatsby's Nick as soon as my business is done. I'll try to be there before your shift's over so you don't have to look for me."

That smile—unnervingly bright. "This time I promise not to be surprised you show up."

"Deal."

ROBBIE RAN down the stairs and almost into two guys who were opening the liquor store on the bottom floor. They had sallow-brown complexions of the Far East, one tall and thin with sort of a stoop and the other shorter, stouter, with a square, capable face. They were both wearing puffy blue jackets in the frosty chill, and Robbie envied them, because the sweater was not cutting it. He could have done with some gloves and a scarf as well.

They smirked when they saw him, and then all three of them froze.

"You guys…," Robbie said, trying to place them. "Don't I remember you from somewhere?"

"Yeah," the taller one said, obviously identifying Robbie as he spoke. "You were the one who brought Finn in."

"That's right!" the shorter one said with relief. "Oh my heavens! I remember now." He smiled at the other one with gratitude. "Thank you, Ravi—it was going to drive me crazy."

Robbie danced from foot to foot in the cold. "So he's going to be okay?"

"Yeah. He broke his ankle, bruised his hip and his knee, and actually broke his wrist," Ravi said. "He didn't even know about the wrist until they got him to the hospital. They kept him two nights because they wanted to make sure no concussion. But you did a good thing helping him—thank you again."

"That was my pleasure," Robbie said, thinking about that kid and how much he'd meant to Adam. It truly had been.

"So, you help Finn," the shorter man said, "and now you do the walk of shame with Cy—is there something else we should know about you?"

"Anish!" Ravi reprimanded, blowing on his hands. "Let him go— he's freezing his ass off, and he's a little bit skinny."

"You're the one who's a little bit skinny," Anish groused, unlocking the padlock that chained the doors together and held the iron grate over the doors. "Don't yell at me because you forgot the gloves that Nana gave you!"

They bickered like they were married, but they seemed to be related in some way, and he would have loved to get to know them better, but cold! Ravi looked up before he could edge away to the curb, and waved.

"Be sure you come back to Candy Heaven, okay? And to Cy's, if he'll let you. He doesn't do encores that often."

Robbie grinned. "He's doing one tonight," he said smugly, and then the crosswalk turned green and he waved back before trotting to the other side of the street, and his truck.

THE DAY went slowly. He did grown-up stuff (adulting, as the Internet called it) like vacuuming his shitty apartment and detailing his truck. After the truck was done, he stopped by Target and picked out shower curtains in blue-gray, along with matching bathroom rugs and a new comforter. When he was done with that, he drove all the way down to Citrus Heights, because that was where Cost Plus was, and he suddenly wanted shit you *couldn't* find at Target.

He came back with a red lacquered end table for his bedroom and some plates that *weren't* Corelle for his kitchen. He also managed a tapestry wall hanging to go behind the futon in his living room, and a runner for his glass-topped coffee table. He put all his purchases in their appropriate places when he was done, and looked around.

And wanted more.

Because it looked like someone lived there—someone different, and maybe a little special. Someone with his own tastes, and someone who maybe didn't follow the crowd.

It wasn't Cy's apartment, of course, with what had appeared to be handpicked fabrics arranged just so, right down to the fleece-lined crazy quilt, but it looked more like Robbie lived here, and less like the Unknown Soldier.

He thought that maybe tomorrow, when he was out with Cy, he'd look into getting a plant. Plants were living, right? People with plants cared about their surroundings. Robbie wanted to be one of those people.

Cy's apartment had been unapologetically *Cyril's*. Masculine, feminine, colorful bed and utilitarian kitchen. He didn't seem to mind bringing people over, and neighbors knew his business—and apparently who came and went from his bed—and they didn't judge. Cy didn't seem to care if anybody judged him. Cy seemed to like himself just fine.

No more Ashleys.

No more regrets.

No more wading through life waiting for his guilt to go away. It wasn't. Robbie would have to live with that betrayal for the rest of his life.

But it didn't have to be the only thing he lived with, and he was determined to make that count.

Which was a really brave thing to think to himself just as he set out to go talk to the man he'd betrayed for real.

THIS TIME he brought gloves and a scarf—and a leather coat that he kept in the car, in case he weenied out when the wind swept off the river, and decided he needed it.

He paused while striding across the boardwalk to Candy Heaven and looked out over the bridge. He could see the top of the pyramid building over the rise of the levee, and something was going on at Raley Field, even in November, because there were lights in that direction too.

Robbie had seen bigger cities since he'd joined the military—the two weeks' leave he and Adam had shared in Berlin came to mind—but sometimes the smallness of Sacramento was comforting. He wasn't sure he wanted to live here all his life, but he didn't mind living here now.

All of that big, wide world out there, he thought now, and none of it was as huge and as scary as the man in the store.

He sighed.

He might as well get it over with now. Ravi and Anish had seemed to like him this morning. The sooner Adam told the whole world what a rat he was, the better.

Adam was counting inventory when Robbie walked in, but Ezra waved at him, a friendly smile on his achingly beautiful face.

"Hey!" he said happily. "Darrin said you'd show—and he wanted me to tell you that you'll regret not bringing your jacket from the garage, so, whatever that means to you, now you know."

Robbie blinked. "That means I'm officially scared now," he said apologetically.

Ezra bobbed his head side to side as though he was measuring how scary that was on the scale of things. "Yeah, no. Miguel says that sort of stuff freaks him out, but it really doesn't bother me. You're not alone, though. Adam pretends it doesn't happen."

Robbie thought about pragmatic, *phlegmatic* Adam. Yeah, not a lot of faith in the unseen in that one. "Doesn't surprise me," he said softly, looking up to where Adam's brow was screwed up in concentration. He turned his gaze back to Ezra, because he didn't want to stare at Adam looking for changes, for any sign, any at all, that Adam would remember Robbie fondly. His attention was caught by a series of drawings behind the counter.

"I didn't see these," he said, wonder tingeing his voice. "Adam's work, right?"

Ezra glanced back reflexively. "Oh yeah—Adam's taking art classes in college. I guess he lost his VA grant in San Diego and came up here and started over. Adam doesn't fuck around when it comes to dreams."

Robbie swallowed. "I should have had faith," he said, his stomach suddenly in knots.

Ezra's hand on the back of his was an unexpected grace. "Yeah—we don't always, even when it's justified. It's why faith is such a rare thing." He looked up then, and Adam had apparently relaxed for a moment, because he called out, "Adam, come put him out of his misery, okay?"

Adam grimaced back and nodded briefly to Robbie. "Yeah. Uh, I've been saving my break so—"

"You guys can go walking if you want."

"Sure, Ezra. Walking in the cold is *exactly* what I'd choose to do if I could order my life."

Ezra laughed like he was used to the sarcasm. "You're just missing the dog."

"Well *yeah*. I mean, we *had* to give him to Rico, right?" The expression on Adam's face then was surprisingly open—surprisingly sad.

"Yeah," Ezra nodded. "Finn's in no shape to get thrown around the house by Clopper. Give it a week. We'll get him back, and like Finn says, it'll all be happy fine."

Adam rolled his eyes. "And then you'll move out and we'll be missing *your* lazy ass—"

"I'll be upstairs," Ezra said, but he looked pleased, like he'd be glad to be missed. Robbie got a nice sense of camaraderie here—deeper than he'd seen when he'd brought Finn inside—and he wondered at

Ezra's kindness, when he seemed to know Robbie's past but didn't treat him like a pariah for hurting someone he cared about.

"Yeah," Adam said, shrugging like it didn't bother him. His gaze fell on Robbie, and some of his bravado fell away. "Let me get my coat," he said softly. "Ezra's right. I need the walk."

"Here," Ezra said, turning around and grabbing a coat hanging from a hook behind the counter. "It fits me, so it'll be a little small, but you won't die from a walk around the block, okay?"

Kindness. These people had it in spades.

"Thanks," Robbie said. He'd struggled into the thick wool peacoat by the time Adam came around the corner wearing a fleece-lined hooded Giants sweatshirt in vibrant orange and black.

"Holy *God*!" Robbie laughed as they started out into the darkness. "*Adam*—who talked you into wearing that?"

"Wha—" Adam looked at the cuffs at his wrists like he'd forgotten he was wearing Day-Glo orange. "Yeah. It was Rico's idea. It was… you don't want to hear this."

"Yeah," Robbie said, surprised at himself, "I do. Because, you know, it's normal. I need some normal before we hit the rough stuff. Do you mind?"

"Sure, whatever," Adam said. He was wearing blue fleece gloves, and Robbie thought fondly that he did not seem to give a shit whether anything matched. "See," Adam continued, "the thing was, last year when I got here, I had… well, less than nothing. Rico—"

"Your cousin?" Rico was the only family Adam talked about.

"Yeah. He was leaving for an internship in New York, and he knew I'd just lost my grant and my place in school and my apartment—"

"*Jesus!* Adam—"

"Oh no, you got no idea. The fuckin' *car* died on the way up here. But I got here and I was, like, starving, you know? Rico hadn't left anything in his apartment but pet food and medication for Gonzo, his cat whom I killed, because yeah, life sucked that bad. But my winter jacket was this blue sweatshirt—"

"Germany?" Their second year stationed together—so, six years earlier—he and Adam had taken leave in Berlin. It was before they'd gotten serious, when they were just convenient orifices and someone to play cards with, but they went to Berlin, and the nights had been colder than they'd expected. And Adam had gone and bought—of all the beautiful things he could have had in Germany—a basic blue fleece sweatshirt.

"Yeah," Adam said, "that was the one." They'd been walking down the boardwalk, and they came to the last street of the little pocket of shops and kitsch that was Old Town. Adam didn't even need to tell Robbie where to cross—Robbie figured out they were doing a big circle around the little four-block area, and he just kept walking at Adam's shoulder. The streetlights worked pretty well in Old Town, and the moon was full, so the place was eerily lit, even with all of the Christmas lights that lined the overhang over the boardwalk. It was pretty, yes, with the pyramid building lit up in gold across the river, but not welcoming.

"So it must have been pretty ratty," Robbie said, suddenly getting it. Adam—he *hadn't* landed on his feet. He'd scrabbled, fought, and kicked to end up where he was.

"Yeah, and it wasn't that fuckin' warm. So anyway, Finn and I, we met right before Thanksgiving, and you know, by the time Rico got home in April, that was it. All she wrote. Me and Finn...." Adam shrugged. "But Finn was still mad at the world, you know? 'Cause... things. 'Cause I wasn't in great shape when I got here. So we went to a baseball game this summer, and Finn told Rico about the jacket, and Rico, he bought me this fucking coat with the lining and the baseball team, and told me that if I ever needed anything or anyone, to not hesitate to ask."

Robbie's eyes were burning, and he had nothing to blame but the fog. "That's... that's awful," he said softly.

Again, that pragmatic Adam shrug. "You see lots of guys on the streets, Robbie. I had it good."

Robbie swallowed. "They try to pretty them up in Lincoln and Rocklin," he said, voice hoarse. "But I keep looking for faces of guys we served with."

"Yeah," Adam said. "Me too. Ain't found any yet, but...."

"They're out there."

Adam's grunt told him all he ever needed to know about the state of the world. "We were lucky," he said.

"*I* was lucky, you mean," Robbie retorted bitterly.

"Naw," Adam said, surprising him. "See... I've had time to think. And... I mean, I don't know if you and me are ever gonna be friends like Ezra and Rico—"

"Ezra dated your *cousin*?"

Adam turned to him, moonlight glinting off his teeth in a wicked smile. "We are one incestuous fuckin' pool of gay here in this little corner of the world," he said with some pride. "You got no idea. But I was saying that... okay, so Finn thinks you're awesome, right?"

God. "He's a sweet kid—"

"Twenty-five, if you can believe that."

Robbie could not. "Seriously?"

"Yup. Gonna have his bachelor's in structural engineering at the end of this year. We're going to be looking for an architectural school, but he wants it close to home."

"Jesus, *why*?"

Adam shook his head. "'Cause, I mean, you know *I* lost out on the parent lottery, and I read your mother's letters, and I don't think you're doing so hot either. But Finn? He got the whole fuckin' enchilada. His family is like... like these weird fairy gnome people from outer space that just sprinkle happy dust on the world and make us all love each other and shit. It's *terrifying*."

"You're yanking my chain." God, this Adam was fun to talk to. The other one had been reserved, almost taciturn, and that man was still there. But Robbie saw humor here, and a sense of playfulness that Robbie had really only seen when they'd been alone in bed together.

This Adam didn't have to be sexual to be himself.

Robbie was impressed.

"God no. Seriously, this thing they did with Rico's mom? You had to have been there to even believe it. It was like... like PFM—pure fucking magic. Anyway, you got that in your corner, who in the fuck wants to leave, right?"

"Yeah," Robbie said glumly, kicking a stray rock with his shoe. The rock skittered at the feet of a horse and carriage. The horse looked down at his hoof, then looked back up at Robbie, and then munched oats.

Well, Robbie was just not making that much of an impact.

"Yeah," Adam said, his voice settling down. "You want to leave."

"Not you," Robbie said, surprised, because this talk should have been all the suck. "You—I mean, I thought you were pretty awesome before, but you're *amazing* now—"

"Taken," Adam barked sharply.

"Yeah, I know." Robbie took a deep breath. "And... see...." They got to the end of the bottom block and turned left at the railroad museum.

They weren't the only people out on the boardwalk—most of the food places were busy, and people trotted through the cold—but that didn't mean the dark didn't mask them and their painful conversation from the rest of the world. "I think I know what I want to say right now, is that okay?"

"Go for it," Adam said, his step not faltering in the least.

"I'm sorry—"

"Forget about—"

"Shut up," Robbie said without heat. "It wasn't small. It was huge. And horrible. And I'm *so glad* to see you landed on your feet, but I know it couldn't have been easy. What you're not telling me is how long it took before you could even trust Finn, and I know that because I know *you* and I know that what I did to you probably broke something inside you for a long time, and it *hurts me*, like physically, to know I did that."

"Oh God," Adam moaned softly, like this was the worst possible thing for Robbie to say.

"So I know this isn't all roses," Robbie persisted. "I could listen to you talk about your life *all night*—and it would make *me* happy to know you were okay, but that would *not* make it all fine between us."

"It doesn't need to be," Adam growled. "Finn thinks you're a hero—I'm not gonna take that away from him." His voice softened. "That kid—I'd let him think Bigfoot saved him if that was what he wanted to believe, you understand?"

"Yeah," Robbie said simply. "And that's fine. You want to let him believe I'm a hero? Man, somebody does—he might be the only person in America who ever will. But... but that doesn't mean I don't look at you and want to *try* to be one for real."

Adam tripped on an icy board and almost recovered. "What in the hell—?"

"No!" Robbie said, although it hurt him, because yeah, he'd had fantasies about making it up to Adam and them being together one day. But part of letting go of Ashley and the fantasy of being straight and loving the kind of girl his parents would approve of had been letting go of Adam and the fantasy of ever getting back together with him.

"I couldn't do that," Robbie said, quieter. "I... look, even if you were ready to break up with Finn—and I don't see that happening, so don't freak out on me—I couldn't. I couldn't wake up every morning next to you and remember that….” His voice broke. “That moment in the barracks and think, ‘I did this to him.’ I—there’s just no way. I couldn’t look you in the face for the rest of our lives. So I’m not going to try to do that. But I want to not be that guy ever again. What you did? Show up here with nothing and end up with Finn and a family and people who care about you? *That’s* what I want to be.”

“Huh.” Adam kept walking, and Robbie fought the urge to kick one of his feet behind the other just to get more out of him.

“That’s all you got?”

Adam stopped, and Robbie almost ran into him, and suddenly they were facing each other in the moonlight in front of the river. “That thing you did to me?” Adam said after a moment.

Robbie was only a couple of inches shorter than Adam—they were nearly eye to eye. “Yeah?”

“That was a really horrible thing.”

Robbie swallowed and looked away. “I know.”

“But I never—I never knew you’d be holding on to it like this. You’d feel so bad you couldn’t look at me.”

Robbie still couldn’t. “It’s the worst thing I ever did, Adam. How do I live with that?”

Adam shifted uncomfortably. “I killed Rico’s cat,” he said after a moment.

Robbie remembered something about this. “Uh—”

“Not on purpose. Thing was old. Took off after people left the apartment. Was sick. By the time I found it, Gonzo was on death’s door. Anyway, cat died, first thing I did—”

“Bury it?”

“After that—hole in the backyard, by the way. Fucking classy. Anyway, I broke up with Finn.”

Robbie hadn’t thought his eyes could go wider. “You don’t *look* insane.”

Adam actually made eye contact, and his teeth glinted briefly. “Fact that you say that after meeting him once—that means you’re a good guy. Anyway, I figured, I fuck up like that, kill Rico’s cat—”

“But it sounds like the cat just—”

“Not what it felt like, Robbie. Rico gave me a place to live, and *weeks* later, I kill his fucking cat. Anyway, I figure I’m not a good enough guy to hold on to….” His lips twisted, so much love and longing and joy all twisted up with them that Robbie's heart sort of thumped in his stomach. "How could a guy who'd kill that fuckin' cat actually, you know, ever be good enough for Finn?"

Robbie closed his eyes then, because he didn't know if he could see any more of this pain on Adam's face. "You're the best guy I know," he said softly, remembering all the times when Adam would crack a joke, or nudge Robbie with his shoulder, or say something brilliant and sweet—and completely unassuming. He'd been a good soldier—smart, competent, gave orders easily, took them when needed. But he'd been— and still was—a truly great man.

"Sorry to hear that," Adam said sincerely. "And I'm still not good enough for Finn."

Robbie let out a cracked laugh. "Well, you were too good for me," he said, and his eyes burned some more, spilled over. He wiped them with his palms, realizing that this feeling—*this* feeling right here—was why he'd had to wait for a chance to deliver himself to Adam's feet.

"That's the problem," Adam said, his voice growing hard. "That's probably why you got afraid that day. Same reason I got afraid after the cat died. You didn't think… didn't think you deserved any happiness then. And now? You're gonna keep hating yourself for that moment and you're never gonna get any happiness *now*."

Robbie thought about Cy waiting for him in an hour, and his chest ached. He wanted that. That beautiful, laughing boy dancing with all the fabulous in his soul. How did he not fuck that up?

"Suggestions?" he asked, voice thick. "Because I mean, I got plans. I talk real big—made a date, keep swearing I'm going to do things different. I'm going to look at schools—"

"All the deadlines are past," Adam said seriously. "You gotta wait until spring."

"Fucking awesome. I'll wait until spring. Now do you got any ideas for how I *not* weenie out like a fucking coward again? Because I am all fucking ears."

Adam didn't even blink. "If you're getting fucked in the ears, you're doing shit wrong."

Robbie sputtered through tears and tried to wipe them away with his hands. "You asshole."

"Here." Adam held his chin and used the cuff of his bright fancy sweatshirt and his palm. "And I am an asshole." The rough scrape of

Adam's sweatshirt under his eyes calmed him down, and he could take a deep breath and not yield to the sobs that lurked a surprisingly shallow depth under the surface.

"You are," he said quietly. "And I guess you don't know the answer to my question either."

Adam stopped working on his face and paused. For a moment they were intimately close, and Robbie's heart beat hard, yearningly.

Adam stepped back with formal grace. "Whatever the answer is? It starts inside you, Robbie. With why you were so afraid. I mean, I get why you were so afraid you didn't want to make that step. I—I mean, for a while, until just now, actually, I thought you hated *me*—"

"I didn't!" Robbie said, almost desperate for him to believe this. "I *don't*. It was just… that moment, I could only think about all the people in the barracks, and my parents, all the people I'd ever known, *hating* me. And then, then they hated *you*—and I realized that being on the other side of that wall from you was *worse*. I *wish* they would have hated me, because I deserved it and—"

He broke, and Adam was there, arms around his shoulders, shushing quietly into his ear. "It's okay," he whispered. "It's okay."

"It's not—Adam, you were so alone—"

"And you weren't?" Adam took a step back and shook him. "Robbie, you went back with Heller and those guys behind the Humvees, and you *hated* them. You think I didn't see that? How much you hated them? How much you hated *yourself* for doing that?"

Oh God. He'd been the unit in-box, the platoon whore, sucking any cock, bending over for any fucker. Everyone's bitch, that was Robbie. He would have exiled himself, like Adam, gone to the other side of the wall—but by the time he realized what had happened, he was the only one watching out for Adam. Pulling wolf spiders out of his boots in the morning, making sure Adam never went out on patrol alone—Robbie couldn't have done that shit if he'd been on Adam's side.

Those last months before Adam had left—and Robbie not long after him, although he'd never told Adam he'd put his papers in too—he'd told himself he was getting fucked so Adam wouldn't end up dead.

"I had to," he whispered, not sure he could keep this to himself. A hero could have. A hero could have been silent and let Adam hate him, because Robbie deserved it. But Robbie had already proved he wasn't a hero. "They… they let me know when they were going to fuck with you if I slept with them. I…."

"You got guys from other units to patrol with me," Adam said. "You kept my shit from being stolen. You watched out for me—did you think I didn't know?"

Robbie wiped his face with his hand, suddenly feeling a little better. "You knew that?"

"I was watching you for a sign," Adam admitted, face bleak. "Any sign that all that shit we said, it wasn't garbage to you. And I saw that shit you did. The times Heller was gonna mess with me and you grabbed his ass. You—it was like you were trying to make up for doing that by keeping me safe." Adam swallowed. "Still sucked. It all still sucked. But it helped. Knowing you didn't hate me. Not really."

"Never." His throat was so swollen he could hardly speak.

"Naw," Adam said, wrinkling his nose. "You saved all the hate for yourself."

Robbie nodded, feeling stupid and weak and helpless.

Adam reached out and wiped the last of the tears from under his eyes. "Let it go, baby," he said quietly. "Just… I have a picture of that time. Of how awful I felt. And every time I have a good memory, I write it on the back of that picture. And about a week after we got back from San Francisco, Ezra was out dancing, and Finn and I got out a Sharpie and I wrote *San Francisco* over the front of that picture. Because that trip with my cousin, that meant a lot to me, and my cousin got over Ezra and so I could get over you. So you need to find good memories of someone *not* me, and memories when you're brave, and you need to put them over that time. The time will still be there—but you know how to make it never happen again. Just keep those memories, the ones you learn from. It'll help."

Robbie nodded. "Yeah? It'll help?"

"Helped me."

"I can't draw," Robbie said, even though Adam knew that.

"It's a metaphor, and I'm late back from my break."

They turned again and started walking. "I've got someone to meet," Robbie said awkwardly as they walked. "Thanks for, you know, stopping the emotional evisceration."

"Yeah, well, I haven't done that in a while. Fuck you for dredging all that up for me again—gotta tell you, not my favorite."

Robbie actually laughed, and by the time they got back to Candy Heaven, his cheeks were chilled, but he felt like nobody would be looking at him weird because he'd been crying.

"I... I'm not sure if I would have gotten it over with sooner if I'd known you were this close, or just run from it for the rest of my life."

Adam grunted. "Yanno, I don't know if I could have lived with that forever if I was you. I'm sort of thinking you owe Finn for getting hit by a car."

"I *do* owe him," Robbie said glumly. "Got any ideas?"

Adam took a deep breath. "I don't know," he said at last, simply. "We're all the same age, it's a college town. Ezra and Miguel go dancing, Rico and Derek, they've got their fingers in *everybody's* business, and this place here?" He pointed his finger up and spun a circle indicating Old Sacramento. "This is not that fuckin' big. We're going to run into each other if you're down here. So how about I don't tell Finn you're *that* guy, but if he figures it out, you need to find a way to make it square with him."

Robbie nodded slowly. "Can I tell him myself?"

Adam shrugged. "Yeah, why not? But... but whatever you do— don't hurt him." Adam's face closed down, and the tender friend who had just helped Robbie pull his shit together disappeared. "That's the number-one rule here, you got it?"

"Yeah." That nod picked up speed. "Don't hurt him. Got it."

The grimace caught him by surprise. "Look, in all fairness to you? He finds out first and I might be carrying him away as he's trying to claw your face out. His sisters taught him how to fight. It's not pretty."

Looking Adam square in the eye came as a shock, because it was something he never thought he'd do again. "If that's what it takes? To make it so this isn't the last time we talk like... like *people*? I'll do it."

"Jesus, you're nuts." Adam shook his head and stomped some of the frost off his feet before opening the doors and barreling inside. "Ezra! Sorry it took me so long! I'm gonna start closing now!" he bellowed before charging toward the back.

Robbie guessed the conversation was over.

Reluctantly he slid Ezra's peacoat off his shoulders and hung it on the peg where he'd gotten it. Even though the walk to the parking garage was short, it had been cold out there, and he was grateful.

"So," Ezra said, appearing by his elbow out of thin air, "how'd it go?"

"Coulda sucked worse," Robbie said gruffly. "But it was cold. 'Preciate it."

"Wait." Ezra touched his elbow. "Look, I had one of these in August. The talk with the ex? I was a disaster. I needed someone afterwards. You got someone?"

Robbie flashed him a weak smile. "Better than someone. I got a guy who had no idea who I am or what I did and doesn't give a ripe shit."

Ezra nodded, his curls waving. "That's nice. But if he gets to be important, you need to tell him."

God, his throat was swelling again. "Right now I'm telling you, if I can just make it to see him, it will all be better."

"Sure." Ezra bowed his head like he was conceding something, and Robbie turned and stumbled out the door.

He kept Cy's picture in his mind during the forty-block drive down J Street. Not Adam's words, not the tears that he kept a leash on—just Cy. Happy, free, not ashamed of a fucking thing.

In his heart, he kept that feeling, the one he had when they were dancing. The one he had when he was free.

He remembered Cy tousled in the morning, sassy, sexy, casual.

But still happy he was coming back. Looking forward to seeing Robbie walk through the door. God, Robbie needed someone happy to see him walk through the door.

Robbie hit the gas a little and the truck fishtailed to the right, up off the curb, and right into a telephone pole. The last thought Robbie had before the airbag released was *Jesus, how'd I manage to fuck this up too?*

Unexpected Pleasures

CY FELT the phone buzz in his pocket as he was clocking out, and when he saw Robbie's name flash across the screen, he was only a little disappointed. Late—or even a no-show—he could deal with. But the guy cared enough to send a message and not just stand him up, so that was nice. Cy rolled up his apron and tucked it under his arm because it was getting a little rank and needed a wash, and since he wasn't getting laid tonight, why not?

It wasn't until he was halfway to the door that he thought to check the message.

Not getting laid tonight? Who said? Maybe Robbie was just running a little late. Give the guy a break, right? Check his text and maybe wait around and have a drink.

Cy pulled out the phone and saw the picture of the smashed truck and then the selfie of Robbie on an ambulance gurney, holding a gauze pad to his nose.

The caption *SORY CANT MAKE IT DONT DANC W/NOONE ELSE* was just icing on the cake.

"Jesus *fuck*!"

"What?" Antony, the busser clocking in to take Cy's place, paused on his way into the back. "You gotta work some more?"

Cy rolled his eyes. "No, your shift is safe. My date can't make it—"

"That hot guy you tongue-fucked on the floor last night? Man, *that's* a *shame*!"

"You don't know the half of it," Cy muttered. "Shit—he wrecked his truck and—" His phone buzzed again. *MERCY SAN JUAN.* "And he's going to Mercy San Juan, which is right down the street! Hallelujah—if I run, I can be there before frostbite sets in!"

"Here," Antony said practically, pulling off his fleece hoodie. "And God, Cy, would it kill you to bring a fuckin' jacket to work, or do you just like rubbing it in that your commute is about a minute and a half?"

Cy grinned at him and checked the pockets. Antony was known to partake, and the last thing Cy wanted was trouble for green shit that wasn't his. He grimaced and pulled out a baggie, shoving it in Antony's front pocket while his friend leered at him. Not that Antony was bad-looking—his skin was palest brown and his eyes were deepest black, and he looked like a naughty angel. He was a sweet kid—but just that. Sweet. Cy needed a little bit of dirty with his sweet, and damn if Robbie didn't qualify.

"Thanks for the jacket," he mumbled, texting quickly. *OMW.*

He was down the block, running briskly, before he realized what he was doing.

This was a *boyfriend* thing, wasn't it?

After a one-night stand? Augh! He wanted to stop right there and take it back, but the phone in his hand buzzed.

Thanks, Cy. Don't worry. If you can wait for me until I get a cab, I won't impose.

Aw, Jesus. Okay, then—Robbie knew what was up. What had he said? Cy was the only person he could talk to about breaking up with his girlfriend because he didn't feel that way?

Well, it wasn't like Cy hadn't planned for him to stay the night anyway.

You can sleep at my place. No worries. Just hang tight.

He trotted down the street a little faster now. It was *weird* how having someone waiting in a hospital just motivated the shit out of you.

ROBBIE WAS sitting up in the ER bed, dozing a little with an ice pack on his nose and a brace on his wrist, when Cy got there. He smiled gratefully as Cy entered, and looked at the nurse next to him. "Am I all signed to go?"

"You sure you don't want to spend the night?" she asked kindly. "You've got your concussion paperwork, right?"

Robbie nodded. "Let me ask my friend—he might not want me potentially hurling all over his couch."

Cy half laughed. "You can sleep in the bed, sweetness—and don't worry. You won't be the first to roll over and toss cookies."

He watched Robbie's eyes widen and could have kicked himself. *Not out, not out, not out.*

But the nurse just laughed. "Well, you two sound like you have a system down, so I'll go get the doctor to sign this and you can go."

She bustled out and Cy flopped into the chair next to the bed. "Sorry," he muttered. "Low-rent move."

"You came here after work," Robbie said, voice muffled. "Don't let my hang-ups make that a bad thing, 'kay? 'Sides. Easier to practice on strangers."

Cy smiled, surprised at how relieved he felt. "You're being a sport for a guy who must have a splitting headache. What in the hell happened?"

Robbie grimaced and then winced, probably because he wrinkled his taped nose. "Ice patch. Good thing the truck is built good. They towed it to a garage—I might have to call...." He groaned. "My *boss*," he said, like this was his last best hope. "God, I can call my *boss*. He doesn't *seem* like a racist douche bag—he can come tomorrow and get me!"

Cy laughed. "So *not* being a racist douche bag is a requirement for picking you up? Good to know."

Robbie shook his head. "Mostly I don't want to expose you to my dad. He embarrasses me."

Yeah, Cy got it, and in return for the honesty, he did an impression of his grandmother from Louisiana. "Cy, are you still dancing? You *know* only *those* people dance. I know your mother says you're happy, but you're not gonna be happy until you get yourself a girl and settle down! By the time I was your age, I had three babies!"

Robbie's eyes, if anything, got wider. "Who was that—?"

"*That* was my nana. I'm telling you, until I turned twenty-one, whenever Nana was coming, the blowout turned into twists and a baseball hat, the skinny jeans and glam tops turned into baggies and giant T-shirts, and there was *no* makeup near little Cyril McVeigh's completely heterosexual face."

"Why twenty-one?" Robbie asked, pretty astutely for a guy who looked like he'd smushed his brains through his skull.

"Because that's when her eyes got too bad for her to notice the makeup. So, you know, a blessing and a curse, really."

Robbie groaned. "Man, that sucks."

Cy shrugged, because it was what it was. "Yeah, but my mom gets it. She knows the boys and the girls—more boys than girls, and she gets that too. I see Nana once every three years, and I'm, like, one grandkid out of thirty. I see my mom three times a week. Guess which one matters most?"

Robbie appeared to be thinking about that for a moment—and then the doctor came in and woke him up.

Cy laughed and blew it off until they were in the cab and headed back for the L Street apartment. "If they didn't like it," he said muzzily, "they wouldn't have to see me that often. So... the person I saw all the time, he'd be more important."

"Simple logic, junior," Cy said affectionately. The boy sounded stoned, and given the prescriptions they'd gotten on their way out, he wasn't surprised.

"You'd think so," Robbie slurred. "But I'm not that smart." Then he fell asleep on Cy's shoulder for the rest of the ride home.

ROBBIE WAS actually a model patient. There was no throwing up and very little whining. Cy needed to help him to the bathroom once and bring him a pain pill at oh dark thirty, but other than that, he slept on the far edge of the bed, stretched out top to tip, like he was trying not to be a bother.

At four in the morning, Cy couldn't handle it anymore and plastered himself along that lean, pale back. Robbie made an "mmm" sound and relaxed into Cy's arms, and Cy could sleep.

At seven o'clock he shook Robbie gently, just to make sure he was okay, and Robbie yawned and stretched and rolled over, pulling Cy into a cuddle that Cy was pretty sure he'd waited all night just to get.

"Why didn't you do this earlier?" he grumbled. "This is nice."

Robbie grunted. "No sex. Swollen brain. This gives me a boner."

Cy laughed a little and scooted his bottom half back so they weren't touching. "Better?"

"Mm... yeah. None of the boner, all of the sweet. This is good."

"Do we have a plan for this morning?"

"More drugs?" Robbie asked plaintively.

"Yeah, let's do this a minute and I'll definitely get you more drugs for your noggin. Anything else?"

"I need to call my boss."

"I can drive you," Cy said, casually throwing his treasured day off to the four winds. "Seriously—my car is parked about three blocks away, so I don't use it for local shit, but I can take you. Where do you need to go?"

"Ugh. Well, the repair place first, for an estimate, and they're right by a car rental I guess, so I can get out of your hair."

Cy gave a sigh and cupped his face. "Look, I won't pretend I hadn't planned on something more exciting than that, but you know what? It's a day with a guy I sort of like. Let's get your shit squared away, then go to lunch, then go to your place and watch movies or something. I know you don't feel like setting the world on fire, but I'm game if you are."

Robbie smiled. "You're something, you know that? That sounds… well, my apartment's sort of a saltine tin with no character, but other than that, it sounds good. I would really love to spend the day with you if you don't mind the no sex and the stupid errands and the boring apartment."

"Well, when you package it with a bow…," Cy said, laughing. Robbie laughed too, and Cy threw himself out of bed to get the pain meds. Yeah, for a second date, it sucked, but this wasn't about that, not really. It was about how Robbie hadn't assumed that Cy would care about him after a one-night fuck—but Cy really wanted to. It was about how much Cy had missed Robbie's cuddling when he was trying to be unobtrusive. And it was about how grateful he was for simple help—not like he'd never known kindness before, but like something somewhere in his past had made him not take it for granted.

These were good things—good qualities in a lover—and Cy approved. Somebody somewhere had trained this guy up and maybe delivered him to Cy's home turf with a pat on the back and a "Go get 'em, tiger!" It wasn't being sentimental to keep the date—and the connection—going. It felt like self-*interest*. This guy—*this* guy—could be a keeper.

Cy remembered that sinuous, needy feel of the boy he'd met when he'd come back from his cruise. He so could have kept that boy, but that one hadn't been for Cy. This one felt sinuous on the dance floor and needy and self-reliant at the same time. Like a really graceful dog— strong and capable, but so happy for affection.

Cy liked that.

This lover might stay a while. He hadn't thought that before— he'd just been thinking about another night, another dance, some more touch the night before. Hard truth was, it wasn't until Cy had seen the picture from Robbie's phone with the wrecked truck that he'd been able to concede that he just might be ready for someone like that in his life.

So what was this, a bump? Hell, from what he'd been told, all long-term relationships had bumps. If this was the worst thing Robbie did to him, he was a lucky boy!

The rest of the day made him feel that lucky. They got something light for breakfast and then took care of Robbie's business. Cy could tell he wasn't feeling great—he confessed that his head ached and his chest ached from the seat belt bruise—but he kept up his end of pleasant, dry conversation in the car.

The insurance business went as quick as those things could. Robbie signed a few pages, tried desperately to concentrate on what the guy behind the counter was saying, and then Cy called an end to it.

"So can he come in tomorrow morning and get his car?" Cy asked abruptly, cutting into the guy going on and on and on about assessments and relative value and shit Cy didn't care about.

"Not the truck!" the guy said, surprised.

"Then the rental—the one it says right here"—Cy found it in the paperwork—"that he gets when his car can't go. Can he get it *tomorrow*."

"Yeah, sure," the guy said. "If that's what he wants to—"

"It's what he wants to do," Cy reassured him. "When do you open?"

"Eight o'—"

"I'll have him in then, and he won't look like he's going to pass out on you while you natter on and on about shit he doesn't give a fuck about!"

"Sir!" The guy was white with a thin, weaselly face under a graying goatee.

"Look at him?" Cy was pulling out his full-tilt diva, and he didn't give a shit. "That white boy is *gray*. Can we maybe just let him go home and get some rest with his concussion and his broken nose, and he can come back tomorrow for the rest of this shit?"

"Yes, sir." The guy—Leon by his name tag—looked down repentantly. "Mr. Chambers, you've signed everything you need to. You can get your rental tomorrow."

"Thank you," Robbie said weakly. "I really app—"

"Appreciate it in the car," Cy muttered, grabbing his arm and hauling him there. "You got any decent takeout places where you live?"

"Yeah, I've got some places on speed dial."

"Good. I'm getting you home to your shitty apartment, getting you to bed, and ordering out. Then you can sleep, I can watch old movies and surf, and we can call it a date. You look like hell, soldier boy—I am *not* okay with that."

Robbie made a little chuffing sound then, and when Cy glared up at him, he had a suspicious smile on his face.

"Are you laughing at me?" he asked, on the border of being hurt.

"I am *in awe* of you," Robbie said, and Cy recognized it then. The smile was pride.

Oh hell. Cy chivvied him into his little Nissan and got behind the wheel, following Robbie's terse directions down Taylor, then right on what was apparently some sort of wormhole to Lincoln, left on a side street, and voila! The characterless apartment complex he'd described, a revenant of eighties architecture where everyone wanted to look the same, was a Seussian concrete eyesore, and Cy grunted as Robbie directed him to the parking slot with 81 painted in it.

"What in the hell?"

"Sorry," Robbie said weakly. They'd stopped at a drive-thru for some soda and Robbie had taken his pain pill. He seemed to feel a little better but was still obviously out of it. "I'm not that good a person. I figured I didn't deserve that good an apartment."

Cy snorted. "I do *not* know what you are talking about. No, don't get out—I'll come get you."

"Yeah, okay," Robbie agreed. When Cy came around to his door, Robbie threw a companionable arm around Cy's shoulders and then ducked his head to whisper in his ear. "You and me can come out to the neighbors like we came out to the nurse," he said soberly. "So someone asks who you are, I say—"

"I'm your friend," Cy told him gently. "'Cause, you know, boyfriends don't happen after a weekend."

"D'oh!" Robbie sighed. "I knew that. I violated the law of boyfriend rule. Sorry."

"That's okay, soldier. I knew I was tempting fate by giving in to the hurt/comfort thing—and you were being sweet. But you know, a few more weekends as exciting as this one—"

Together they began walking, Robbie guiding on unsteady legs, toward one of the little cave-like stairwells. "A few more weekends as exciting as this one, you'll be finding someone to dance with who's not quite this pathetic," Robbie muttered. "I swear, I'll step up my game."

"Yeah?" Cy was curious. "Where you going to step it to? You know we've got Christmas in three weeks. I don't know about you, but I've got some shit to do!"

"What sort of shit?" Robbie asked, sounding legitimately curious. They came to a staircase, and Robbie, leaning heavily on the wrought iron rail, began to crawl up. When Cy spoke next, his voice echoed down the stairwell.

"Well, besides bussing for my Christmas cash, I've got to help some friends move next weekend. Then I've got two recitals with my kids—"

"Do you perform too?" Robbie asked. He fumbled with his keys for a moment before Cy steadied his hand with the key in the lock, and Robbie let him.

"Yeah, I do. There's instructors' numbers, and then the kids go up. I'm on the gym team too, and we do competition routines—we've got special numbers worked up for the holidays. It's going to be a nice show."

He spoke with pride—he loved seeing his students succeed, and *damn* but he loved dancing with his peers. A number of the people who had danced for Anna as children had grown up and become instructors. They could practically read each other's minds on the dance floor, and Cy wouldn't trade those performances for the world.

"I'll come see your show," Robbie said, bursting through the door. Cy caught him under the shoulder and helped him to the couch. Robbie groaned and sat down, and Cy helped him wriggle out of his jacket before helping with his shoes.

"God," Robbie muttered, "I'm fucking useless!"

"Naw, man—you're hurt. Now hang out here, I'll go get you a pillow and the remote. What do you want for lunch?"

"Rubio's, but they don't deliver."

"Out by the galleria? That's not far at all. I'll go get it. Now just chill."

He came back in a few moments with the remote and a pillow and a glass of water—and Robbie's phone charger, since it had run out of juice that morning. Robbie took everything and settled in, tired but composed, on his own couch, but he caught Cy's hand before he could bustle off.

"I mean it," he said softly. "I love watching you dance. I want to see you perform. You're beautiful."

Cy melted a little. "I will go get you Rubio's any time," he murmured, kissing Robbie's forehead. "I'll be back. You sit and watch whatever manly shit you have to have on a Sunday, and I will be back with lunch. I'll give you my performance dates then."

Robbie's smile lit up fountains of gold light inside Cy, and he just couldn't deny them. "That's a deal. Thank you. I can't wait to see you dance."

All in all, not a bad day. Rubio's was one of Cy's favorites. When he got back, Robbie was semidozing in front of *It's a Wonderful Life*, and Cy, like everyone else in America, was a sucker for that one.

After that they watched *Elf* and *Arthur Christmas*, and then Cy laid him down wearing his boxers and the T-shirt Cy had lent him and pulled out a paperback he'd snagged that morning. He'd had time to look around the apartment, and although not *thrilling*, it had some touches here and there, and Cy had spotted a few more thrillers on a little shelf in the living room. He thought maybe with a little more time of Robbie working to find out who he was, there'd be a little more evidence of Robbie's personality in his living space.

"Your place isn't as bad as you said, you know that?" he asked softly.

"It's got everything but a toaster," Robbie said sleepily. "Ashley threw the toaster against the wall."

Cy groaned. "Baby, whether I stay or not, you need to get a better class of friend in here!"

"Not arguing. You're the classiest thing in this place since I moved in, at the very least."

Cy resisted the urge to pat his cheeks. Flattery was a beautiful thing. He read in bed next to Robbie for the next hour or so, reaching out to pat Robbie's well-muscled arm every now and then. When he put the light out, he snuggled up from behind, the big spoon, and Robbie snuggled back.

"This is good," Cy said softly, liking the company. "I haven't done this much."

"Me neither," Robbie mumbled back.

"One-night stands?" Cy asked, thinking that he'd been missing out.

"One relationship," Robbie told him. "In the military. Not a lot of sleeping in."

Oh. "I... I've had a few," he understated. "I got off a cruise ship in August after a three-week relationship—one week on the ship."

Robbie laughed a little, and suddenly Cy felt compelled to honesty. "But like, as soon as I got off the ship, I met a guy—I mean, we were great on the dance floor, you know?"

"Jealous," Robbie mumbled, and Cy clutched him a little tighter.

"Yeah, that's what the guy with him was," he admitted. "I just... I could have made a move, I think. But the guy with him—I mean, they weren't even together, but I could just tell. I could walk away, and it would hurt a little. It was the other guy's entire world. He wanted it more."

"Mm." Robbie's chest moved under Cy's hands. "I'd want you more."

"I'm starting to see that's important." And he was. "I'd want you more too."

Robbie captured Cy's hand against his chest and placed a sleepy kiss against his palm before his breathing evened out completely.

Nice. So very nice. *Way* worse ways of spending the day.

Ankles-Deep

"So I can go back to work?"

Robbie's boss hadn't been mad about him needing time off, but he had been worried because three weeks before Christmas was a nutso time for *anyone* to go missing. This was Tuesday morning, and Robbie was hoping he could get in a little bit of overtime so he could make up for the past two days.

"If you're a good boy," the doctor said, giving his eyes one last check with the flashy light. "No heavy lifting, no serious manual labor. I know you work in a warehouse—"

"Boss okayed me for forklift duty," Robbie said quickly. He'd been certified for a month, but they hadn't had an opening. Matt said he could move one of the drivers down on the floor if it would get one more functioning body back into the warehouse.

"So you're not cleared to lift over twenty pounds, but we're going to let you manipulate a five-ton machine," the doctor said slowly, eyeing Robbie with mock suspicion.

Robbie grinned back and swung his bare legs underneath him. He'd bruised his hip, his stomach, his shoulder, his chest, his wrist—all the things needed to be checked out when he got his eyes checked and concussion assessed. God, he couldn't wait to get back to work! "Yup," he said now. "That's the idea!"

"Sounds good to me!"

They both chuckled, and then the doctor, a stooped, thin man with sagging jowls and a surprising sense of humor, turned sober. "The first hint of dizziness, you pull yourself off duty. Remember, the concussion clock resets ten days after your last symptom. You say your head stopped hurting yesterday, so you've got until *next* Thursday before you can pretend you never smacked your face."

He nodded and then—"Oh, hey! Wait! What about sex! Isn't that exertion too?"

The doctor laughed. "Well, yes. So nothing too acrobatic—slow and sweet if you can manage it, and if your head hurts, call it quits."

Oh. Well, damn. He felt like he'd *wasted* his one day with Cy—he wanted to make it up to him.

The doctor must have sensed his disappointment. "Don't worry. I'm sure the young lady can wait a few days."

"Man," Robbie mumbled, flushing. Very carefully, he studied his bare knee, which was purple and green after the impact with the steering wheel. The coming out was part of his new resolution. Baby steps. People he wouldn't see too often. The nurse. The weasel-faced guy at the insurance place when Cy took him back to get his rental. This guy. He was coming out incrementally, one member of society at a time.

"Oh," the doctor said, hardly surprised. "A young *man*." He checked his notes and frowned. "So, do you know where the lab is?"

Robbie nodded. "Uh-huh. Like, second floor, to the back, right?"

The doctor raised his eyebrows and smiled, all teeth. Then he grabbed a pad and scribbled on it and ripped off the top sheet. "So...."

That flush could *not* be good for his healing brain, he just *knew* it. "So, uh, you would like me to go get tested?"

The doctor nodded. "I don't see any tests on your records here, and, you know...."

"A tested boy is a safe boy," Robbie said, losing to embarrassment and talking to his knees again. He'd been planning on it anyway, but hey! Nothing like your doctor's gentle but firm direction.

"You *are* recovering from your concussion! I knew it!"

The guy gave another toothy grin, and Robbie chuckled. He had a sudden thought, an intense wish that cramped his stomach, and he slid off the paper-covered examination table so he could change.

"So, anything else hurting you?" the doctor asked, and Robbie shook his head, turning around so he could gather his clothes.

"No, sir. Thank you—I'm glad to go back."

He heard the sigh behind him. "Son?"

Robbie cast a quick glance over his shoulder and turned away from the man's sympathetic look. Making unnecessary noise, he started to scramble into his pants.

And the doctor didn't move. "I thought we were getting along so well," he said, his voice jovial but gentle.

Robbie nodded. "You're great for a nice doctor man I met on Sunday." Because he'd lucked out and gotten the same guy Tuesday morning that he'd had Saturday night. He'd asked—Dr. Llewellyn had been covering for a friend that night. Robbie had more blessings than he deserved.

"But...."

"My dad's not so great and doesn't know it's a boy," he said in a rush. "I'm sorry. Not your prob—"

"Give him a chance," the doctor said softly. "Not all dads get the whole coming out thing right, especially not out of the gate. Parents, they want the world for their kids, so they assume that all the stuff *they* want is the stuff *you* want."

Robbie swallowed and fumbled with his belt. "It's just... it's... I know how he feels about gay people and...." And black people. And brown people. And any people not white, Christian, and American.

"Yeah, but you don't know how he'll feel about them when he finds out *you're* one."

Oh God. Robbie took a deep breath and pulled on his T-shirt and sweater as one entity, then he turned around.

"Doc, I appreciate what you're trying to say. But I'm not going to bank on... on my dad being a good guy about this. I'm just going to keep practicing coming out with the rest of the world until I can remember my parents are only two people and as long as I stay out of, like, eighty other countries in the world, I'll be fine."

"Well, we can't do anything about them. I mean, we *can*, but it's not like waving a magic wand." The doctor's dry humor was like a superpower.

Robbie found himself smiling. "It would help if we stopped sending our lunatics overseas to spread the hatred, but yeah, I see what you're talking about. My little corner of the world is not as bad as it could be."

"No, sir. No, it's not. So you keep practicing and getting brave. But remember, however he reacts, you have the means to make your life okay." He looked meaningfully at the health fliers on the walls, including one box that was covered in rainbow stickers for a local LGBT community center.

Oh. Without prompting, Robbie thought of Ezra and Darrin and the people at Candy Heaven, and the dancers at Gatsby's Nick. "I've got places," he said, almost surprised. "But thank you. You have a really good point."

"Well, I *am* a highly underpaid health care professional in a city hospital," Dr. Llewellyn said wisely, and Robbie laughed again.

"I forget—do you get sainthood for that, or do you just get to wear the pope hat for a little while?"

"I get a *hat*?"

Robbie had to laugh. "Yeah, sure. Next time I come in—"

"Stop by the front desk and get an appointment for a regular physical next year. Fifty-dollar co-pay and I'll check your prostate for free!" He nodded as though unhinged, and Robbie agreed.

"Fine. If I'm going to be a grown-up with regular checkups and blood tests, then I guess I can start now."

Dr. Llewellyn extended his hand. "Very good, young sir." His grip tightened. "Adulthood can be uncomfortable," he said meaningfully, "but necessary."

Robbie nodded and squeezed back. "I hear you. Thanks."

He made an appointment for his yearly on the way out and then followed his own directions to the lab. Adulthood—perhaps a bit delayed, but he was on it.

ON THURSDAY he called into the medical office on his lunch hour and got his test results, and even though he'd been careful with condoms, the negative results (and the reminder that he had a three-month window for another test) still gave his confidence a little boost. He asked Micah his opinion on plants, and after work they drove to the nearest hardware store and he bought a mini Christmas tree and an icicle plant as well.

"These are cool," Micah said, nodding. "You feel like you're doing something, but seriously, hardly have to water them at all."

"So… anything else that won't make me feel like a loser in my own apartment?"

Micah thought about it. "Do you have a mat in your kitchen? And area rugs? My mom bought them for me when I moved out—I'm telling you, it made me feel like a total grown-up." He grimaced and rubbed his buzz-cut hair. "Well, that could be because I'm a loser, but still."

Robbie liked him—it was impossible to stop. Yeah, he was a good-looking kid, and Robbie could have crushed, but mostly he just liked his gentle sense of humor and the way he and his family stuck together without shame.

"Well, you're younger than me," he said with a wink, "so I'm probably the bigger loser."

"Yeah, but you served." Micah nodded soberly as they pushed the cart with Robbie's plants toward the department with rugs and welcome mats.

"You want to know why I served?" Robbie asked, because God, it would be great if someone besides Adam knew this truth, and he wasn't ready to fuck up his relationship with Cy yet.

"Because you wanted money for school? Because I was totally going to do it for just that reason, but my mom...." He grimaced. "She sort of, you know."

"Wanted you here at home," Robbie filled in. "No shame in that. See, my parents wanted me to join the service, and I figured if I die, *great*. Nobody knows I'm gay."

Micah stopped right in the middle of the aisle, and Robbie thought, *Oh well. It was nice to imagine friends of my own.*

"Dude," Micah said, trotting down the aisle to catch up. "You gotta *warn* a guy before you spring something like that on him! I mean, it's not like I give a shit, but we're three bro-dates shy of the mandatory sexuality conference!"

Robbie couldn't help it. He burst out laughing. "You mean there's a *protocol* for coming out to friends? Dammit, nobody tells you *jack* when you get out of the Army!"

Micah held up a fist to bump, and Robbie went for it. They followed with the intricate male slapping ritual that really depended on who led. Micah led. It was all good.

"So, rainbow row?" Micah asked, clarifying.

"Yeah," Robbie said. "Folks don't know."

"That's gotta *blow*." Micah nodded.

"Won't it, *though*?" God. Adam should have warned him about this. About talking to a perfectly normal person who liked you and didn't care who you slept with. It *rocked*.

"I can't rhyme no *mo'*," Micah announced and then jumped on his toes. "Wait! Wait! No, I got one! And it's real, 'cause remember? You introduced her once? I saw you dating a *ho*!"

Robbie groaned. "Oh God! You remember her?"

"Oh yeah!" Micah nodded and rubbed his buzz cut again, his wide gray eyes earnest as fuck. "She was *cray-cray*. Oh my God! That girl was like… I mean, like *Psychos 'R' Us*! You introduced her and Teddy told me he was going to have dreams where she was chasing him with an ice pick, and then *I* had them!"

"Oh Lord. Well, I wish you two would have told *me*, because I was *not* prepared for the breakup."

"Bad news," Micah asked, nodding for details.

"She broke my toaster. It's the next thing on the list."

"Oh *dude*. That's *heinous*! Oh my God. Tell me it's easier to break up with a guy, because crazy women, man—they scare me."

Robbie grimaced. "I wouldn't know," he said softly. "I'm taking, like, baby steps, right? So, first I break up with Ashley, then I go meet a guy I like, then I try to make things right with…." Oh hell. "With a guy I sort of fucked over. My ex, but, you know, I blew it."

"Cheating?" Micah asked, like he was being totally nonjudgmental.

"I wish," Robbie said grimly. "I… he came out because our CO was being an asshat, and he looked to me for backup and…." Yeah. This was the real test. "I called him a faggot." His voice dropped so low he was surprised Micah could hear him.

"Aw, man." Micah clapped him on the back. "That's rough."

"Rougher for him," Robbie said, trying to get him to understand how bad the thing he'd done was.

"Yeah, but… I mean, it's like… like my mom figured this out. My little brother and I used to beat the holy hell out of each other 'cause… boys, right?"

"Sure." Robbie hadn't had a brother, but he could imagine. Military wasn't much different—too much energy, too little to do.

"So, like, three times, one of us would be at school, and the teachers would see bruises or, like, I couldn't use my wrist because it was broken, or once I broke Teddy's nose when we were walking to school. And like, CPS came to our house, man."

"Dude!" Robbie looked at him, aghast. "Seriously?"

"Right? And that was no good, 'cause you've met my dad."

"Nicest. Person. On the planet." Robbie nodded sincerely. He'd believed that *before*, but now, after talking to Micah, he thought it was probably an understatement.

"Right? And my mom, she's good too. And so CPS shows up, and me and Teddy just start babbling about how we were playing bloody knuckles or uncle or whatever, and CPS glares at us until we shut up, and then glares at my mom. 'Ms. Harris, you need to control your boys!' And then she leaves, and Mom is like, 'You *idiots*. If you'd just *told* me you hurt yourselves, I could have *explained* it and told your teachers myself!'"

"But you didn't," Robbie said, seeing where this was going.

"Yeah. Being afraid of what's going to happen—it makes you do horrible things, you know?"

"Yeah."

Micah patted his shoulder again. "Hard lesson, man. Relationships, that shit's *rough*. Someday I'll get drunk and tell you about my ex-girlfriend." His voice dropped. "And her kid. I was there when he was born, but she went back to his dad."

Aw, man. Robbie patted his back. "Tomorrow night?" he said. "Bar or my house?"

Micah brightened. "That depends on what carpets you get. If they're fuckin' ugly, it's gonna be the bar."

"I'll pick real good," Robbie said. He had a friend—not a gay friend, but a gay-*friendly* friend. "Last time I was in a bar to drink, I came home with the girl who broke my toaster. I had to live without toast for weeks."

Micah's laugh came from his belly. "Man, you have *got* to tell me how that conversation went!"

By the time Robbie was done with the story, he'd picked a runner for his hallway and a matching rug for under his coffee table, as well as a mat to put under the end table next to his bed.

And towels for the kitchen to match the hot pad he hung from the refrigerator.

And a toaster.

"How did you know about all this shit?" he asked Micah as he pulled out his credit card at the cashier.

"My mom. I'm telling you, she's awesome. Didn't your mom want to help you out with this stuff?"

Robbie thought about it. "She… she never offered. I don't know. I guess she just assumed I'd find a girl to do it for me."

Micah grunted. "If I ever assumed a girl was going to do *anything* for me, my mom would skin me, my grandma would cook me, and my aunt and my cousins would *eat me*. It'd be ugly. Dude. The nine-year-old cousin would get in on it. She looks sweet, but she's crafty."

"Man, I *wish* nobody had assumed *jack* about me," Robbie said bitterly, thinking of Cy and Adam. Neither of them had assumed—but that meant they were the people he had the most to lose by hurting, and he'd already fucked that sitch up once.

"I can assume you're a good guy, right?" Micah asked guilelessly.

Robbie was going to say no, because *Adam*, right? But then he realized Micah *knew* about Adam, and he'd hung out through the entire trip to Lowe's.

"You know the worst things about me," Robbie said. "If you can deal with that shit, I'm a hero."

"Right on." Micah grinned, and Robbie felt a yearning for Cy in his stomach.

He wanted to see Cy again. He wanted to tell Cy about himself. He wanted to be a hero.

THAT NIGHT he got home and put away all of his apartment stuff, and the rugs, they really *did* something for the place. When he was done, he broiled himself some pork chops and cooked some green beans, then put the leftovers in the fridge for the next day.

Then he sprawled on the couch, turned the TV on without sound, and called Cy.

"Soldier boy?" Cy said, sounding tentative. He'd left Robbie at the car insurance place with a kiss on the cheek and a promise to be in touch. Robbie hoped that went two ways.

"The one and the same," Robbie said, the comfort of Cy's voice hitting him right in the stomach. "How you doin'?"

"I should ask you the same. I mean, I left you on Monday feeling like I'd abandoned a puppy!"

Robbie laughed, warmed. "Naw, man. I got my car, called in sick to work, drove home, and slept another day. The truck'll be ready next week, by the way, which is great 'cause the rental *sucks*. Anyway, Tuesday, I went in and got the all clear and…." He felt himself get shy.

"Got tested. So I'm negative, but you know, windows and shit, but so you know—"

"Odds are good I can swallow," Cy said dryly.

"Well, didn't think you wanted to get that serious that soon," Robbie told him, feeling humble. "But… thought maybe you'd want to know."

"Yeah." Cy's voice got rough. "I'm actually really sort of proud you'd tell me. I mean, I'm still waiting for *my* window to clear, but maybe in the future—"

"There will *be* a future," Robbie said triumphantly, and Cy's laugh on the other end felt like vindication.

"Yeah, Robbie. Yeah. I mean, I actually *nursed* you to health, sort of. I don't do that shit. I'm… I mean, I'm the least nurturing person I know!"

"Well, I didn't notice any plants in your apartment," he acknowledged.

"Right? And I'd *love* a cat, but God, my life is so crazy right now—bussing, dance, gymnastics. I'd have to have a roommate to have a cat and right now—"

"No time for a, you know, roommate."

"Just sort of a string of… well, like I thought you were going to be," Cy admitted. "And then you turned out to be a *really* great lover and a really decent guy."

Robbie's stomach twisted. "I'm not that decent a guy," he said, feeling like shit.

"Yeah? Where are your bodies buried?" Cy asked playfully, and here they were. This was it. Time for Robbie to confess how bad he could be.

"Candy Heaven," he answered heavily, right when someone on Cy's end started talking.

"I love that place!" Cy said distractedly. "My friends who are moving, they work—*yeah, Anna. Sorry! Off my break now!*"

"Oh God, you're at *work*?" Robbie felt bad.

"Well, we do back-to-back classes. I was out for a cigarette—"

"You smoke?"

"Only when dancing," Cy muttered, like this fact irritated him. "But I gotta go. Look, do you want to get together tomorrow?"

"I got a friend coming over—sounds like he wants to drink."

"So about that test—"

"Not that kind of friend," Robbie reassured him. "Boss's son. Nice guy. Very straight. But he wants a buddy, and after eight months out of the military, I'm ready for a brother, you know?"

"Yeah. Didn't mean to get catty." Cy grunted. "I just... nnngg...." That last sound was pure frustration. "I just sort of *missed* you, that's all!"

"Me too," Robbie told him, being honest. It had worked *swimmingly* this past week, after all.

"Well, then, Saturday? I work again, but Sunday I'm helping friends move."

"Yeah, I got it down in the phone. Saturday night's great, and I can come help move on Sunday."

"Really?" And he sounded *really* grateful. Robbie felt like a hero again.

"Promise," he said staunchly. "I'll be... like, perfect boyfriend... I mean... shit!" Oh God—too soon, too soon, too soon!

"We'll call it boyfriends," Cy said. "I mean, you and me, we both know it might not last, but it makes us sound less like assholes—" The voice on the other end of the line intruded. "I'm *coming*, Anna! Dammit! Okay, see you Saturday night. Don't crash the car!"

Cy hung up, and Robbie thumbed the sound on the television, smiling to himself. Yeah. He'd tell Cy about Adam on Saturday night or Sunday morning. He'd be honest, and straightforward, and make things right. Adam was behind him on this, said it would be okay.

Robbie could do it—he was sure.

TRUE TO his word, Robbie hosted beers and tears at his apartment on Friday night—although he quit after one beer in deference to his head. He was gradually beginning to hate the apartment less. He'd been happy to have Micah, his younger brother, Teddy, and their cousins Truman and Conway come over, and it had been a good time. They talked about sports, commiserated with Micah on his recent breakup, and kicked Teddy's ass in beer pong. Robbie woke up not-quite-hungover, with Micah asleep on his couch and the rest of the guys asleep on his floor, and wondered why it had taken him so long to just go out for a fucking beer.

Because you were afraid.

Oh yeah.

Well. Damn. Turned out that being afraid hadn't just cost him Adam and his self-respect in those last months in the military.

It had cost him friends—or even the opportunity for them—since he'd gotten out too.

Beer pong—he hadn't played since his first leave after boot camp. Dumbest fucking game on the planet, but freaking hilarious if you were playing with the right guys.

Even if *these* hadn't been the right guys—and they were. Truman was a frickin' *pro* at getting the damned ball in the cup and ruthless about making his opponent drink. Teddy was hilarious drunk, and how was anybody supposed to stay sober when playing with a pro like that? But even if these guys hadn't been awesome, Robbie would never have known that, would never have known to keep looking, if he hadn't tried to have friends.

They could have been awful to you.

Yeah. And that would have hurt.

With a little bit of an epiphany, Robbie realized that he was going to have to come out every day of his life, and for a moment, that *terrified* him. Congealed his stomach and stopped his lungs. *Every* day? *Every* new relationship? *Every* time he talked to someone?

Then he remembered something Micah and Teddy had been saying the night before.

"Yeah—my Aunt Stacy—she's like, scary liberal. Like, ObamaCare bumper stickers, feminist diatribes and shit on her car. Like, scary *fuckin' liberal."* Micah shook his head, half in admiration, half in disbelief.

"Here?" Robbie asked, aghast. *"Like—people don't throw shit at her car?"*

"Oh yeah!" Conway nodded. *They weren't real cousins—the family connection was too odd and tenuous for Robbie to follow, but it was easy to take their word for it. Conway and Truman were dark haired and dark eyed, while Micah and Teddy had light gray eyes and the kind of hair that had been blond when they'd been kids but was pretty dark now. Related or not, they all knew the same people, right down to Aunt Stacy.* "She's had people scream at her on the street, nasty notes left on her car—it's freaky."*

Teddy laughed. "Didn't stop her and her kids from flipping off the people protesting Planned Parenthood."*

"Kids?" Robbie asked, sort of entranced.

"Six," Micah said. "But dude, she's all, 'Just because I wanted a zillion kids doesn't mean anyone else has to get stuck with any more than they want.' She's fucking militant."

"But...." Robbie thought about that, how much he'd just love for his sexuality to be his and nobody else's. "She's gotta advertise? Doesn't she lose friends and shit?"

"Yeah." Teddy nodded. "Grandma and Grandpa give her shit. But you know, she couldn't shut up if she tried. I don't see her hiding that from the world."

"And seriously," Conway said, taking a swig of beer, "if people don't like her for who she is, she's only going to piss them off anyway."

"True that," the rest of the guys agreed—and the next game of beer pong was on.

So Robbie woke up with stories of someone else's aunt Stacy ringing through his head and the realization that yes, he was going to have to come out *every* day of his life.

And no. It wasn't fair.

Not even a little.

But that if people didn't like him for something he couldn't change about himself—didn't *want* to change about himself—then he couldn't fix that.

It wasn't his job to try.

He spent the morning cleaning up the apartment after his new friends left, and the afternoon Christmas shopping.

He didn't buy much: a sweater for his mom, a new flannel shirt for his dad, some scotch—*good* scotch—for his boss, since he knew Micah and Teddy would probably get them some of that. He found a felted Christmas tree that he hung up near his kitchen, and some light stuffed cotton ornaments to go with it—it felt more like the holidays already.

And then, feeling foolish because they'd known each other for barely two weeks, a brilliant scarf in sapphire, emerald, and magenta for Cy. Maybe it would get hung in his apartment, or maybe he'd drape it around his neck. From what Robbie had seen, he didn't get hung up on what boys wore or what girls wore, he just liked his colors deep and bright and eye-catching.

Robbie was content to buy it and wrap it and put it under the little plant on his counter and hope. Since Cy seemed to like Robbie just the way *he* was, he figured hope couldn't hurt, right?

Right?

Focal Points

Cy HAD apparently gotten off early and was working the crowd when Robbie got there. As he checked his coat, Robbie watched him shamelessly using every body on the floor as a chance to showcase his moves.

And his moves were so pretty.

Sinuous, powerful, sexy—God, the guy was a full-tilt diva, and Robbie would worship at his feet.

He was wearing black jeans and a full-sleeved blouse in shimmering emerald green, and Robbie pictured that scarf around his shoulders.

Maybe he'd get to see it. Maybe, if he didn't fuck this up.

As Cy saw him walk in, he danced his way out to the edge of the dance floor and did the one-finger thing to get Robbie's attention. Showy? Yes. But Robbie bought it and danced right to where Cy swayed, running his own hands up along his chest, under his hair, and allowing it to cascade out and down. He was just stunning and so full of himself Robbie would do anything to be full of him too.

They didn't kiss this time, maybe because they both knew that would cut the dancing short, but Robbie put his hand out and allowed himself to be tugged onto the floor and immersed in the music, in Cy's sweating, muscular body, in the beat that abducted their autonomy and forced them to move in time to driving audio-percussive sex.

Cy pranced and whirled, every move he made a throwback to something classical, something precise and effortless, made dirty and alluring, and Robbie pulled out every move he knew in an effort to get his hands on that amazing body and move with it.

When he pulled Cy back against him, their hips moving suggestively, he thought he could close his eyes and simply lock himself into that rhythm, caught in the foreplay of dance, for hours, days—*weeks* at a time.

And then Cy leaned his head back on Robbie's shoulder and ground back against him.

"Soldier boy," he moaned over the sound of the music.

"Yeah?"

"Man, take me home and fuck me."

Something in Robbie released, and he was both looser and needier than he had been until just that moment.

He nuzzled Cy's ear. "You want it?"

"Please?"

"Really? From me?"

"No one else," Cy whispered.

"I'm dying to fuck you."

Cy pulled away and grabbed his hand, and they got Robbie's coat and slid into the night. No playful laughing or skipping to their destination like children—not this time.

This time they had a purely adult intention in mind, and Robbie, at least, was not playing the fuck around.

They strode through the light drizzle with purpose, and when they got to the top of the stairs and Cy let them in to the apartment, Robbie waited until he'd turned around and locked the door before he fell upon Cy like a wolf on a kitten.

He needed the taste of Cy's mouth on his the way he needed to breathe, or needed his heart to pump blood.

Cy devoured him, both of them frantic in an effort to taste *everything*, to feel *everything*, to chew boldly and suck the flavor from every brush of skin upon skin.

Robbie ran his lips down the side of Cy's neck, sucking and nibbling, while Cy turned his head and let him.

"You're gonna leave a ma-ark," Cy sang, and Robbie made sure his chuckle echoed in the mystery of Cy's many-bangled ear.

"Do you care?" he asked, darting his tongue out along the whorls and teasing the little studs and their attached charms.

"Mmm... *no*...."

Robbie kept nibbling, kept scraping his teeth along that tender, delicious skin, and Cy struggled desperately with the buttons on his shirt.

"No!" Robbie grabbed his hands when it looked like he was just going to rip the buttons off.

"No?" Cy asked, looking bemused.

Robbie turned him around and bent studiously over the shirt, unbuttoning each of the tiny pearl-shaped emerald buttons. "No," he whispered, stopping to kiss a dark triangle of skin as it came into view. Cy waxed, whether for vanity or necessity as a dancer, Robbie didn't know.

"You don't want me to rip off my shirt?"

"I love this shirt," Robbie whispered, kissing another wedge of skin. Cy shuddered and relaxed against the caress. "It's a beautiful color, and it looks beautiful on *you*."

Another uncovered bit of skin, this last one below Cy's navel, and Robbie took his time and licked the line under the waistband of Cy's jeans.

"You're good for my ego," Cy breathed, tilting his head back in surrender. Robbie undid his belt and then the top button of his jeans. And kept on cruising that skin with his tongue.

"You just like me because I wanna suck your cock," Robbie teased, shucking Cy's pants as he squatted on the solid base of his thighs.

Cy hissed in arousal as the air hit his erection, and then again as Robbie licked him, balls to tip, playing with the foreskin and making sure the bell got plenty of attention.

"I…," Cy breathed as Robbie repeated the maneuver. "I… I will do a *lot* for a man who wants to suck my dick."

"I'll take it all," Robbie whispered, and then *did*, down his throat while rubbing his palms up the outsides of Cy's thighs and kneading his backside too. Cy groaned and pushed up into Robbie's mouth, letting out a little half laugh as Robbie grazed his pucker with a kneading finger.

Oh, he liked that!

Robbie had never cared about topping or bottoming—all things had been good. With Adam especially, each one had been his *very favorite* when he'd been doing it. But with Cy he felt the need to lead—to show Cy that he was worthy.

Cy knotted his fingers in Robbie's hair, and the sting drove Robbie on. Ah, yes, he was making his lover *want*. Robbie pulled Cy's cock farther back against the constriction of his throat and tightened his lips.

Oh! He wanted!

He and Adam—they'd talked about it. They'd been tested, had been waiting until they cleared the service to commit that way.

Robbie wanted to be the man who could do that now, when the time was right.

Cy made another strangled sound of pleasure, and Robbie squeezed him hard and slow from base to tip, teasing his asshole with playful fingers.

"F—*fu*… oh God! If you fuck me, I'll come!" Cy, naked above him, tugged Robbie's hair until it hurt, until Robbie stood up from his crouch at Cy's feet and plunged into a ravenous, starving kiss.

"Like that?" Robbie taunted, so, so proud he could have a man like Cy at his mercy.

"Fuck me," Cy demanded, dragging Robbie to the bed.

Robbie hurried up with the rest of his clothes, pausing only for the strip of condoms he'd shoved in his back pocket. Cy's lube was on the nightstand this time, and yeah, he probably only had it there in anticipation, but what if he'd been stroking himself, thinking about Robbie?

Robbie reached over Cy's head to grab that bottle, a sudden flash of heat washing his skin, pulling it tight over his cock, contracting his sphincter and his balls and *Jesus* almost making him come. So much desire, just from the thought of Cy in his own bed, his hands wrapped around himself.

He retrieved the object, then plastered his body against Cy's back, biting the join of neck and shoulder while rutting up against his backside in an effort to contain the desire that swamped him.

"Biting's kinky," Cy moaned. "Fucking's better."

Robbie bit him again but managed to push himself up to his knees between Cy's spread thighs.

Deftly, with strength honed in the military and bulked from hauling boxes around, he manhandled Cy so he was flat on his back, knees over Robbie's shoulders. That quickly Robbie was sheathed, slickened, and breaching Cy's asshole with missile locked and all systems go.

Cy used one hand to tweak his nipple and the other to squeeze his cock.

"Squeeze it," Robbie commanded, spreading those thick, muscular dancer's thighs and shoving himself inside.

"Yeah," Cy panted, moving his hand sinuously.

Robbie kept pushing, kept pushing until *ah*, bliss! He was seated all the way inside Cy's ass. For a moment he possessed all of him through that one orifice—Robbie held all of his lover, his heartbeat, his joy, his pure physical presence, in the seat of his balls.

He pulled back, just a little, and thrust forward, just the same.

Cy tilted his head back and arched his spine. "Soldier?"

"Yeah?" Robbie moved again.

"It's time to pull the trigger. I'm primed to explode."

Horrible metaphor, but who the fuck cared? Robbie's blood rushed in his ears and his breath labored in his chest. He stroked his cock inside Cy, banging, pounding, every thrust reverberating through Robbie's body, every long, hard squeeze bringing him closer to skyrockets and explosions behind his eyes.

Cy gibbered shamelessly, begging, demanding, *pleading* to be fucked, and more, and harder, and please, and more and harder, and please, and *God, Robbie, fuck me harder*! Until the light behind Robbie's eyes washed bright purple, gilt with gold, and his entire body lit up like his nerve endings were fireworks and he blew, shiny sparks of pleasure pulsing down the base of his spine, through his clenched balls, and out his cock.

Cy cried out as Robbie locked in place, thrusting as far as he could inside Cy's ass without disappearing. As Robbie blinked his eyes open, he saw the whiteness of come spray over Cy's skin, and the picture was so wanton, so pretty, Robbie closed his eyes again and felt a second, slower orgasm roll through him.

When climax had finished squashing him flat, he fell forward, head pounding, vision black.

"You okay?" Cy asked, stroking his sweaty hair from his forehead. "You went pretty gray there at the end."

"Wasn't supposed to be this physical," Robbie mumbled. Oh hell—they still had him on the forklift at work. It was making Matt crazy because they had to pay for two forklift operators when one of them was just a standard hump doing hauling.

Cy gave a fractured laugh. "God, you broke your brain having sex with me? That's... well, freaky, but sort of sweet."

Robbie groaned. "My head hurts," he confessed. Hell. He was going to have to call Dr. Llewellyn, wasn't he? "Pounding.... Jesus."

Cy breathed out and kissed his ear. "Well, did you bring your painkillers?"

"Yeah. In my pocket."

"I'll get them for you, don't worry. After a fuck like that, baby, I will wait on you a little."

"Aw, man." Robbie had wanted to be strong for him. "I was gonna take care of you...."

Cy's chuckle rocked both their bodies. "That's okay," he said softly, kissing Robbie's temple this time. "You took care of me for the big bang, I'll get the rest of it, deal?"

But Robbie's vision was black—he didn't have much more of a choice.

THE ON-CALL doctor made sure there wasn't any nausea or vomiting and told Robbie he was on sit-down duty for the next twenty-four hours.

"Dizziness, ringing in the ears, dark spots in your vision—"

"Got it," Robbie muttered. "No more shaking the brain like an egg in the shell."

"And if you lose consciousness, do not pass go, do not collect friends, and do not call us again—come in. Immediately. Understand?"

Robbie would have nodded from his place flat on his back in Cy's bed, but he was trying really hard to follow orders. "Hear you. Concussions. Don't fuck with them."

God, how embarrassing.

"You broke yourself during sex," Cy said as Robbie hung up the phone.

"I'm sorry," Robbie mumbled.

"Why did you break yourself during sex?"

Robbie closed his eyes, grateful that Cy didn't do air freshener or patchouli or even music in the background. "Because it was *really good* sex, with *you*. I don't know how much more of that I'll get in this lifetime—I wasn't going to turn that shit down!"

Cy laughed throatily. "God. There is just no downside to you, is there?"

Robbie made a hurt sound. "I've done some shitty things in my life," he said.

In response, Cy thrust two tablets into his hand and followed it up with a cup of water with a straw. "Well, haven't we all. Care to share?"

Robbie swallowed his medicine and then drank more water, which was cool and soothing. "Yeah. I was going to have confession time tonight, but then—"

"You broke yourself during sex. I get it. Well, tell you what."

"What?"

"You lie here, I'll turn out the lights, and we'll just have a quiet postcoital cuddle and sleep. Then, tomorrow, we'll go help my friends move and you can come with us—as long as you *don't move*."

"I'll hang out and be useless," Robbie agreed.

"Play with the cat. Ezra's roommates have a great cat and a helluva big fuckin' dog. So you sit on the couch, hang with the furry things, and drink no beer, and when we've welcomed Miguel and Ezra into their new apartment, you and I will go have some dinner and you can tell me all about it."

The name Ezra pinged something, but Robbie's head hurt too much to explore it. "Dinner? Afterward?"

He still had his eyes closed, but Cy dropped a kiss on his lips. "Yeah. You made it three times—"

"Two," Robbie muttered.

"Three. I count the car wreck, moron. And you've made it and been on time, and good company, and…." Cy was leaning close enough that Robbie felt his breath across Robbie's closed eyes. "I'm just *really* liking you. I mean… like, dangerous amounts. I like you in my bed—and even now, when we're not doing the thing, I'm not planning to kick you out. So just calm down about the sex you're afraid is gonna go away, and stay. We'll have sex again at this rate, you know?"

Robbie kept his eyes closed and cupped Cy's cheek. "Just… just don't want to take this for granted," he said, liking the almost kittenish way Cy leaned into his hand. "I… I've learned the hard way—I could fuck this up so easy, and when it's gone, it's gone."

"Mmm…." Cy sprawled across his chest, and Robbie palmed the back of his head until his cheek was pressed along Robbie's shoulder. "I've got to tell you," Cy said when they were situated, "the idea that you don't want to take me for granted? That you think I am all of that? I find that *really* attractive in a lover, do you know what I mean?"

Robbie smiled, knowing the expression was probably wistful, even as it crossed his face. "I do," he said, thinking Adam had felt that way once. "I do. When you're young and stupid, you can lose that shit. I'm older now—I want to learn."

"Amen." Cy was falling asleep even as they lay there, and Robbie's painkillers were kicking in.

"If I asked you to turn off the light…?" Robbie begged.

"I'm on it." There was a shift in the bed, and Cy came back in the deeper, stiller darkness. "Night, Robbie. I'm not glad you broke yourself, but damn. I'm so glad you came back to me again."

"Ditto," Robbie murmured. God. Just some stillness, some quiet, and he could figure out why tomorrow filled him with so much dread.

THE NEXT day Cy drove Robbie's rental down J Street and then across 11th to F, and turned on a row of Victorians that had been converted into multiapartment houses. The area wasn't swank, but it wasn't a slum either. Robbie saw a number of cars and a small moving van parked in front of one of the Victorians, as well as two guys moving a bed frame down the walking ramp of the U-Haul.

"Oh!" Cy said excitedly as he parked across the street. "Miguel's already here with his stuff! His mom usually cooks them breakfast on Sunday mornings, but I'm guessing they were in the mood to start early."

Robbie took his hand and was led across the street, his head still pounding as everybody greeted Cy with warmth and excitement.

And then he realized that the people greeting him all looked familiar.

The two guys hauling a couch across the lawn and awkwardly up the stairs, one tall and one short, both of them with golden brown skin and brown hair and eyes—oh Lord, that was Ravi and Anish, who had been unlocking the liquor store under Cy's apartment.

And who had been in Candy Heaven when Robbie helped Finn.

And the pretty boy with the dark curly hair who was running down the stairs was… oh crap. Ezra, who had held Robbie's hand and told him it was going to be okay.

God. Ezra—Finn and Adam's roommate.

Robbie remembered Adam waving his finger like a magic wand and saying they were the same age, they were in the same city, and the world wasn't that big of a place, but Robbie hadn't expected…. God, he should have expected… why hadn't he expected the people who should hate him most to know the guy he wanted to hate him the least?

Oh motherfucking *hell*.

"Cy!" Ezra said, going for a quick, unself-conscious hug. The kid moved like he didn't know people were going to want to be all over him, and Robbie wondered how irritating *that* would be to his boyfriend.

"Ezra!" Cy said back, voice warm and a little wistful. God. Ezra was Cy's crush—Robbie could hear it in his voice. Great. Ezra was Cy's crush, Adam was Robbie's ex, and Robbie wanted to fucking *die*. "Ezra, hey, I brought a friend. He was going to help us move, but then he almost broke his brain last week, and then made it *worse* during sex, so, you know, mostly he's just going to keep the furry things company."

Ezra nodded earnestly. "Someone in Adam and Finn's room to chill Clopper out until Rico gets here? That would be *stellar*! Thanks a lot—" And that was when Ezra looked at him. "Robbie?" he chirped, and Robbie grimaced.

"Heya, Ezra," he said, keeping his voice low-key. Just don't make a big thing, nobody will get embarrassed. He could do this. Confession time later—he and Cy had a date.

"You and Cy?" Ezra said, wagging his fingers between the two of them like he was making sure.

"Yeah," Robbie confirmed. "Uh, recent, you know? But...." He blushed. Flat-out, like a girl, hot face and all. "It's a good thing," he said, voice weak.

Ezra's confusion dimmed and that open, compassionate look Robbie had gotten used to took its place. "And you were clearing shit up, weren't you? So you could let it happen?"

Robbie shrugged, feeling stupid and miserable. "Not enough for this," he said softly.

Ezra nodded and then smiled at Cy, who looked a little confused. "Okay, so Cy, Miguel and his brother are going to break everything they own if someone doesn't tell them how to lift shit. They need you at the moving van, my friend, and that's all there is to it."

Cy looked at Robbie with worry, his brow furrowing. "You'll be okay, right?"

"Yeah. Ezra will take me to the dog and cat room, and I'll chill with the rest of the animals." His head throbbed again, and Robbie was pissed at himself for starting the whole concussion clock moving one more time. But he was also grateful for the chance to crawl into a bedroom and be forgotten. He liked cats, right? The *cat* at least shouldn't hate him.

"Wow," Ezra said as Cy skipped off. Cy had put his hair in a ponytail and worn a gray hooded sweatshirt and baggy jeans today, but nothing could hide the sinuous movements, the swagger, the simple joy to be freely moving that was Cyril.

"Yeah," Robbie said wistfully, watching him. Robbie was already tired, and some of that was the concussion, but some of it was the sudden stress. "This is uhm...."

"Awkward," Ezra agreed, nodding. "Sayin'. Well, here. Adam and Finn are out getting doughnuts for all the helpers—and it's like we got more helpers than furniture, you know? But follow me and I'll stash you in their apartment while the rest of us ruin the fucking house."

"Yeah, uh—" They both winced at the crash, the rapid patter of Punjabi, and the frantic barking from inside what sounded like the apartment in the middle on the left.

"Anish and Ravi have dropped *everything* they tried to carry," Ezra said frankly. "I think Miguel gave them the couch because he wasn't sure if they could actually do anything to it that his mom's place hasn't already done."

"His mom gave you a couch?" Robbie asked, feeling stupid. Parents did that?

"Well, Miguel's sister and her husband and their four kids were moving in, so Miguel and his brothers all got to move out—she figured the couch from the family room got to go with us." Ezra shrugged. "I don't know *why* with us, because Jaime and Berto, they still had to buy all of *their* furniture, and we got the queen-size bed and a new mattress and a couch and the microwave and...."

The list of things went on as Robbie followed Ezra up the staircase and around familiar people holding various boxes and domestic items. Everybody nodded at Ezra and gave an even smaller nod to Robbie, while behind them, Robbie could hear Cy yelling.

"Dammit, Mik, you're gonna fuckin' throw your fuckin' back out if you don't listen to me. I lift big women for a living, now fuckin' listen!"

Ezra grimaced even as he opened the door to the apartment where some of the people and all of the dog noise was coming from. "Yeah, Miguel's not going to listen," he said on a long-suffering note. "He's still sure Cy wants to get in my pants, even though he thinks that about *everybody*, but Cy in particular."

Robbie barely kept a smirk off his face, because Cy had told him that. He'd also told Robbie that he'd known enough to back off when Miguel had staked a claim. It was cute, the way Ezra had no idea. But probably not so cute to Miguel, who was apparently beating guys away from Ezra with a baseball bat.

"So, Miguel's mom gave you all sorts of shit," Robbie said, pulling his brain back on track. "Because why?"

"Because Ezra's her favorite." A handsome—*more* than handsome— man with dark hair, dark eyes, and gold-brown skin was tromping up the stairs, apparently following Robbie and Ezra inside. Robbie hurried after Ezra and turned around just in time for the newcomer to close the door with a little bit of forcefulness.

"You're supposed to be moving the furniture," Ezra said, but he had a smile on his face like he didn't mind the fact that this guy wasn't doing as he was told.

"Cy wanted to be in charge." The guy—obviously Miguel—moved past Robbie like he didn't exist, put his hand on Ezra's waist, and kissed him sweetly on the lips. "I decided to let him. This is the guy?"

"Which guy?" Ezra blinked at him and smiled complacently. "Lotta guys here, Miguel. You gotta—"

Miguel gave him a flat-eyed gaze that didn't seem to bother him at all. "*Cy's* guy! The one who he's seen two weekends in a row. Ravi and Anish can't shut up about it. They seem to think the sky's gonna explode."

Ezra's playfulness faded, and he sent Robbie a level look. "This here, he's a lot of guys. He's Cy's two-weekend guy, he's the guy who helped Finn when he got hit by the car—"

"*That* guy?" Miguel stared at Robbie like this was inconceivable, and then he seemed to pick up on what Ezra had been about to say. "*And....*"

"And he's the guy that me and Darrin dreamed about," Ezra said, big blue eyes searching Miguel's brown ones like he was waiting for ridicule or disbelief or something.

What he got was dismay. "But no...."

Ezra nodded. "But yes."

"Does Adam know?"

"We talked," Robbie said, hating that they were doing all the communicating without him. "Me and Adam. We're okay. I... he and Finn

are good. I didn't mean to be here, I was just gonna help you guys move
'cause you were Cy's friends, but I hurt my head, so—"

Miguel held his hand up and waited for Robbie to stop. "You need
to go lie down. You're gray."

"Awesome." His head had started to pound again, and he fumbled
in his pocket for his pain pills. "If I could get some water—?"

Ezra stepped forward and took his elbow. "Miguel?"

"Yeah. He'd better not hurt Adam."

"Adam's not the fragile one," Ezra told him, sounding distant,
and both Miguel and Robbie let out little *pffts*, even as Ezra conducted
Robbie down the hall and into the back bedroom, where all the barking
was coming from.

The dog—and holy wow, Cy wasn't kidding about him being a
big fucking dog—was a gray cross between a bull mastiff, a boxer, and
some sort of giant farm animal. Ezra said, "Clopper!" warningly, and the
barking—blessedly—stopped.

Ezra petted the giant horse-dog while Robbie looked around
Adam's bedroom.

Which was… charming.

Not bright and bold but more… well, ink drawings and watercolors,
which were actually what covered the walls. Lots of greens and blues
and yellows, whimsical colors, the occasional complex line with simple
blocks.

Robbie liked those paintings very much. It was this combination of
sensitivity and strength that had always appealed to him.

Ezra let go of Clopper, who curled up at the foot of the bed like all
the barking had been loneliness and nothing else, and helped Robbie sit
down on a sunshine yellow comforter as a revelation penetrated Robbie's
thick, aching skull.

"Adam did these," he said softly.

"Yeah," Ezra said. "He's still in school—wants a degree in art and
advertising, I think, but yeah. He sells paintings in one of the galleries in
Old Town—paints and draws at the kitchen table when his brain is about
to explode from schoolwork. It's impressive."

Robbie swallowed. "He always has been."

"Yeah. Adam's a… a focal point in the universe, you know? Sort of
pulls people along in his wake—doesn't even try. But it's reassuring that
the world has people like that."

Robbie didn't even question what he was saying. Darrin was weird, but *Ezra*—well, he was weird too, but he seemed to speak clairvoyantly in a language Robbie could understand.

"Why reassuring?" he asked, acutely aware that he was in his ex-boyfriend's bedroom. Finn and Adam—they'd made love here.

There *was* love here.

"It's like… like old stories? The ones that get done in movies again and again? Batman movies, or superhero movies, or Queen Elizabeth movies. It's like people pick stories that mean something special about being *people*—and then want to find out why that is. Adam's one of those people—and it's reassuring because he's just a guy, in a way. But that doesn't mean he can't be sort of awesome too. So our heroes, they can be just guys, and it's all good."

Robbie nodded. He agreed, but God, he had nothing to say. Instead, he reached over to a *ginormous* orange cat lying stomach-up in the one sun spot on the covers. Carefully—'cause you never knew with cats—he scratched the animal's stomach and was rewarded by a luxurious, toe-curling stretch, and then the cat hugged Robbie's hand tight, licking his arm. Robbie laughed a little and picked the thing up, relieved when it just sort of sagged against him, purring.

"That's my buddy Jake," Ezra said fondly, leaning over to scratch the cat behind the ears. Jake closed his eyes and motorboated drool. "He's going to keep you company. In fact…." Ezra pushed gently on Robbie, who lay down on his side, cat in his arms. "He's gonna be your nap buddy." Ezra pulled at the stupid dance loafers and set them down next to the bed.

"You and Cy tore up the floor last night," Ezra said fondly, ruffling Robbie's hair.

"How'd you know?" Robbie asked, so relieved to be in this quiet, peaceful spot with his pounding head and his aching fears that he could almost cry.

"'Cause Cy loves to dance, and those are dancing shoes. You like to dance too. You can keep up with him. That'll be pretty cool."

Ezra smiled again, so sweetly, so at peace, that Robbie felt some of his fear lighten up. Someone would forgive him. He had Micah and his family. He had Ezra and Darrin. Robbie might not end up with a guy to *love*, but he wasn't going to end up alone.

He didn't hardly hear Ezra as he slipped out.

HE WOKE up to Clopper's barking and an apologetic kid stumbling over his own bedroom.

"I'm sorry! I'm sorry! I didn't mean to—crap! They told me you were in here sleeping, and I just wanted to hang up my jacket and—dammit, Clopper! Could you calm down!"

Robbie grimaced and looked at the clock on the corner end table.

"I slept an hour and a half?" he mumbled. "God, I'm sorry. Finn, I didn't mean to just crash on your bed. That's rude."

"Naw—no. Clopper, sit *down!*"

Robbie laughed and stuck out his hand for Clopper to lick. "He's okay. He's good, in fact. I gotta say, I never pictured Adam with a dog."

He didn't even realize what he said until he sat up and saw Finn staring at him.

"Wait—you're the guy who helped me across the street, right?"

Oh God. "Yeah," Robbie sighed. "You're doing okay?"

Finn shrugged and waved his wrist, which was still wrapped, and then stood on one foot and waved his ankle and knee, which were braced. "Yeah—I'm alive and mending, but... but how do you know *Adam?*"

Adam, please get in here before he rips my face off.

"We, uh, knew each other from the service," Robbie said, and watched Finn's eyes go wide.

"Robbie?"

"Yeah."

"*Robbie?*"

"Yup."

"*That* Robbie?"

Robbie closed his eyes. "I'm so sorry," he said, just as Finn swung his braced leg around and thumped out into the hallway, screaming, "*Adam!*"

The Line

CY ENJOYED bossing people around, so he enjoyed the hell out of helping Miguel and Ezra move. *They* obviously had no idea where their shit was supposed to go, and Cy? He was all for fixing that situation.

The apartment itself was *awesome*. Lots of floor space, with sloped ceilings. They'd painted the rooms different brightly tinted colors and then painted the trim off-white. The result was like a candy barrel, and given that their furniture was eclectic by necessity and Ezra seemed to gravitate toward teal/magenta/sky blue/orange, Cy couldn't think of a better place for them to start out.

He directed Ravi, Anish, Ezra, and Miguel with the big stuff and let the girls—Darby, Katya, Joni, and Mari—do the smaller objects, and yes, it was sexist as fuck, and no, he didn't give a shit.

The girls had common sense and the boys did not, and he thought maybe wearing themselves out with big objects would keep them from doing stupid stuff like sticking the television toward the west-facing window, which would ensure that nobody in the apartment *ever* would get to watch a television show near sunset for as long as they lived there.

So they had *just about* gotten everything in place, and everybody was standing around looking for that one last box or that one last lamp to put in the appropriate spot, when Finn's voice, raised shrilly, drifted up from the apartment Ezra had just vacated and penetrated the floor, the walls, and the stairwell of the apartment where he now lived.

"I don't *care* if you're fine with it now! Does *he* have any idea what he did? *Does he?*"

Ezra grimaced. "Shit. I'm resident peacekeeper, that's my cue!" and while Finn continued to yell, the tears in his voice evident through walls and furniture and bodies, Ezra turned around and bolted.

Cy followed, practically hip-checking Finn's sister Mari out of the way. Dammit, he'd brought Robbie here as a friend—in a safe place—and a guy Cy had always thought of as an overgrown puppy was now making *very* overwrought noises over Cy's hurt and gallant suitor. Until Cy realized Robbie was under attack, it hadn't occurred to him that for all his capability and stoicism, Robbie might need to be protected.

When Ezra and Cy burst into the back bedroom of the apartment, Adam was holding Clopper and trying *hard* to keep Finn from imploding.

"*How could you not tell me!*"

Adam and Robbie both cringed like this was aimed at both of them, but Adam answered. "Because," he said while Clopper barked like mad.

"That's an answer?" Finn demanded, and Adam growled, then looked up at all the new people in the apartment.

"Ezra, could you take Clopper upstairs or outside or somewhere besides here?"

Ezra turned, looking for Miguel, Cy was sure, and then frowned, realizing he'd gone to return the truck. "God*dammit*," he murmured. "I told Darrin I'd take care of this." But he grabbed Clopper's collar and left, snagging the lead hanging off the door as he went.

"Finn?" Mari said, one hand on her hip. She and Finn looked a lot alike—same curly hair in almost the same color, same little heart-shaped face and wide, full mouth—but Mari gave the impression of being just a little more grounded. "Why are you throwing a tantrum so bad that we had to remove the dog?"

Finn glared at her and held up a picture, charcoal drawn roughly on tattered art book paper.

Cy took one look at the picture and gasped.

A figure—blurry and dark, but the outline of fatigues could be seen crystal clear—huddled nearly fetal in the center of the page. He was surrounded by other silhouettes in uniform, yelling, screaming, mocking, making that central figure small. Across the page, in sharpie, someone had scrawled *San Francisco* in big black letters, and the back was littered with a list of some sort—but that's not what bothered Cy.

What bothered him was the way the things in the picture seemed to make Adam and Robbie both look small, and young, and sad in real life.

"Finn," Adam said, voice strained, "I love you, baby, but I would have paid a lot of money not to have anyone but you see that."

Finn gave a strangled cry like he'd just realized what he'd done. "*He* did that to you," he said, voice breaking. "He did that to you, and then he just strolled back into your life like it wasn't a thing—"

"Because it wasn't," Adam said, standing up on obviously shaking legs from where he'd been crouching with the dog. "It wasn't a big thing, because I'd let him go. Because of *you*. And because... because you were hurt, and he carried you across the street and to safety, and... I would have lived that again, I would have done it for *years*, just to have you be okay."

Adam paused to take a shuddering breath in the excruciating silence. Cy could hear his own breathing, and Robbie's breathing, and Finn's strangled sobs, and God help them all, Adam's suppressed crying.

"I'm sorry," Finn whispered, not looking at anybody. "I'm sorry, Adam. This is beyond private, and—"

"I'll leave," Robbie said, but Finn glared at him.

"No. No—stay right there." He glanced around the room beseechingly, and everybody *else* left, including his sister. But Cy stayed. Because Robbie was his—he'd brought him here. He'd started to care for the guy. It was his job to know what he'd done.

Mari was the last to leave, and she shut the door quietly behind her.

"I'm sorry," Robbie said, looking pale and in pain and embarrassed. "I... I made things... well, as right as they could be with Adam, Finn." He looked ruefully around the room, and his eyes made contact with Cy's, and for a moment, they stuck.

Cy saw a sort of earnestness, a sincere remorse, that made him want to reach out and grab the guy's hand—but they'd been dating, what? Two weeks? And Cy didn't even know what he'd done.

"Well, you need to make it right with me," Finn said, voice broken. Adam reached out a hand, and Finn shook his head and waved him away. "I can't do this if we're touching." Finn gave a broken smile. "Touch me when we're done."

"Any time." Adam's voice was low and raspy, and Cy's heart hurt for both of them.

"So?" Finn said, wiping his eyes with the back of his hand.

"What do you want me to say?" Robbie asked bitterly. "I... I fucked up. We'd made all those plans, and then Adam outed himself in front of the entire unit and...." Robbie closed his eyes. "I abandoned him. I let them... *do* that. I ran away like a fucking coward and pretended I wasn't—"

"Shut up," Adam said, voice thick. "Finn, there is shit you don't know, okay? About what he did to protect me once it all went down. About how he had my back."

"Yeah." Robbie sneered at himself. "I had your back so good I let that shit go down—don't try to soften it, Adam. I'm the fucking bad guy."

Adam shook his head. "But that's the thing," he said. "You weren't *bad*, you were *afraid*. And you're not that guy anymore. Or you're trying hard not to be. I... have to work every day to be the guy Finn thinks I can be, you know?"

"It's not that hard for you," Finn said, giving a broken laugh. "But for him—"

"But we can't judge him on who he was then," Adam told him. "Because I'm with you now, and you're... you're the thing that gets me up in the morning." Adam's wrecked smile hurt Cy's chest. "You're... you're my angel. You're my bright and shiny, and nothing can make you dirty for me. Don't you see? Robbie could have *shot* me and I still would have forgiven him, because when you needed someone, he was there."

"Oh Jesus." Finn's chest heaved like he was gulping air. "Adam...."

And Adam took the two steps in and wrapped him in his arms. For a moment all they could hear were Finn's noisy hiccupping sobs, and then Adam looked over his head, straight at Robbie and Cy.

It was only then that Cy realized he'd gravitated close enough to grab Robbie's hand. Long and bony and cold from sweat, Robbie's fingers clenched around his, and Cy found himself clenching back.

"You're both welcome here," Adam said, sending Finn into a fresh wave of sobbing. "As far as I'm concerned, you and me are square, Robbie. Cy, you're here to be a friend to our friends. I'm good with that. Maybe not *today*—" Finn's broken laugh echoed against his chest. "—but *some*day, we can try this again, without the drama."

Robbie nodded. "One thing," he said quietly, voice rasping. He broke away from Cy and bent gently, grabbing the picture—that terrible, painful indictment of past wrongs—from Finn's unresisting fingers. "This shouldn't have to be yours," he said, wiping his eyes on his shoulder. "This should never have been yours."

He wiped again and turned toward the door, and Adam whispered urgently to Finn before he broke away.

"Robbie, wait a sec." A sketchbook—Cy surmised it was probably the book the first page came from—was lying on the floor behind the door. Adam bent down and started flipping pages, and he tore off four or five. He folded them neatly down the middle and then stood and wrapped Robbie's fingers around them. "You should keep these too," he said before he turned away. Obviously he was done with anyone not Finn.

Robbie opened the door again and strode purposefully down the hall. When they got to the living room, *all* the people were there, regarding the two of them with neutral eyes.

"Hey," Cy said, holding up his hands and giving his best stage smile. "Adam said we're welcome back. Maybe not *today*—"

"Thanks for coming to help, then." Mari hopped up off the ground and walked them to the door, giving Cy a one-armed hug. "You're the only one moving with any sense. I'm sure Ezra would agree."

Cy smiled at her, so grateful for the friendliness and the effort at normalcy that he felt his eyes burning. "Is he upstairs with the big fuckin' dog?"

"Yeah. I have the feeling that dog is gonna be the most confused animal on the planet—between Rico's place and Ezra's and here—"

"Rico needs his own dog," Ezra said, coming through the front door. "Hey, everyone. Miguel's here, and he brought pizza and beer—if you all want to take that shit up to our new digs, we can eat there!"

Ezra turned around, and Cy didn't even realize how effortlessly he managed to walk Cy and Robbie downstairs while directing everybody else upstairs until they got out on the lawn.

"Hey," Ezra said soberly, "Robbie?"

Robbie blinked dead eyes at him. He hadn't said a word since they'd left Finn and Adam's room.

"When this has faded, you know, you're still welcome—here, my place, Candy Heaven—"

"Adam said we were welcome too," Cy said hurriedly. God, they'd already caused such a scene! He didn't want to cause a rift too! "Just, you know—"

"Yeah," Ezra said with a head bob. "*Now* would be a good time to take off."

He shivered. The long afternoon shadows had drifted over the lawn and the street, and it was now about the time when the dead grass got icy. They were all wearing sweatshirts, but Cy had seen Ezra's breath on that last word.

"Bye, Ezra," Cy said wistfully.

Ezra smiled, all the sweetness that had first attracted Cy still there for the world to see. But only for Miguel to possess. "Bye, guys." He closed his eyes. "Uh, Robbie?"

"Hm?" Robbie pulled his attention away as though from a great distance.

"Remember to keep fighting."

And with that, Ezra turned and trotted toward the stairs, where Miguel was waiting with a big stack of pizzas on one arm and a case of beer under the other.

And that was their cue to go.

CY WANTED to ask a *lot* of things. "What in the fuck?" ranked number one, followed by "What did you *do*?" followed by "I take you to meet my friends and you've already fucked up with them?"

It wasn't until they were almost home, after he'd run through the entire list in his head, that he realized how furious he was, and just as he opened his mouth to say something—

"I'm sorry," Robbie said quietly. "I didn't even realize you knew them."

"Yeah," Cy responded on automatic. "How could you? I mean, it's not like you ruined the lives of every other gay man in the city, is it?" Oh God. That came out *way* bitchier than he'd intended it, and he bit his lip.

"Just the one who apparently *knows* all the other gay men in the city," Robbie responded, sounding bitter and resigned—but not mad at Cy for the bitchiness.

"Can I… can I just ask—what did you *do*, specifically? Because that picture…." Cy had felt that. He'd *been* that kid in grade school, in junior high. It was something you looked back on as an adult and said, "Yeah, that was rough, but I got by," but you never really *did* get by, did you? Those taunts, those words—they stuck in your craw. Until every time you touched a lover, or executed a dance step, or had a moment when you felt on top of the world, a tiny little part of you was thumbing its nose at the people who told you that you were nothing so often, and so loudly, that you'd eventually started to believe it.

"We were making plans for the future," Robbie said, his voice wooden. "And the CO of our unit—he was a real piece of work. We… I mean, Adam and I, when we started out, we were like *half the unit*, giving each other blowjobs and hand jobs back in this space between the Humvees and the garage bay. I know most units aren't like that, but this guy—he made it part of the hazing, and then we got bored and… whatever. But Adam and I, we got leave together once, and then we made it a point, and then…."

"It was a relationship," Cy said, feeling the pain in his gut. Finn's Adam. Everybody had that boy who broke their heart—Cy's had been in eighth grade, because he was precocious that way. But Adam, big, strong, stoic Adam, who the rest of the people at Candy Heaven seemed to orbit around like he was their sun—*his* heartbreaker had been Cy's handsome soldier, the one who was earnest and sincere and who worked hard to keep his promises.

Cy was not sure he was ready for this.

"Yeah," Robbie confessed quietly. "And we made plans. We were going to turn in our retirement papers and leave the Army and go to school and be a couple."

"So what happened?" Cy could see soldiers screaming and laughing and Adam in the middle.

"What happened was our CO made one too many cracks about gay people, and Adam snapped. He said the thing that *nobody* said, which was that we fucked each other silly when the brass wasn't watching. And then everybody's looking at me, because I'm Adam's boy, and they all *know*, and they're all *judging*, and me, instead of saying, 'You guys are the ones blowing that guy, 'cause Adam and I ain't been with any of you in *months*,' I look at Adam and I call him a faggot. And that was all she fucking wrote."

"Oh *Robbie*," Cy said, as appalled as Robbie wanted him to be.

"Did I mention I was the fucking bad guy?" Robbie snarled, and then lapsed into wounded silence.

Cy tried to figure out what to say. "How long ago was this?"

"Two years ago," Robbie said quietly. "I put my papers in about a month after Adam but got out nearly a year after he did. I sort of planned it that way." His voice sank. "I think I was hoping I'd get taken out before I retired, but no such luck. Our unit got shipped stateside and we just sort of… cooled our heels here until they set me loose." He let out a sigh. "First thing I did—and I mean, I barely had a couch in the apartment—was go out and pick up Ashley to prove I was still a man."

Cy sucked in a breath. "Until…."

"Until I saw you," Robbie said, voice throbbing poignantly. "And I realized that a real man wouldn't let anything stand in his way."

"Augh!" Cy snapped, slamming his steering wheel repeatedly until his palm stung and his wrist ached. Because he didn't know what to *do*. "God, that was the perfect thing to say," he muttered.

"Yeah," Robbie said as Cy pulled up near his rental car. They'd fed the meters ad infinitum that morning, and the rental was sitting, cold and unmolested, in the descending darkness. "But you can't trust me, right?"

"I didn't say that," Cy protested, because he was still on the fence, dammit!

"But you're wondering. You're thinking, 'Yeah, this guy fronts good, but I don't know—he could have not changed a fucking bit.' I get it. Why would you want to put your heart in the hands of a guy who did… *this*." Robbie shook the picture still on his lap, accusing him with every tattered edge.

For a moment Cy almost protested. His heart? His heart was nowhere *near* engaged. But as he sat idling and studied Robbie's averted face, he realized that if he said that, the only real liar in the car would be *Cy*. Robbie hadn't told Cy he was an angel. In fact, Cy figured they were having pretty much the same conversation now that Robbie had planned for them that morning.

The only difference was, Robbie had been embarrassed by an overdramatic Finn, and his self-loathing had been kicked into high gear.

Cy was surprised to find himself reaching for Robbie's hand once again. This time Robbie didn't clench around him, because that would have meant he'd have had to give up his death grip on that damned picture. So instead Cy just stroked Robbie's tense knuckles slowly.

"I don't want this to end us," he said, so surprised when it came out of his mouth that he almost looked behind him to see who just said that.

Robbie nodded and then—and only then—seized his hand, bringing Cy's knuckles up to his lips so he could plant a wet, salty kiss on the backs.

"Space," he said. "You need space to decide if you can live with me."

"And you?" Cy didn't like this idea—not at all.

The face Robbie turned toward him was swollen with tears. He held up the other pictures then, the ones *not* written on.

He was a handsome soldier, with a wide mouth and laughing gray eyes and an easy, sprawling grace on the barracks bed.

"I'm going to think hard and see if there's enough of this guy left to love you like you deserve."

Cy gaped, and Robbie leaned over and kissed him—really kissed him—slow and aching and bitter and sweet.

When Robbie pulled back, Cy's eyes stung, and Robbie wiped the tears away with his thumbs. "I'll call you," Robbie whispered. "Even if I'm not there yet. I'll call you. I won't leave you hanging."

Cy nodded, his throat swollen too, because out of nowhere, it hit him. Now that Robbie might be bailing, Cy wanted to keep him. Wanted to keep him so bad, his whole body already ached at the thought of letting him go.

"Soldier boy, you'd better not be saying good-bye," Cy interrupted. "This is a Robbie needs a deep breath—this isn't good-bye. Because I don't *do* a relationship like this. I don't just *care* like I'm caring now. And it hasn't been long, but we could be... we could be so damned much more. So don't give up on yourself, okay? Don't give up on me—"

Robbie's mouth was hot and needy and greedy, and Cy gave him everything back with interest. Robbie pulled away, panting, and his voice sounded tortured and harsh in Cy's ear. "*You* are nobody to give up on," he said. "You're a reason to pull my shit together and make that fucking call."

One more kiss, hard and frantic, and Robbie pulled away, gathered his painful reminders of shit long settled, and left. Cy stayed to watch him start his car and pull away, and then he toodled toward his parking garage, trying hard not to get maudlin about a guy he'd known less than two weeks.

But had been hoping to know for a really long time.

The Burn of the Lash

"ROBBIE, YOU look like shit," Micah said as they were clocking out. "What happened—are you still hungover?"

Robbie shook his head and winced. Nope, concussion clock hadn't started again. "Naw, but drinking with you was a bad idea."

Which was true. He had no business drinking with a concussion— even one beer. But then he'd had no business fucking Cy until his head felt like blowing off or even being with Cy in the first place.

Nope. Robbie just seemed to not fuckin' learn.

Micah nodded like he knew. "Concussion clock, right?"

Robbie blinked. Sort of, he did! "You know about that?"

"Yeah—football in school. Mom made me stop." He grimaced and then grinned. "You know, you were really nice about not saying anything Friday, but I really am a mama's boy."

Of all things, that made Robbie feel a little better. "I'm jealous," he said, completely sincere. "I... I haven't told my parents anything meaningful since I said I was enlisting. The way you and your brother and your dad hang out—I mean, you brought your *cousins* to my house to party like friends." He remembered the big moving-in party that he'd inadvertently crashed, and his throat closed. "Jealous," he finished, shoulders sagging.

"Hey," Micah said, a friendly hand on his shoulder. "You know, we don't need alcohol for you to pour out your troubles. You go home and take some painkillers. I'll be there in an hour with dinner."

"I don't want to...." Intrude? Impose? Lean on a friend any more than he had to because he didn't deserve one in the first place?

"Yeah, but I owe you." Micah's smiles had dimples in them, and Robbie almost wished *Micah* was gay. It would be easier to fall for someone who'd already forgiven you, right? But maybe you had to have been—or fear being—that person on the inside center of Adam's picture. Not that a straight boy couldn't, but Micah *hadn't*.

But that didn't mean he couldn't listen.

"Dinner?" Robbie said plaintively. God, he'd gone home the day before and cried. Just cried, for *hours*. If his head hadn't hurt already, *that* would have guaranteed a shitty day. But right now he felt like opening a tin of soup was beyond his capabilities, and ordering drive-thru might be a cataclysmic decision.

"Yeah," Micah said gently. "My stupid brother has a date, so it'll just be me and the television remote. It'll be good."

Surprisingly enough, it wasn't bad.

Micah showed up with a two-person casserole dish of lasagna, as well as some salad in a bag. It was so far from the pizza box Robbie had expected that he felt his face heat.

"Did you make this?"

"Naw. Mom had it ready—I knew she would. Here, take it."

Robbie reached out and grabbed it automatically, cradling his hands around the old towel wrapped around the bottom to keep the heat in.

"She also sent these—Grandma got them from a neighbor."

A bag of mandarin oranges swung from his hand, and Robbie's mouth watered.

"Seriously?" he asked, eyes big. "My parents used to put them in my stocking when I was a kid!"

"Right? Better than potato chips." Micah nodded earnestly. "So here, let's set the table and eat!"

God, it was good. Home-cooked lasagna was like, the ultimate in comfort food, and Robbie ate all the salad, even if he normally wasn't a salad kind of guy. It felt like he was being taken care of by proxy, and he wasn't going to turn down a smidgen of comfort at this point.

They dug in without a word, because hey—not a date—and Robbie put the extra food in plastic butter-ware while Micah washed the dishes. They retired to the couch, the bag of mandarins and a bowl between them, and watched mindless television for about an hour. Robbie felt almost human.

"So," Micah said, putting the TV on pause between shows. "What happened? Why'd you look so shitty?"

Robbie grunted and for a second wished for the military, where guys didn't ask and didn't tell. But then, look how well *that* worked out. "Well, I broke my brain having sex," he said with a half smile. "So that wasn't so bad."

Micah's chuckle went low and evil. "That's epic—I'm telling everybody. Teddy'll think you're a god."

"Teddy's too young to have sex," Robbie said, half-affronted. Yeah, he was twenty-one, but he had those guileless blue eyes, and Robbie felt a little protective of the guy.

"Teddy's been having sex since Dad gave him condoms at sixteen. Don't worry about Teddy, he's fine. So, you broke your brain with sex." Micah paused delicately, and Robbie thought about what a good friend he'd put off having for months. "So how'd you…."

"Break my heart?" Robbie said with a crooked smile. "There's where it gets complicated."

He told the story, appreciating Micah as an audience if nothing else. When Robbie told the part about the dog, Micah grimaced like he knew what was coming, and then when Robbie talked about the picture—

"Can I see them?" Micah asked. "I draw. I want to see the pictures."

Well, why not. It wasn't like an entire apartment full of people Robbie *didn't* know so well hadn't already, right?

Robbie went to his bedroom, where he'd dropped them on the end table, and then brought them out.

Micah took his time looking at the big bad, and when he looked up, he seemed unbearably sad. "There was a girl at school—you know, the bullied kid?"

Robbie nodded, his heart one big, sore, abscessed wound.

"Yeah," Micah said. "I was part of the outside people."

"You?" Because he'd seemed nothing but decent.

"Kids," Micah said simply. "We're stupid. But this girl, she was in drama, and she was good—and my first year at junior college, my girlfriend at the time kept talking about this girl and how nice she was, and funny, and talented." Micah shuddered. "You know, confessing to my girlfriend—that was the hardest thing in the world. I thought."

"What was worse?" Robbie ached to know.

"My girlfriend made me *apologize* to her. It was nonnegotiable. And it was funny. I thought it was the dumbest thing in the world—because even when I was doing it, I could tell the apology was never going to take it away, right? That horrible feeling of being hated for just being *you*?"

"I know the one."

Micah nodded, understanding. "But my girlfriend, she said that afterward the girl had been really... really *happy*. Like the apology, it hadn't been bullshit after all. So yesterday probably sucked—I mean, *huge*. I can't even imagine. Modern science can't measure. But... the way your ex and his boyfriend feel now?"

Robbie blinked, something in his heart shifting. "Better?" Was it insane to hope?

"I'm sure," Micah told him sagely. "Hey—what's this scrawled over it?"

"San Francisco," Robbie told him. Then he remembered. "Adam said they tried to write down the memories on the picture that made it not hurt so bad."

"Yeah—most of them are on the back."

"Huh." Micah turned it over and put it on the coffee table, and for a moment, the two of them got to read the best moments of two people on the other side of the city.

"So, we've got *Christmas at Finn's Parents*," Micah read. The phrases were roughly in order, but some of them were scattered like rain in the margins. Well, happiness wasn't always linear.

"That's Adam's handwriting," Robbie confirmed, because Adam's almost perfect printing was unmistakable. "And this one says...." He smirked.

"No, what, seriously—what's it say?"

"It's sorta personal—"

"*Finn tops*," Micah read. "*Not great. We'll try again.* Wait—tops what? Like a cake?"

Robbie snickered helplessly. "Uh, no, straight man. Not like a cake."

"Uh...." Micah squinted at him, and then those dark-lashed eyes got really big. "Oh! Like, uh, like *tops*."

"Yeah," Robbie said, covering his laugh. Oh dear—he hadn't meant to grab Adam's diary. "Maybe we should—"

"Oh, hey," Micah said, squinting closer at the writing. "Here—different writing. *Finn tops. Got better.*"

Robbie giggled a little, and his voice softened. There, in Adam's handwriting, was written: "*Way better.*"

"That's good," Robbie said, nodding at Micah, who nodded back soberly.

"Take your word for it. Wait—what else we got?"

The moments ran the gamut. *Way better* was followed by *Happy New Year, Adam* was followed by *Clopper loves Adam best*.

"What's the thing with vegetables?" Micah asked after they swapped phrases for a few moments. "*Finn ate salad. Time down to ten minutes.*"

"I don't know, but oh—look! Adam's cousin came home."

"And he met somebody," Micah said, grinning. "This is—this is *great*. I mean… I mean, I know you took the bad picture for a reason, but… I hope they're doing this with other pictures, you know?"

"Yeah," Robbie said, tracing his fingers along the random scattering of good moments. His body felt transformed, like it had been leaden, but now it was dynamic, muscle and bone, fit and ready to live. "It's… this feels good." He smiled at Micah and remembered the guy's heartbreak on Friday. He'd loved his ex-girlfriend's kid like a son, but he'd let him go so the boy could love his father. A big decision for a kid who hadn't hit twenty-five. "You were right on Friday, that it's the knowing the people you love are happy because if you really love them, that's important."

"Yeah?" Micah grinned and pointed both thumbs to his chest. "I'm a genius." His grin softened. "What about… you know. Your friend. Cy."

Robbie sighed and leaned back. "I… here." He pulled out Adam's other drawings. "Do I look like this guy?"

"Huh." Micah studied the pictures and then studied Robbie. "Well, you look older. And wiser and shit—"

"Don't be stupid," Robbie muttered.

"No. Seriously. This guy here—he looks like someone who would bail. The guy sitting next to me, he looks like he's stronger than that."

"God, you're wasted on women," Robbie told him, laughing.

"I hope they don't think so." Micah grabbed his crotch and thrust his hips. "It has been a *while*."

Micah crashed on the couch and left early to shower before work. After he left, Robbie fielded a call from his mom—she wanted him to come over for dinner the next day and bring Ashley.

"I broke up with Ashley, Mom. I'm seeing someone else now."

"Oh, that's too bad. We liked Ashley, Robbie—why the breakup?"

It could have been the opening for the big dramatic out—but Robbie thought that maybe he should be a little more subtle. "Well, we disagreed on a lot of stuff, Ashley and me."

"Really? Like what?"

"Well, politics, mostly. Civil rights, gay rights, women's rights, funding for schools, healthcare—I'm sort of *for* all those things, and she was sort of *against*. It just… you know… made it really hard to be around her."

"But Robbie, your father and I… I mean, you know how he feels."

"Yeah, Mom. It makes it hard to be around you sometimes. But you're my parents—I have to." He laughed to soften it. "But I just didn't want to feel that way about the person I'm dating."

"Robbie… gay rights? Civil rights? What does that even mean?"

He really wished he was having this conversation with his father. "It means that just because the guy who moved your refrigerator was rude it doesn't mean *all* the guys who have the same skin color are rude."

"I never said—"

"Yes, Mom. Yes, you did." He pinched the bridge of his nose. It was a losing battle. "But don't worry. Like I said—you and me and Dad, we don't have to agree. But I don't want to fight about this with the guy I'm dating."

"Wait—the who?"

Oh hell. "Gotta go, Mom. See you tomorrow night! Bye!"

He hit End Call with a clammy finger, heart thundering in his ears. Oh God. Oh hell. Oh shit. What had he said?

He pondered it all the way to work, and the only thing that got his mind off it was the knowledge that if he wasn't careful on the damned forklift, he could kill somebody.

Had he really just come out?

No, not really.

Yes, sort of?

His heart stopped pounding in his throat around lunchtime, and Micah and Teddy got an earful. They thought it was *hilarious*.

"So you *sort of* came out?" Teddy asked, as confused as Robbie felt. "How does that work?"

Micah glared at him. "I think it's a safety net," he muttered. "So Robbie can bail."

"No!" Robbie said, and just that quickly, he knew that it was true. "I'm not going to bail—not on them, and not on Cy."

"Then why the sorta?" Teddy spoke through a mouth full of french fries—God, Micah's little brother could eat.

"I want them to think about it," Robbie said after a moment. "I want them to think—like, you know." He looked at Micah. "Like, now, whenever Dad makes a joke, I want him to think, 'But what if my son is….' Every time he makes fun of someone because of what they believe, I want him to take a breath and say, 'But my kid thinks this.'"

"Yeah," Teddy said doubtfully. "But Grandma and Grandpa know Aunt Stacy is a liberal, and they say shit just to push her buttons."

Robbie looked at him levelly. "At least they're going to have to look at me and wonder where my buttons are," he said. "And wonder if they want me in their lives, buttons and all."

DINNER WITH his folks in Sun City was exactly as awful as he'd feared it would be.

"So your mom says you're a socialist now," his dad blurted as he sat down to the table. Robbie, impressed after watching Micah and Teddy take care of themselves, was helping his mom bring stuff from the stove in spite of her halfhearted objections.

"Sure, Dad. I'm a socialist."

"And you were in the *service*!"

"You can believe in civil rights without being a socialist," Robbie explained, trying to be patient. "And you can believe in healthcare for everybody without being a communist, and—"

"And you're dating a *guy*!" Don Chambers slammed his fist down on the table, spilling the gravy and knocking over a milk glass.

"Don't worry, Mom, I'll get it," Robbie said quietly. "I was wondering if she caught that." He wasn't great in this new house, but he knew where his mom kept the towels. His father barked at him the whole time he went to fetch them.

"Stop trying to yank her chain. She was so upset I had to come home from my golf game yesterday to keep her from just losing her fucking mind."

"Sorry," he said humbly. "Mom, I'm sorry. I should have waited until tonight to even talk about it—"

"But your father said you were just pushing our buttons, sweetheart." His mother smiled happily as she came to the table and set down a big bowl of bacon beans.

For a moment Robbie closed his eyes and blocked out his parents' retirement home kitchen. Cream-colored tile, red walls, and a cream-colored stove—Cy would approve of the color choices; they were certainly modern enough. His mother was wearing stretch jeans and a cardigan, and his father was still in the leisure suit he'd put on that morning to go play a round of golf.

Yes, the kitchen was modern, but the people in it… not so much.

"I'm gay," he said with his eyes closed.

"Bullshit," his father snapped, and Robbie opened his eyes and saw that nothing had changed.

"If you can't see that about me, you can't see *me*," Robbie told him quietly, sitting down.

"My son who served in the US military is *not* gay." Don threw mashed potatoes and chicken on his plate and let the green beans alone.

Robbie served himself on automatic and wondered how he was supposed to counter that. "Your son sitting across from you at the dinner table *is*," Robbie told him, trying to keep his humor. "And even if I wasn't, I still couldn't date a girl like Ashley, because she believes all the stuff I really hate about the world."

"Oh, Robbie." His mom's voice had tears in it. "Not this again."

Oh hell. He'd made his mother cry.

"Look," he said, pouring himself some milk, "we can talk about something else. *I'm* certainly not comfortable. But it's not going to change the fact that I'm gay and I don't believe a lot about what you believe in. So let's talk about football or basketball or how *Castle* is a really good show."

"Too fuckin' liberal," his father said meanly.

Robbie let out another breath and felt his anger and his embarrassment burning behind his eyes. "Or how nice it was for Mom to cook."

"That's her fuckin' job."

"Or how it needs to snow some more."

"Global warming is a fucking myth fed to us by the liberal media!" his father roared.

"Or how your son is gay and is going to go eat alone because his dad's being an asshole." Robbie stood up and kissed his mom's cheek. "Sorry, Mom. Don't worry, I didn't taste any of the food. Even if gay *was* catching, you can still use it for leftovers."

And with that, Robbie turned around and walked out of his parents' nice little retirement ranch house and drove back home to his steadily improving apartment. On his way home, he stopped at In-N-Out, because he was starving, and then he stopped at a craft store, where he bought a frame.

After a double-double and fries, he washed his hands and very carefully selected one of the pictures of himself—one of the ones where he was laughing, carefree, a goofy smile on his face. Adam had caught him in a candid moment, and in that crystal in time, nothing was going to keep Robbie Chambers down.

He wanted to be that guy again.

But braver this time. Stronger. The guy who always told the truth, no matter how it hurt. He figured he'd made a good start that night, but he had some more stuff to clear up.

When he had the picture framed, he hung it in the living room, to the side, and wondered if he could commission Adam to draw another one of Cy. Not even as a gift, but just because if Robbie could be brave, maybe he'd have the right to have Cy's picture up in his apartment.

It seemed so little to ask. Robbie hoped he could earn it.

Before he went to bed that night, he checked his phone. Yup: Friday night performance, Cal Expo.

Seven thirty to nine.

Robbie would be there with bells on.

Diva Pants

CY HID behind Exhibition Hall C with the other grown teachers of Anna's Dance, and they all shared a communal cigarette while the volunteer mothers took care of the costumes and organized the kids for parent pickup.

"God," Kyle said, taking a deep draw and exhaling a plume of smoke straight into the air, "that sucked."

Kyle was a year or two older than Cy, straight, going to school and struggling under a day job as a restaurant dishwasher. A thick-chested Hispanic man, he clung to Anna's because his nieces and nephews danced and learned gymnastics there. It was a family thing—his sister's two kids were enrolled, and every year at the big recital, she worked backstage.

Like Cy, Kyle loved teaching, he loved performing, and helping the kids made him feel good—but that didn't mean that when shit went wrong, it didn't go horribly wrong.

"Augh!" Heather echoed, pulling off her bright red glove and stealing the cigarette from Kyle. She took a quick puff and shuddered, partly from cold and partly from reaction. Kyle put a purely platonic arm around her shoulders and pulled her close. *Not* Anna's finest hour.

"You all!" Oh Lord, there was no mistaking that thickly accented Russian voice. "You are all finished, I take it? The children are all with their parents?"

"No, Anna," Heather said humbly, looking at their mentor with gigantic kohl-rimmed amber eyes. "We're sorry."

"Be sorry later," Anna said, and then she looked furtively around. "Give me cigarette now. Quick, before Mikhail comes back here. We need to get those kids out of the exhibition hall before I am forced to kill somebody. Hopefully that swine—" She spat. "—who told us we would have room to set up on the fucking stage."

In the summer during the fair, the stage was bigger. After the dance numbers, the gym team would spread the mats and perform their competition numbers, usually to a lot of applause. While the dance classes were open to everybody—no kid who wanted to work and who could behave like a human being was ever turned down—the gym team was the one class of Anna's in which the spot had to be earned by both hard work and ability.

In the summer the normal-size stage was actually pretty small. It was not unknown for kids to fall off because the spacing was cattywampus, and Anna had gotten to be a pro at having parents sign a release for injury liability just so the kids could have a chance to perform.

It was a stage parent's dream, really—the kids performed on the main stage between professional hypnotism acts and high schools with truly ambitious glee clubs. The four exhibition halls formed a two-story square, and there was a combination of brick platforms and stairs that formed a large four-sided spiral around the quad and acted as festival seating when the folding chairs were all filled. For summer shows, the students chasséd, pliéd, and sashayed across the stage to the same grand recital numbers that Anna had them work toward every year. For the winter show—and this was the first year Anna's kids had been invited—she put together something simple and easy to learn, and the students performed during the Winter Wonderland Exposition—at night. In the cold.

On the much smaller stage.

Which meant that the gymnastics performers couldn't actually put their mats down. The already small makeshift stage for summer had been diminished by about twenty square feet, which was just enough on every edge to send someone catapulting off the stage and to the bricks four feet below.

But Anna had promised her gym team would perform.

Their solution had been to spread the mats on the bricks in front of the stage and perform there—and on the one hand, in spite of the cold, there were no strained muscles, no broken bones, and no snapped tendons.

On the other hand, they had all just performed some really tricky shit on cold mats stacked on top of hard bricks, and for the performers over the age of ten?

They felt it in every sinew, every bone, every corpuscle of their bodies.

For the performers over the age of sanity (whenever that set in—after teaching for the past eight years, Cy believed it was different for each kid), they had the additional pain of pure freaking terror.

There had been *so* much potential for shit to go wrong.

As soon as they'd taken their bows and run the kids off the stage and to the staging room with the supervising parents, the core knot of teachers had slipped away to take shaky drags of forbidden drugs and calm the thundering of their hearts.

And fear the voice they all heard next.

"Yes, yes, I can smell the stench of cowardice from here."

Anna grimaced. "I thought my old taskmaster was a pain in the ass," she muttered. Well, he had been, but compared to Mikhail Bayul-Perkins, he was probably a pussycat.

The man who stalked around the corner in his gym leotards with no sweater did not *look* that imposing.

Standing at five feet six inches of slender muscle, Mikhail was a dancer through to every follicle of his curly blond hair. He worked Renaissance faires and taught at Anna's, and, in his spare time, helped his husband with their halfway house for runaways out in Levee Oaks.

And, Cy was sure, in every capacity, he inspired his victims with the same terror they were all feeling now.

Anna took one last drag of the smoke and put it out under her tennis shoe. "My bad, Mikhail," she said almost ingratiatingly. Cy wasn't sure when the balance of power between them had shifted—Mikhail had been her student since he was in his teens and had been allowed to teach her more advanced classes. Cy understood that he'd been hot shit back in the old country before his body had been ruined by overuse, but other than that?

Well, he was a blond-haired angel-faced harridan who let no dancer rest until they'd wrung every last bit of their best performance out of themselves. And then he smiled gently and told them they'd done well.

He was not smiling now. "I realize we are all frightened, children," he said grimly. "That was a scary brave thing we all did in the name of art. But our students need us, and we have duties."

He scowled at them until they all smiled back sheepishly and walked by him, shrugging in their embarrassment. He stopped Cy with a hand on his shoulder, though.

"There is a young man waiting outside the exposition hall. He was there through the entire performance, and he had eyes only for you. If you are going to rip his heart out, tell me. I know of several young men who would love to help put it back."

Cy gaped at him, his heart tripping like a dancer on an ice rink.

"I... uh... what did he look like?" Because it wasn't like Cy had a score of young men who were ready to come back and fight for him.

Yes. Yes, he would fight for me. I never should have doubted.

But Cy *had* doubted.

God, he thought he would have died for Mikhail's smiles as a young man; he would have died a thousand times over to have Robbie's name pop up on his cell phone, or to see those gray-green eyes staring at him from across the dance floor this past week.

He'd squashed that yearning down. Functioned, danced and bussed and taught and rehearsed.

But this past week had been a gnawing in his stomach. A tightness in his chest. A hollowness behind his eyes. His apartment—his haven, his pride—had felt empty and cold. He'd had friends he could invite, but not the will to do it.

And he'd driven the people at Gatsby's Nick batshit. "Should I call? No, I shouldn't call. I mean, he looked so sad! But...."

"Oh, for fuck's sake!" Antony had finally burst out. "Either call this guy or fucking own up that you're going to wait for him to call. Jesus, Cyril—I get that you like to think that you're God's gift to manwhores, but it's not going to kill you to admit you *like* this guy. We all saw you making out! There's making out with an available body and making out with someone you give a shit about, and guess which one you were doing. *Twice.* So calm the fuck down!"

"Sorry," Cy had muttered, grabbing his bar cloth and leaving the back of the house so he could make the place all shiny. They had just been so new, and Cy hadn't let himself want things like this in so long....

"What does he look like?" Mikhail asked slowly, pulling Cy back into the now. "He looks like a pale young man with big gray eyes who is eating his heart out. Do you have many of those in your history? I certainly thought better of you."

Cy felt his face heat, blushing like a caught-out toddler. "No, Mikhail," he said humbly. "I treat people square." Mikhail had never talked about his personal life—until he changed his name, many of his students had no idea he was in a relationship or even gay. But being scrupulously honest with people—*that* he had drilled into them. Cy had been his student for a long time. When he'd started dating, all it had taken was one or two arch words about being a player but not an asshole, and Cy had learned to be upfront and honest about no attachments.

There were three people you didn't disappoint in your life—your mom, your nana, and your terrifying Russian dance teacher who seemed to think you were special.

"Then he should look like somebody you remember," Mikhail said, that little fuck-you snarl he kept handy pulling his lip up. "Now let's hurry and deliver the children and load the mats. I have a home to get to, you know. My cop was not able to come see me perform, but that does not mean there is no hot chocolate waiting."

Cy smiled shyly. Ah, the rare reference to his "cop"—who had apparently retired a few years before. The fact that persnickety little Mikhail could have a "big, strong cop" waiting for him had given Cy some hope over the past eight years of young adult dating. The fact that he now had someone waiting for him, when for so very many years he had seemed to be so much alone—well, it made Cy optimistic.

It made him think of Happy Ever Afters.

"We wouldn't want to keep him waiting," Cy said soberly.

"Did I hear you laughing at me?" Mikhail asked, all suspicion. "Because if so, I should have disciplined you more as an impudent child."

"No, sir!" Cy mock saluted. He dropped his voice. "It's just good to know you're afraid of disappointing someone too."

Mikhail grunted thoughtfully, and they began to walk, shoulder to shoulder, to the empty exposition hall that served as a staging area. "It is frightening, is it not?" he asked into the unlikely quiet. "Having someone you can disappoint. I know for too long it made me keep people at arm's length."

Cy swallowed. "Yeah," he agreed. His mom thought he was an angel, and his grandma assumed he wasn't. But the human beings in the middle—was that why he'd spent so much time insisting on freedom? So he didn't have to deal with simple human expectation and disappointment?

As he rounded the corner, he drew up short, seeing Robbie standing, lanky and uncomfortable, among the wandering throngs of reunited parents and children who were running off to see the rest of the expo.

Was that how Robbie had felt asking Cy out? Was that how he'd felt when suddenly asked to declare his sexuality in front of his peers? When he'd had to go back and face what he'd done?

Cy had thought Robbie was all forgiven, but as Robbie turned his head and their eyes met, he realized that there had been nothing *to* forgive. That person that Robbie had wanted to be, the one who was honest and brave and fair—he was standing right *there*. He had been from that first dance on the boardwalk. Whoever Robbie had been, whatever sins he'd committed, the person Cy had known—had been, moment by moment, falling for—was the one looking at him with that terrible combination of hope and shyness that Cy had come to care for.

Without realizing it, Cy separated from Mikhail and changed directions, brushing past a broad-chested, sweet-smiled man with graying brown hair as he did.

"Oh, I see," he could hear Mikhail bitching. "Yes, Cy, I will go and round up your children and do your job just so you can ease the pangs of true lo—*Shane!*" The joy in Mikhail's voice made Cy turn his head. "You made it!" For just a second, Cy paused to watch his little Russian diva run into the arms of the big man with kind brown eyes, who lifted him up in a mouth-on-mouth kiss without even trying.

Then Cy only had eyes for his own man, who was smiling slightly in hope.

"Hey," Cy said, walking into his space, hoping he'd take the hint.

"Hey." Robbie put his hands on Cy's shoulders and urged him a little closer.

Cy grimaced. "Anna doesn't like us to get too… handsy." He cast another look over his shoulder to where Mikhail still had his legs wrapped around that big cop's waist and was kissing him silly. "And usually *Mikhail* is the first person to kick our asses—not sure what that's about, but the parents get—"

"Weird." Robbie rolled his eyes. "Yeah, I know all about weird parents. So, uh… you done here?"

Cy risked the wrath of Anna and Mikhail and stood on his tiptoes to kiss Robbie's cheek. "Not yet. Let me go check my kids and give them candy canes and shit, 'kay? I'll be back."

Robbie nodded. "I'll go get us some chocolate."

Nice gesture, but—"The hot chocolate is no bueno—get us some cider and we'll go out to Starbucks or something!"

Robbie's face lit up, and Cy grinned back. Yeah. They were going to have a date and they were going to kiss, and they were going to make plans for the future.

As Cy rounded the corner into the exposition hall and started checking on his students and the sign-out sheets and the equipment, he couldn't think of a better Christmas.

THE WINTER Wonderland expo was really a big light show, with giant silk balloons lit up from the inside against the frosty dark sky. Two different bubble machines simulated snow, and inflatable light tunnels were lit up for people to walk through. Vendors hawked hot honeyed almonds and hot chocolate, and some even sold toys that glowed as the kids walked the carnival area oohing and aahing over each new sculpture.

Robbie had paid the fourteen dollars to get in and see the show, and after Cy had put the last mat in Anna's minivan and the last box of costuming into Mikhail's big purple serial-killer van, he was bound and determined that Robbie get every penny out of it.

"You are sure you don't need a ride?" Anna asked before he slammed the hatch shut on her Odyssey and took off to meet his soldier. She'd picked him up that night so he could help with the setup.

"Yup," he said, grinning. "I've got a *date*."

"Huh," she muttered, starting the car. "Is he the same guy you've been mooning over all week?"

Oh God. "Yup."

"Make sure he treats you right. Mikhail got lucky."

With that she pulled slowly away.

Cy ran back to the performance area and found Robbie waiting patiently, two cups of steaming cider in hand.

"You free?" he asked impishly.

"Yes." Cy had never *felt* so free. And then Robbie, careful of the hot cups of cider, bent forward and brushed their lips together, and he thought he'd soar.

"Then let's enjoy the fair," Robbie said softly.

Cy took one of the cups in one hand and Robbie's hand in the other, and they set out to wander the night.

"This is fun," Robbie said, although his teeth were chattering. He had his leather jacket on, but he'd forgotten a scarf and a hat or gloves. Cy took off his bright green hat with a little shake of his hair and pulled it on over Robbie's ears.

"It's more fun now that you're not freezing," he said, huddling deeper into this thick, wooly scarf. Cy didn't screw around with winter—when it got below forty outside, he had a big puffy parka, in purple, with white fur around the collar and sleeves. Yeah, sure, it was from the women's section, but it looked *amazing* on him, and he couldn't give a shit.

Robbie grinned and took a fortifying sip of cider. "Yeah, well, I was stupid. My friend wanted to talk after work, and he's been really decent to me, so I gave him half an hour. Then I realized I had *no* time, so when I got dressed I forgot, like, *everything*."

"You didn't have to get here for all of it," Cy told him, still warmed that he had—or had at least tried.

"Well, I missed some of the little kids," Robbie admitted. "Which is too bad, because they were *hilarious*. I've never seen so many kids watching each other's feet. It was like, one kid—maybe—knew the entire routine."

Cy grimaced. "Yeah, well, four-year-olds in tutus. They usually get by on their looks."

Robbie's laugh was deep and unfettered, and Cy drank it in to keep himself warm. "You can say that again. But...." He took a sip of his drink. "It was good. I mean, most of those kids aren't going to dance after high school, but until then...."

"Yeah." Cy squeezed Robbie's hand. "It gives them an identity, you know? They don't have to be a troublemaker or a bad student—they can be a *dancer* instead."

Robbie smiled at him like he was smiling at Cy's soul. "Like you. It's... it's part of your heart. Like when I first saw you dancing on the boardwalk. It wasn't your skin color or your hair or your sexuality—those weren't the things that made you glow. It was the *dance*. That's why I fell for you, right there. 'Cause that thing inside you that made you shine, it was real and beautiful, you know?"

Cy had trouble breathing. Flat out, his chest wasn't working, his lungs had stopped, and all that came out of his throat was a pathetic sort of "nnnnnn" sound.

"You fell for me?" he asked, sounding needy and wistful and not caring.

"Well... *yeah*." Robbie tossed his empty cup in the trash can next to him and turned from his contemplation of a giant beehive made entirely of recycled brown medicine bottles. "I...." Carefully he pushed the hair back from Cy's ear. "I just... you know. I wanted to talk to you... see you again. *Be* with you. The good guy, the happy guy I thought I'd left behind in the fuckin' desert—he came out and wanted some play when I saw you."

Cy captured his hand and kissed his palm, warmed from holding the drink. "I... I was so scared you weren't going to call me again," he confessed.

Robbie stepped into *his* space this time and pushed gently until Cy's head was leaning on his surprisingly broad chest.

"I had to do some things," he said softly. "I had to say good-bye to Adam once and for all, but find the part of me who was brave enough to love him then."

"Did that guy show?" Cy asked, wrapping his arms around Robbie's waist and holding tighter.

"I hope so," Robbie said dryly, "because *somebody* came out to my parents on Monday night."

Cy gasped and pulled back. "Oh, Jesus, Robbie—how did that go?"

Robbie shrugged and the skin on his face seemed to tighten, leaving his high cheekbones and aquiline nose in stark relief from the glowing light sculptures. "Well, it's a good thing my coworker's grandma takes all comers on Christmas Eve, 'cause otherwise it would sort of suck."

"Oh." Cy cupped his chilled cheeks and pulled him down for a hard kiss. "Baby—I'm so sorry."

Robbie shrugged, keeping his face averted, but Cy could see the shine in his eyes. "Well, I knew it, right? But the thing was, when I was afraid it was going to happen, that's when I did the stupid stuff. Now that I *know* it's happened, I can *deal* with it happening." He looked at Cy and flashed an almost-smile. "I'll deal."

Cy's own eyes burned. Yeah, there was a reason he didn't come out to his nana, and a reason his mom didn't tell her either. But his *mom* knew, and that meant the world to him.

"I'm sorry," he said softly. "I... I mean, a lot of us have been through it—"

"So I can survive." Robbie gave another one of those lip twists. "But I thought, you know, I did it, the bad hard thing. So coming to see you dance, that was my reward."

Cy smiled—a real smile—and kissed him again, this time softer. "Soldier, I am not sure where you get your moves, but you manage to say *the* best shit sometimes."

ROBBIE HAD apparently gotten his truck repaired and back, which amazed Cy to no end because it was so quick. But it was also handy, because it was easy to spot in the crowded parking lot. They made it to Starbucks, closing the place down as they nursed a few hot chocolates apiece to ward off the cold that had seeped into their bones as they'd wandered the fair.

And they talked.

Cy heard about Robbie's coming out, about his friends' easy acceptance, about his research into local schools for the fall semester of the coming year. In turn, Cy told Robbie about teaching, about the fuckup with the mats, about...

Missing him.

"See," he said, talking matter-of-factly as they stood up and stretched, "the thing is, I've always thought, you know, there's got to be someone better coming around the corner."

"Ouch!" Robbie said, that slight smile in the corners of his mouth twisting something in Cy's stomach.

Cy grabbed their cups and threw them away, heading for the door and avoiding Robbie's eyes.

"No," Robbie said, catching up to him as they trotted through the frost to the truck. "No—what? I'm not asking for marriage you know—I mean... I just—"

"Don't you get it?" Cy asked, turning to him and feeling foolish. "I walked around the corner of that building tonight, and the only person I wanted to see was you. There was *nothing* better waiting for me around the corner. What do I do with that?"

Robbie's smile got bigger, a little lopsided, a little radiant, like the sun on snow. "You let me take you home," he said, drawing close to Cy and framing his face, sliding his fingers through Cy's hair and making him remember again why he liked it long. "You let me touch you."

Cy wet his lips unconsciously, and the frost of the night bit into him.

And Robbie covered his mouth with his own and everything was warmth. Cy's hands shook as he brought them up to cup Robbie's jaw, his cheeks, the back of his head. The pulse of the kiss rocked them both, and Robbie kept his lips and tongue slow and hard, the slide and glide of their mouths together being the point, the whole point, and nothing but the—

"Ahhhh!" Cy pushed his groin against Robbie's, aware they were making out in a Starbucks parking lot. He buried his face in the hollow of Robbie's neck and begged. "Your place," he whispered. "You can take me to work…."

"I'll bring a book and watch you," Robbie told him, like he'd planned it. "I'll watch you dance tomorrow night."

Cy blinked at him with shiny eyes. He'd done pretty damned much everything in bed with as many people as he could handle—but having someone watch him dance? That was an intimacy he'd never thought of.

It made his chest clench and ache with want.

"You like watching me dance?" he asked, sounding plaintive to his own ears when he'd always thought he could go out into the world and get himself anything he wanted.

"You're beautiful," Robbie breathed, and claimed his mouth again. Their bodies tried to meld together, to cling, in spite of Cy's puffy coat and Robbie's leather jacket, but Cy let the kiss go one breath longer, one heartbeat longer, until he felt Robbie shiver.

"Your place," Cy said again.

"Your place is cooler," Robbie said, his eyes crinkling at the corners.

"Yeah, but we haven't done your place before. I want to wipe out the girl cooties with our sex funk."

Robbie laughed and stepped back, clicking the truck open and walking around to the driver's side while Cy tried hard not to just hold on to the handle and swoon.

Never in his life had he been so close to just abandoning all common sense and going at it with the same guy in public twice, not even in high school, when he'd been a walking erection.

"Your place has girl cooties," Robbie said after he'd started the car and they were waiting for the windows to clear. "You told me that!"

Cy rolled his eyes. "Yes, but I *wanted* to have sex with those girls. That was *willing bisexual* girl cooties. *You*, on the other hand, went out and skimmed the girl tank to see what would float into your pad."

Robbie's deep-throated laughter actually warmed Cy more than the heater did. "That's mean!" he protested. "She might have been a perfectly nice girl if I hadn't—"

"Picked her up at a bar and tried to tell her you weren't going to marry her? Yeah, I'll believe that."

Robbie grunted. "How do you know it was like that?"

"Because," Cy answered, realizing this was important. "You're good to your word. I can't believe you ever committed anything to this girl that you didn't mean to deliver."

Robbie sighed and peered through the windshield before putting the F-150 in gear. "Yeah," he said after a moment. "Yeah, you're right. But… there's this quote from a book in high school—*The Crucible*, you remember it?"

"No," Cy said, rolling his eyes. "No, because if it was a class that involved actual work, I was trying to find a way out of it. But go on."

"It said that there were promises in sweat—and it was, you know, *that* sweat. That even if a guy says, 'No, this is not a commitment,' if you're doing the thing, the other person is bound to get the wrong idea."

"So you're saying…?" Cy asked, suddenly interested.

"I was looking for a way to break up with her that wouldn't have been ugly," Robbie said after a moment. "And there *was* no way to do that. I was just looking for a way to cover my gay, right? But she was looking for a person. I started it out on a wrong. It wasn't going to get any righter."

"Huh," Cy said, thinking about it. "You know, it would have been easier to just write her off as a crazy bitch who broke your toaster."

"Yeah," Robbie said, sucking his teeth in thought. "Well, she was sort of. But I brought her home." He stopped at a light and turned to Cy, winking. "And now I'm bringing you home, as proof that even *I* can grow some smarts."

"God, have you," Cy said with a mock shudder. Then he perked up. "So, have you at least gotten a toaster?"

"Of course." Robbie flashed a grin. "How else am I going to heat up my Pop Tarts?"

Cy groaned. "Ugh. How about wheat toast? Pop Tarts are disgusting!"

Robbie nodded soberly, like he wasn't even going to question this. "Understood."

"God, you're obliging," Cy laughed. "I'd think of a sexual favor or something to hit you up for, but I don't think there's anything you haven't done for me already."

"And enjoyed!" Ah, that enthusiasm was gratifying, Cy had to admit.

"I'd be happy to reciprocate," he returned primly and then grimaced.

"What?" Robbie didn't glance at him, because it was foggy, but Cy felt his concern.

"Man, I want all the sex in the world, but… can I take a hot shower first? I'm telling you, my joints hurt—that thing we did on the mats on the ground, that was *not* easy!"

"Yeah, absolutely." Robbie nodded. "I can give you a rubdown or something, you know? Don't worry—I'll take care of you."

"Yeah," Cy said, his lips parting and his entire face going slack. "You will." God. He was so gone. He'd never laid himself so open for heartbreak in his life.

He'd damn well better get some decent sex out of it.

Something Real

CY TOOK him up on the shower, and Robbie felt a little bit of pride in having a clean bathroom and an apartment ready for company.

While the water ran, Robbie went and fetched him a T-shirt and his one pair of briefs, since Cy didn't seem to wear boxers, and set them on top of the toilet for when Cy got out. While he was waiting, he took off his outer clothes, and after *way* more deliberation than was probably necessary, he took off his jeans and folded them up on top of the hamper.

The socks he left on. He knew it was probably unsexy as hell, but his heater was just kicking on, and he figured frigid feet would be *way* less sexy than socks. On that note, he put the condoms and lubricant on the pillow next to him. Because sex. Sex would happen there.

He'd slid into bed and pulled out his Kindle to start reading before it occurred to him to *actually* read porn instead of *pretend* to read something else.

But then he thought, *Cy is coming out of the bathroom to get into bed with me and have sex*, and his boner shot out so hard it almost made a hole in his boxers.

He found himself staring blankly at his Kindle page while he was clenching his asscheeks and thighs together and pressing his groin against his flattened palm, spurred on by just the *thought* of sex with Cy.

Oh God. I bet he likes to top sometimes too.

Robbie made a strangled little sound in the back of his throat and reached under his T-shirt to pluck at his nipples. Oh, he hadn't counted on this when he'd gone to see Cy dance. He'd *hoped*, of course, because hey, *sex*—but he hadn't counted on it. He'd assumed there would be talking and he'd *hoped* there would be kissing, but Cy… Cy seemed to be all in, and Robbie was going to have sex with… well, someone he was in a relationship with.

Like, he could say boyfriend for real.

The thought was almost erotic. He pinched one of his nipples especially hard, tilting his head back and exploiting that magnetic connection between his tender nipples and his erect and aching cock.

He was so immersed in the sensation of his own hands on his body that he didn't hear the water shut off or Cy pad in from the connected bathroom.

"You reading porn?" Cy asked, startling him.

"Nope," Robbie breathed, letting the Kindle balance on his chest while he ran the hand not playing with his nipples down his stomach to the waistband of his shorts.

"If you're going to start without me, you need to let me see!" Cy protested, and Robbie looked up to see he hadn't made use of the T-shirt or briefs *at all*.

A few droplets of water clung to his mostly dry hair, and he loosely clutched one of Robbie's new towels—pale blue—against his privates.

Robbie wanted nothing more than to slide his palms and fingers along that smooth skin and the defined muscles underneath it.

"C'mon, soldier," Cy taunted, dropping the towel to the floor and standing back with his arms crossed. "Strip."

"Nungh…."

Oh God, Cy was naked. And beautiful. And half-erect.

Robbie set the book down on the bed table and slid his boxers down his hips and his T-shirt over his head. Shivered.

"Cold?" Cy asked, squinching his nose teasingly, like a cat. "You don't *look* cold. Your balls ain't shriveling. Your cock is *big, full, and hot*."

"Uh-huh," Robbie agreed, and he ran a finger from his balls to the dripping head, shuddering when the rough pad of his forefinger skated in his precome and abraded the soft skin of his crown. "Yeah."

"Do it again," Cy whispered, stretching out sideways on the bed with his head at Robbie's hips.

Very slowly, Robbie complied.

When his finger got to the end of his cock, Cy stuck the tip of his tongue out and lapped gently at the tip.

Robbie's brain shorted a fuse or two, and he let out a long, shaking breath.

"Here," Cy whispered. "I only teased you. Let me try it again."

"Yeah, sure."

"Maybe you could squeeze it a little, you know, aim that thing where it needs to go?"

Oh, he was wicked. Robbie complied—would have complied if Cy had sat on his face and said, "Rim me!"—but now, when Cy was the one about to—

"Oh yes!" Cy breathed, licking again. "Squeeze it some more, really slow. Let me see what you want tonight."

Long. Hard. And slow.

They'd done hard and fast—a couple of times.

This time was all about slow.

The pressure of Robbie's fist coupled with the evil teasing of Cy's tongue were enough to push another drop of precome through the slit. And another. And another.

Cy groaned and wriggled around on the bed until he was lying on his stomach between Robbie's legs. He cupped an inner thigh in each hand and pushed gently until Robbie was spread wide, a willing playground, cock throbbing to his thundering pulse while his asshole and balls were dusted by Cy's thoughtful breaths.

That clever tongue darted out again, this time tickling the base of Robbie's balls.

Cy looked up the length of Robbie's body and gave a Cheshire grin. "It's like I've had a playground across the street from my apartment. And I finally get a chance to play."

He followed it up with a long lick from the edge of Robbie's pucker up under his balls and along the underside of his cock. By the time he was pushing inexorably into Robbie's slit, Robbie could barely breathe.

"Nunnnnnnghhh...."

He tilted his head back and closed his eyes, and Cy did it again. This time Robbie put both hands on his stomach to *force* his hips to stay on the bed.

"*You* are sensitive," Cy laughed. He ran a finger in the slickness by Robbie's asshole and pushed in, just the tip.

Robbie's eyes rolled back in his head, and his thigh trembled under Cy's palm as a cold sweat sheened his body. "Yes...," he hissed.

Still wiggling the end of his finger, Cy licked again, this time stopping to nibble on the taut little string of flesh and nerves of the frenulum.

"Oh," Robbie moaned, his hips jumping, everything in his groin and ass begging, *grasping*, reaching for *more*. "You… uh… God. Wanna… please…."

The finger sank in to the first knuckle, and Robbie felt the spurt of precome heat his glans—and then the roughness of Cy's tongue as he licked it off.

The burn in his asshole was *exquisite*, and his cock was so swollen and hot, Cy's tongue felt cool.

"Nipples," Cy whispered, blowing breath across Robbie's cockhead.

"I might come," Robbie told him truthfully, because *God*.

Cy took one of Robbie's testicles in his mouth, gently, like he was breathing, and rolled his tongue around it. Robbie pinched his nipples hard and rhythmically, in the same pulse his hips were trying to thrust off the bed.

Cy let go of his ball and slid two fingers inside him, then covered Robbie's cockhead with his warm, wet mouth.

Burn, pressure, ache, caress—

"*Yes!*"

Robbie convulsed, his hips arching off the bed as he pressed his feet down, his hands flailing at the covers, the light behind his eyes exploding into red and black and gold. He keened, gasping, and was still gibbering, just sounds, when he felt the blessed, blessed warmth of Cy's naked body covering his and Cy's mouth on his own.

He tasted his own come hot and slick on Cy's tongue, and the kiss went long and slow while Robbie's body still trembled, rocking continuously from the shock of climax, from the shaking demand for *more*.

Cy gave him more. More kissing, drugging, building, until he sat back on his knees and fumbled with condoms and lube while Robbie stared at him, body humming, brain stuck on "stupid."

His rim was stretched and relaxed, and his body hovered on the threshold of aroused and compliant when Cy began to thrust inside of him. He closed his eyes and let the burn and the ache roll through him, allowed another person's flesh to push into his own. Allowed Cyril to thrust inside his heart.

The colors behind his eyes went golden, bright, like sunshine, and he moaned softly and lifted his legs around Cy's hips, clutching his biceps and shoving down with each thrust up.

Cy's breathing rushed in his ears, and sweat from exertion spattered Robbie's forehead. Still, in his mouth, he could taste that combination of Cy and come that tinged his sense of smell with musk and amber.

"Open your eyes, Robbie," Cy whispered against his temple. "I need to know you see me."

He punctuated that with a sharp thrust and a long, slow withdrawal, and Robbie opened his eyes and watched Cy's face as he worked.

"So beautiful," Robbie said, moving to trace a broad cheekbone with his thumb. Cy's hair hung to the side like a curtain, and Robbie loved the hair, because it was how Cy saw himself, what he wanted to be, and Robbie loved *him*, loved the man fucking him. And how could he not? How could love not happen, their bodies pounding slow and hard, the sweat sliding between them, rolling off Cy's skin like diamonds?

"My eyes, soldier," Cy rasped, lips twisting into a smile. Robbie looked into them, lost, the pressure, pleasure, and pain in his ass swelling, growing, pushing out all other thought, taking his body over like a wave took a well-tumbled beach. His dick lay between them, untouched, aching for release, and Cy licked the outer rim of Robbie's ear, his rhythm faltering for a beat while their bodies melded together. "Stroke yourself," he ordered softly before pushing up again.

Robbie's hand felt unfamiliar around his own cock, he'd been so lost in the haze of possession, but as soon as he wrapped his fingers and began to stroke, the sharpness of the cliff's edge pressed along his nerve endings. Cy began to move faster, and Robbie kept up. Together they pumped and pounded, thrust and squeezed, until orgasm crashed down Robbie's spine, squeezed his balls and his taint, and clenched his asshole in the glorious name of release.

His hand grew hot and slippery, and Cy's gasp and scream of climax echoed in the brightly lit little room, rolling through Robbie's once barren apartment, filling it with the two of them, the sound and smell of their sex.

Cy gave an *oof* and collapsed on top of him, licking his shoulder desultorily, both of them lost in comedown.

Robbie closed his eyes, sleepy and disoriented, and made a disappointed sound when Cy pulled out. His body felt empty, vacant, because in those moments of sex, he'd had someone inside him who had filled him to his heart.

Then Cy came back with a warm washcloth, and after some cleanup, he put the towel on the bed stand and turned off the light.

Robbie rolled into him almost at once, and Cy responded with an arm over his shoulder and soft touches of his lips against Robbie's temple.

"Good?" Cy asked, but it didn't sound like he had doubts.

"Glorious," Robbie said, throat thick. He felt a little weepy, and he couldn't remember ever feeling like that when he'd bottomed, not even for Adam. "You... you sort of rocked my world."

He expected Cy to laugh, but he didn't. "You are telling *me,*" Cy mumbled, and his voice sounded thick too.

Remember, Robbie, you're gonna be brave.

"I feel sorta...." God, this was hard.

"What?" Cy asked quietly against his ear.

"This is serious already," Robbie said apologetically. "I'm sorry. I don't want to scare you." He closed his eyes, burying his face into the sweaty hollow of Cy's body.

"Robbie?" Cy said delicately into his ear.

"Yeah?"

"If it hadn't been serious, I don't think we would have gotten past the second date."

Robbie half laughed. "Wasn't that when I crashed my damned car?"

Cy crushed him hard in those deceptively slender, muscular arms. "Yup. It's serious. You're not alone."

Oh. Dammit. He swallowed hard against the tightness in his throat and behind his ears. "I'm so glad," he rasped, closing his eyes against the unwelcome emotion burning there.

"Yeah." Cy kissed his temple. "Me too."

Robbie didn't remember falling asleep after that. Everything, every shadow in the darkness, every breath he took, seemed saturated with the man in his arms.

Even his dreams.

HE WOKE up the next morning to the buzzing of his phone by the bed, and he picked it up blearily, snuggling back into Cy's warm body.

"'Llo?" he mumbled.

"Robbie? I'm sorry, sweetheart, did I catch you sleeping?"

He blinked hard. "Yeah, Mom. Day off. I sleep in."

Cy grumbled behind him. Robbie had figured out from their other sleepovers that he wasn't a quick riser.

"Sorry, honey," she said again, her voice quavering.

"'S no worries," he said through a yawn. "Wha's up?"

"Well, honey. I was… I mean, your father was wondering… if you still… you know. Felt like you did on Monday night."

"Like I'm gay?" he said, wishing he could laugh about it.

"Oh—we really don't like that word."

He could picture the uneasy look on her face then, as though just hearing it meant she had committed a sin.

"Sorry you don't like the word, Mom," he said, resigned. "Because that means you don't like me."

"But Robbie!" And he heard a bit of panic in her voice.

"What? I mean, I know I'm an only child, but seriously—"

"You were an only child because we couldn't have any more," she said tearfully. "We wanted a houseful. Are you telling me I'm not *ever* getting grandchildren!"

"No," he said, wondering if there was a rule or something about discussing kids when you were in bed with your newish boyfriend after sex. "I'm saying that I'll have to adopt or surrogate or something."

"But it won't be your child if you adopt!"

Robbie's brain hurt. "I think it will be," he said softly, thinking of Micah and the heartbreak of exiting his girlfriend's son's life. "If you want to be the mean grandma that we don't talk about, then that's your problem." Okay, so that wasn't nice. Sue him. Cy was nuzzling the back of his neck and stroking his stomach softly—not even sexually, but in a comforting way that told Robbie he was awake for this too.

"You and *who*, Robbie? I mean, how do you even know this gay thing works yet? You just broke up with Ashley!"

"I've been gay since…." He closed his eyes and had to think. "Since I first thought about boys. I never thought about girls."

"But Robbie—you would have said something!"

"I'd need to get it in between Dad's jokes. You remember the charming one about steers and queers? He told that to everyone he knew when I was twelve. That was awesome."

"Oh, Robbie, you can't blame us for not knowing—"

And that quickly, he was angry. "I can blame you for not *listening*. Every time you pushed someone to the edges of your little world, Mom, you were doing the same thing to *me*. Don't worry, I know *exactly* how you feel about me now. I'm every queer Dad's ever made fun of, every fag he's ever sneered at when he turned his back. Believe me, Mom, I'm *really fucking aware* of how you and Dad feel about me now."

For a moment there was just his pained, suppressed breathing—and her pained, suppressed sobs.

"We didn't know," she wept. "How could we know we were saying those things about you?"

"Because you were saying them about *somebody's* son," he snarled. "Why not your *own*?"

And then he hung up on his mother.

Cy didn't say anything for a minute, just stayed tight against his back, cheek against his shoulder blade.

"Sorry," Robbie said, burying his face in the covers. "Shitty way to start the morning."

"But not your fault." Cy smoothed his hair from his temple, and for a moment Robbie allowed himself to fall into that comfort.

"So," he said briskly, like he wasn't falling apart. "Do you want Denny's or oatmeal? I'm up for both."

Cy let out a low whistle. "Well, we may have to settle for McD's—and soon—if I'm going to make it to work on time. I didn't realize we'd slept in so late."

Robbie felt a smile glow in his chest, and he pulled one of Cy's hands up so he could kiss the palm. "Had to warm you up after all that cold last night," he said softly, and Cy groaned.

"Oh God—we're doing it again *tonight*." Cy rolled away from him to fling his hand dramatically over his head while he sprawled on his back. "Man, I need to take some Advil before I even get to work. *Augh*—I don't know how pro dancers do it!"

"A lot less hot chocolate," Robbie said, winking.

Cy smiled back and sighed, stretching and rolling out of bed. Robbie looked at him for a second—just looked, enjoying the view. His body had been honed, yes, but as much as Robbie loved—uhm, liked— him, he could admit that Cy had a few more pounds than that Emory guy who had torn out his knee and had been on all the news feeds the Christmas before.

"Why *aren't* you pro?" Robbie asked, suddenly curious. Cy had amazing moves. The other teachers had been confident and graceful, but Cy had been *mesmerizing*, and not just because Robbie thought he was pretty special off stage as well. "I mean, you're amazing—why...?"

Cy shrugged and reached for the T-shirt and briefs he'd brought from the bathroom while Robbie had been pretending to read the night before. "I've auditioned for Music Circus a few times—made it too." He pulled the T-shirt on first, his nudity apparently not bothering him in the least. "But the teaching...." He slid the briefs on. "The *teaching* just, you know, does something for me that the dieting and competition doesn't. Can't explain it. I mean, I'm sure someday soon I'll have to get my shit together and find a way to make better money than bussing and teaching—"

"Hard on the body," Robbie agreed with concern.

"Yeah." Cy nodded. He'd left his jeans over the bedroom chair, and he reached for them next. "And nobody sets out to be a busboy his entire life, you know?"

"Feel ya." Robbie pulled a clean pair of boxers and a T-shirt from his dresser, and his jeans from the night before off the hamper. "I don't know if I want to work in a warehouse for the rest of my life, but there's guys that do, you know? My boss, he's got a degree in *theology*, if you can believe that. And he loves working in a warehouse. Is good with the employees, likes moving his body. I can't see him as a reverend or whatever, and his kids are fun as hell. But he has a life that's not the job." Micah and Teddy had talked a *lot* the night they'd come over to drink, and Robbie liked being able to just pull that shit out of his ear. "So, you know, if I go back to school, it'll be to become a better person, maybe not to do a thing with it."

He hesitated in the doorway and checked on Cy to make sure he had everything he needed before Robbie disappeared into the bathroom. "What?"

Cy just looked at him with sort of a surprised adoration. "That's…
that's really smart," he said, sounding puzzled.

Robbie grinned. "Man, I'm not an *entire* fuckup—"

"You were in the Army for eight years!" Cy half laughed. "Not a
fuckup."

Some of Robbie's excitement drained away. "Yeah," he said, feeling
empty for the first time since he'd seen Cy dancing on the boardwalk.
"But I did some of that to try to escape the gay."

"You could have done it by fucking every girl who breathed," Cy
said, taking the few steps to cross the room and kiss him on the cheek.
"Your way is braver."

Robbie smiled again, knowing time was at a premium. "Well, right
now it has more perks. But go make us some coffee while I'm in the
shower. I've got a couple of stainless steel travel mugs in the cupboard
over the sink. I like mine with lots of cream and sugar."

Cy let out a low chuckle, and Robbie rolled his eyes.

"No coffee puns," he warned. "They're beneath us."

And with that, Cy let out an honest guffaw and Robbie retreated to
the shower, still chuckling.

FORTY-FIVE MINUTES later they pulled up to the tiny grammar school
off Watt Avenue, across from what used to be McClellan Air Force
Base. Robbie found a parking space next to one of the islands that ran
parallel to the school. The other vehicles ranged from new minivans
to old sports cars, and his wasn't the only truck parked there either.
A truly eclectic mix—and the population inside the school cafeteria
reflected that.

"This is the beginners' class," Cy told him as they walked through
the doors. He'd bought five giant iced coffees at McDonald's to make
up for getting there too late to set up. Now he winked at Robbie and
hustled to the other side of the cafeteria, where a sort of office was set
up on the long narrow half of a cafeteria table. He set down the coffees,
smiled ingratiatingly at the fiftyish woman with the graying curly hair
sitting at the table, and started shucking his outerwear to the pile in the
corner.

The woman said something Robbie couldn't quite hear, and Cy
shot Robbie a sort of embarrassed smile and replied.

Suddenly Robbie was the victim of a seriously skeptical once-over. He smiled weakly and waved, and the woman at the table dismissed him and turned her attention back to Cy.

"Hurry! Help the second mat with stretches!"

Laid out in the cafeteria were two rows of red and blue gym mats long enough to dominate three-quarters of the length of the room. Each row of mats sported a row of children ages two to maybe twelve, wearing everything from track pants to tutus, sitting down and stretching. The same teachers who had danced the night before either sat at the front of the room and stretched, showing the kids what to do, or, like Cy, walked from kid to kid and helped with form.

As Robbie had noted the night before, some of those kids needed a *lot* of help. One of the boys, an awkward blond who kept having to be called back to attention, apparently had tendons tight enough to launch missiles, and Cy spent a lot of time helping him stretch out while the boy smiled back and said... not a word.

Another boy kept getting up and taking off, screaming until he was caught and calmed down in full-body pressure hugs that appeared to reassure him. A little girl with the facial features of Down's syndrome smiled as she tried valiantly to touch her toes.

By the time the kids all lined up to take a warm-up lap around the gym, Robbie had an inkling as to why Cy would rather teach dance than dance professionally.

Because he was—like the gruff woman who shouted encouragement to the children and asked for high fives from behind the ledgers—a true teacher at heart. Maybe not in school, which Cy showed no interest in whatsoever, but at *this*, which all of the staff seemed to really love.

This was important to Cy. He'd confessed he didn't make a lot of money here, but Robbie watched him and thought that maybe, like his gray-haired mentor, he could do this happily for the rest of his life.

As long as he could have his time in the spotlight too.

The children finished their warm-up laps and split into two groups. One group faced the east wall and lined up at the end of the mats, and the other group moved *to* the east wall and faced the west wall in a line at the end. The instructors all sat equidistant apart, and each line of mats worked on a different skill. The line by the door worked on back rolls, while the line by the wall worked on front rolls. The students would execute the move three times with each instructor and, at the end of the mat, go wait in the next line to work a different move. When all the kids had been through, the move changed and the spotters switched position accordingly.

Robbie liked this format. Each kid got individual time, each instructor got to interact, and every skill was learned as thoroughly as possible for having forty kids of such varying degrees of ability in the room. He sat at the cafeteria table with a terrific assortment of moms, dads, and grandmas and listened to them talk about one another's children, getting excited when one of them learned a new skill or executed a new trick or even made it from one end of the mats to the other without tantruming or screaming or running away.

"Which one is yours?" asked a stick-thin woman with deep laugh lines around her eyes. "My grandson is the instructor there with the long braid and the beard—see?"

Robbie smiled at her and nodded. He recognized the guy from the night before. Broad and solid and hirsute, he was still an excellent dancer and a very able tumbler. He and Cy had run about on the mats making sure the other performers were in place. Today he was all attention on the tiny fluttery little girl with bright plastic clips in her hair and skin maybe a shade lighter than Cyril's. She tumbled like she was made of springs, and the young man laughed with her, clearly delighted.

"Yeah—he must like kids."

"Oh yes—he's so good with them. So which kid is yours?"

"That one," Robbie said, nodding to where Cy was working patiently to help the awkward boy bend over backward and catch himself.

"Owen?" she asked, sounding puzzled, probably because she knew the boy's parents.

"No, the one behind him—I just came with Cy to hang out."

Her eyes widened. "Cy brought a friend?" she asked, her voice hushed.

"Yes, ma'am, he did," Robbie said, hoping that if they kept this at "friend," Cy wouldn't get in trouble.

"Well, good for him." She smiled tentatively. "I watched him grow up here, you know. He and Corbin, they were in the same dance class as kids."

"He's an amazing dancer," Robbie said simply.

"He really is. You should have seen him at twelve—all of the boys go through this stage where they *have* to break something when tumbling. It's like a plague—I think it happens because, you know, boys grow so fast and their center of gravity shifts so quickly, but one month it was Corbin, and the next Cy, and six months later it was Mike. It was like all the boys, boom boom boom! I thought Anna was going to lose her mind! She works so hard to have boys dance, you know, because they really love it, but it's so easy to get discouraged."

Robbie thought about his dad allowing football and not dance, and how happy the kids—all of the kids—had been to be on stage. "That's really awesome," he said sincerely. "Not that they get discouraged but that people, you know, work to make that not happen."

He chatted with Corbin's grandmother for the rest of the class, and after that it was the mother of an eight-year-old named Kelsey, who probably *didn't* suspect that Robbie and Cy were dating but who was happy to tell him about how *all five* of her children were enrolled in at least one class of Anna's. And in soccer. And GATE. And choir. And some other shit that Robbie completely forgot, but *damn* did that woman have his respect. After Kelsey's mom it was Carter's dad, who coached soccer during the season but was happy to switch activities with the last tournament.

And after that it was gym team rehearsal, and Robbie watched with interest as some truly talented young people flipped, tumbled, ran, hopped, and flew, all in time to music. The little guy with the Russian accent, Mikhail, came in after the teaching and just in time for the tumbling rehearsal. Shane ambled in too with a sulky-looking blue-haired teenaged girl at his elbow, and together they sat and watched the little tumbler work.

Robbie had to admit—in spite of being older and smaller, the guy was better than Cy.

"He's showing off," the girl said, rolling her eyes, but the man next to her grinned.

"He's a diva," Shane said besottedly. "It's his due."

The girl snorted and then gasped as Mikhail jumped off a board and over a girl held on Cy and Corbin's shoulders. He landed on his hands and rolled forward, then came to a stop just at the edge of the mats.

He threw his hands up to indicate he was done, then turned abruptly and let the next tumbler do the same thing.

"Jesus," the girl breathed. The man next to her chuckled.

"That's my Mickey," he said mildly.

They watched until the finale, when Anna played the number from beginning to end and the performers threw their heart, soul, muscle, and sweat into practice, much the way they had the night before but *without* the fear. When they were done, right down to the practiced bows, Anna turned off the music.

"Was better?" she asked dryly, and a chorus of affirmatives littered the air. "Good. Be proud. We will *not* be performing it again tonight. The dance, yes, but this? No. They could not get us a better stage, and my joints ached just watching you. Be proud—and be ready to work on the pyramid sequence for the competition next month. My God, that part sucked."

There was some relieved laughter and chatter, and Cy went to help with the mats while "Mickey" walked up to chat briefly with Anna. He came back to his boyfriend right after. "She says yes, our Miss Serena may perform some moves to see if she can participate." He turned around for a moment. "Cy! Wait up—leave half a strip of mats out for me, yes?"

"Here?" the blue-haired girl said. "In front of—"

"Look at them," Mikhail said practically. "They want to go eat lunch and get on with their day. I know you have proper leotards on under those appalling clothes, so strip and warm up. I shall spot you."

"But…." The sulky teenager was suddenly a vulnerable child, and Mikhail took her hand.

"Listen to me, little one. Not everything about your life has been painful—*this* I know was a thing that set you free. Let it set you free again, yes?"

A frightened smile flickered across the girl's elfin features, and she stripped to a set of black footless tights and leotard before running barefooted across the cracked tile of the cafeteria and beginning stretches on the mats.

"She's scared," Shane said.

"It will go away," Mikhail said pragmatically. Then he smiled up at the man next to him with a look of such beauty it made Robbie's heart ache. "Someone to believe in her—this is what she needed."

Shane's smile was just as beautiful, but a little bit sad. "It definitely helps," he said softly.

Mikhail bit his lip. "We do our best, *lubiyime*."

Robbie had to look away. Whatever was between them, it was like the thing between Finn and Adam, and what he hoped he and Cy would have some day. Something time-tested and laden with a thousand everyday moments.

Something real.

He looked up and saw that the mats were put away and the girl had finished her stretching. "Mikhail?" she said hesitantly.

Mikhail called out, "Cy!"

Cy trotted across the cafeteria, and together they spotted the girl through some basic tumbling passes—and then through some advanced tumbling passes, because she moved like people moved in their dreams.

When she was done, Anna pulled her and Mikhail over with a jerk of her chin, and Mikhail turned to Cy. "Thank you," he said briefly. "I will see you tonight?"

"With bells on," Cy said, turning around.

"Bring your young man. Next time he can sweat a little and help us move mats."

Cy grinned at him quickly, a brief, brilliant flash of white teeth. "Can he get a performer's pass?" he wheedled.

Mikhail rolled his eyes. "Yes, sure. Go get one from Anna, they are on the table."

When Cy returned, he had a computer printout in his hand, and he grinned. "Gold!" He waved the paper around. "I got you in for free!"

Robbie laughed and stood, stretching. "Then the least I can do is buy you lunch," he said on a yawn. "C'mon. When do we have to be back?"

"Cal Expo at 6:30 p.m. sharp." Cy turned and waved at everybody left in the cafeteria, including the girl who was putting her street clothes on over her leotard. Almost everybody but the instructors had already gone. Cy's fellow teachers waved back, and Cy grabbed his hand and pulled him out into the cold, bright December day.

"Hey!" Robbie protested. "Don't I get to meet them?"

"We'll go out after the show," Cy said, practically skipping. "But for now, I'm starving, and I want takeout, and then I want to go shopping, and then I want to go back to my apartment and get my backup leotard, because last night's is too funky to wear."

"Shopping—"

But Cy was already ahead of him, and Robbie didn't have a chance to ask another question.

SHOPPING TURNED out to be Christmas shopping, because Cy hadn't gotten anything for his mom yet and Christmas was barely more than a week away.

"So," Cy said as they were wandering around the Hallmark store at Arden Fair Mall, "what did you get me?"

"How did you know—?" Oh God. Robbie couldn't look at him.

"I *knew* it!" Cy crowed, laughing. "I knew it. I got you something too."

Robbie smiled shyly. "My thing's not that good," he said quietly, looking at a series of picture frames that had cats on them. Cy glanced at the picture frames and then paused.

"Okay, these are awesome. Let's see... one, two, three, four— *perfect*. My mom's favorite sister, Bonnie, she's got four little girls. I call Aunt Bonnie, get their school pictures, one of me in the middle...." He grabbed one with a happy leopard on it and grinned hard at Robbie, the playfulness of his smile doing something *amazing* to the expansion in Robbie's chest. "*I* am a hero. I score points not just for giving a present, but *also* for communicating with family, and I've got my recital portraits, so I am *gold*!"

Robbie laughed and helped him gather the rest of the frames. "That's great," he said sincerely. Then he paused. "Uh, when are *we* going to give each other our presents?"

Cy winked at him gently. "Well, you've got Christmas Eve with your friend's grandma, and *I've* got Christmas Eve with my mom and Nana and the whole lot of us." He worried his lip with his teeth. "I... I mean, I've *never* introduced a boy to my mom. My nana doesn't know *who* I date. I, uh—"

"Not yet," Robbie said softly. "I get it."

"But, you know. Soon. I'll talk you *up* on Christmas Eve, at least to my mom. Then she'll be ready to meet you sometime when it's not so—"

Robbie thought of the whole moving-day fiasco and shuddered. "Public. Yeah, I've got it."

"C'mon, let's get these wrapped so we can have some downtime before the show."

They were walking out of the store and back into the mall for a few more items before Robbie realized Cy hadn't answered his question.

"So, uh, Christmas. Us. When?"

"Oh yeah!" Cy gave Robbie a rather heavy bag with three of the wrapped frames in it. "I was going to tell you—Ezra texted me this week. Wanted to ask us if we'd come to their Christmas night shindig. I guess both apartments are in on it, and there's going to be a fuckton of people. You know, Candy Heaven, Adam's cousin and his boyfriend, Finn's family. It'll be…."

"Oh my God!" Robbie shuddered. "Huge!"

"Well, *yeah*." Cy's grin faded. "But, you know. After that party, we can go to my place and…."

And *now* Robbie got it. "So, some happy big party time and some us time."

"Exactly!"

"Sounds great," Robbie told him. "In fact, that'll be perfect."

They took a few steps. "Are you freaking out yet?" Cy asked.

"About what?"

"About us planning Christmas together?"

Robbie thought about it. "No," he said quietly. "Not even a little."

THAT NIGHT he got to watch Cy dance again, and the charming children, and Cy's talented fellow teachers, and he had the strangest thought.

His parents would *love* this sort of thing. His mom hadn't been able to pass a damned fair without looking at all the exhibit halls and watching the school performances. This sort of thing would just charm the crap out of her.

But it wasn't something they'd see—because according to his dad, these weren't his kind of people.

Robbie got it then, that thing about forgiving people and being sad for them. His parents were going to miss out on a whole lot because they couldn't see.

But not Robbie. He was going home with someone he cared about, and they were going to have hot, slow, sensual sex, and Robbie was going to dance in private with as much grace as Cy showed in public. Robbie was the lucky one—he knew that now.

All I Want for Christmas….

CY'S MOTHER owned a small house off Truxel in Natomas. The little suburb between Del Paso and San Juan was actually not bad. It wasn't *rich* like the area across the freeway, but there were a lot of homeowners who took pride in their small patches of land and neatly painted homes, even though almost everyone had hurricane fences up to make sure their lawn ornaments weren't stolen by careless teenagers from the nearby high school.

But Helene McVeigh was doing all right. Her house was a little bigger than her sister's house in Levee Oaks and the area was better than her brother's house in Del Paso Heights, and the other siblings all had apartments, so she usually ended up hosting holidays. Cy didn't mind. His cousins would come over to play, running over one another like puppies and trying *so hard* not to tell what they'd gotten one another for the big name-draw gift exchange that they'd instituted since the number of grandkids had exceeded six.

This year Cy had drawn his youngest cousin, Stella, who was two. He'd bought that gift after the picture frames, and remembering Robbie's wonder that they were buying for a little kid made Cy smile now.

Yeah, Cy had been *an* only child, but he'd never been *the* only child, and he thought that made a big difference. In spite of Robbie's military experience and his friends from work, there was something exceedingly *lonely* about Cy's boyfriend, and Cy sort of loved that Robbie gravitated toward him. He'd never lacked for family, always reveled in friends, but being Robbie's one person made him feel special in a way he'd never anticipated. *This* was why people picked one person forever and ever amen—because that one person mattered more than anyone else. There was no democracy in monogamy, and Cy got that now like he never had before.

The conversation in the living room had reached fever pitch, which was usually when Cy liked to sit back and watch the chaos. The McVeighs were putting on a good show tonight. Cy had one uncle who was always in a get-rich-quick scheme, and he was trying to get everyone to invest in something marginally legal while, in a completely separate conversation, Nana declared loudly that marijuana dispensaries were the devil's work. It wasn't quite holding Cy's attention tonight, though. He moved restlessly. This was fun and he loved his family, but he wanted....

Wanted Robbie there to share it with. He wasn't sure if corn-fed Robbie Chambers was quite ready for this much *loud* in the same place, but he sure would love to see Robbie in the middle of all these people, being honest, being kind, maybe escaping to play with the kids when the argument in the living room got too out of hand.

One of the best things about crowds was how easy it was to slip away, and Cy walked from the overheated space of his mother's living room and down the hallway. She liked pictures with dark brown and black backgrounds, and it tended to make the room claustrophobic when there were only two people there, let alone twenty-two, plus the kids running in and out.

His mother's room had been forbidden when he was a kid, probably because she'd had boyfriends and, like any adult woman, had things in there that no kid needed to see. But now he didn't give a crap about her porn or who she was seeing now. Whoever it was, it wasn't serious enough for her to bring him to Christmas, so he didn't need to worry about the guy.

All he really wanted was a quiet place to sit and a chance to text Robbie.

Hi, Soldier. How's tricks?

He waited, hoping he hadn't pulled the guy away from some vital family powwow—or, maybe an adoption into a family that didn't seem to hurt him quite so much. But apparently not, because Robbie got back within the minute.

I was hoping to hear from you. Tricks are good.

He sent a picture then, of the white rural equivalent of what was going on in Cy's mom's front room. Happy kids running around a cold twilight yard, a couple of big dogs, and grown-ups in conversational clots, beverages in hand. The centerpiece of the picture was two boys, pale cheeks red from the cold and identical blue-gray eyes staring out from black lashes. Pretty, pretty boys—brothers, probably—and smiling at the camera like Robbie was a friend.

Nice guys—Micah and Teddy?

Yeah. This is a good family. I like it here. Maybe I can bring you sometime.

Cy's heart jumped in his throat. He wasn't sure if he could bring Robbie here *any* holiday. Yes, the cousins knew and didn't care, but his mom's generation was not so forgiving. And God forgive his nana know.

I'd go. He swallowed, hurting. *But I'm not sure I can bring you here.*

Pause. Well, he'd said as much. Better hurt now than not know what was coming.

That's okay. We'll work it out.

Cy blinked, suddenly pissed, and not at Robbie. *Well, if you're not welcome, I'm not coming. We'll do the friends-are-family thing. I can do that. As long as we have brunch with Mama once in a while, I think we can deal.*

I love that you call her "mama." Mama's boys are good boys.

Cy laughed. *Not too good.* And then, because Robbie had been wonderful and Cy was starting to realize he was one lucky bastard: *I really miss you tonight. I didn't expect to.*

I knew I'd miss you. But then I'm pathetic and needy, so, you know.

Oh, hell. *No. No I didn't. I never expected this, and I never expected to need you.* A dance. A dance on the boardwalk. A phone call. A date. A one-night stand. Another. A *relationship*. Was this how it happened? How you fell in love—

Oh God.

His hands shook so bad he fumbled the text twice. *I never expected to love you.*

His phone rang.

"You love me?" Robbie sounded so hopeful, but Cy had just put it in writing, hadn't he?

"Yeah," Cy whispered. "I so do—"

"'Cause I've loved you since… God. It just settled into me. It's soon—"

"But I've *never* felt like this!" Cy almost wailed, feeling a little betrayed. "A day, a week, a month—I've had those relationships, and *none* of them felt like this. *None* of them felt like you should be *here* next to me when I'm in the middle of family. How did that *happen*?"

"I've got no idea," Robbie said softly. "Are you sorry?"

"No." That was the truth. "But I lied. I know how it happened."

"Yeah?" Some of that humor that made Robbie so much fun laced his voice. "How?"

"You looked at me like I was beautiful and you let me be free."

"You are beautiful. I wouldn't want you any way but free."

Cy's eyes were watering, and he remembered how Robbie had tried to hide his face that night in his bed. "This is good," he said thickly. "This is a really good feeling. But it's scary as hell. Don't fuck this up, soldier."

"I won't," Robbie vowed. "I promise."

Cy needed the moment lighter—he just did. He took a deep breath, and another. "So, you eaten yet?"

"Not yet—we're lining up now. Everybody brought, like, potluck and stuff. I bought rolls because I'm afraid of making lasagna or potatoes au gratin."

"Oh! No! That shit is easy! Like, New Year's or something, we'll have to cook." He paused, because this was sort of tradition. "Unless you wanted to celebrate New Year's at the club. It's sort of a blast—everyone's a little wasted and there's, like, big exoduses from one club to the next. Fun shit, really. We could stay at my place, you know?"

"Yeah!" Robbie sounded genuinely excited. "I haven't done anything like that in forever! It would be really great to do the countdown and the dancing and the...." His voice dropped. "The kissing someone awesome at midnight."

Cy laughed gently. "I'd like to kiss someone *special*," he said, because he'd gotten laid a *lot* on New Year's Eve, but never with someone he kept longer than the next day.

"That'll do good too—yeah! Sorry, Micah—coming!"

"You gotta go," Cy acknowledged. "That's okay."

"Yeah. I love you, though. We can say that now, right?"

Oh yeah. "I hope so. Love you too."

They signed off, and Cy belatedly wondered if Robbie had heard from his folks. Not a good time to ask, he decided, because if no, that would hurt, and if yes and it had been awful, well, that would hurt worse. He looked at his cell phone for a moment and suddenly wished he'd thought to catch a snapshot of him, anything, because it felt wrong to not have any proof at all but the emptiness of the room now that the conversation was over.

The door creaked open, startling him, and his mother gave a little squeak. "Cy?"

"Sorry, Mama."

"What are you doing sitting here in the dark? It's almost time for dinner."

His mother clicked on the light and smiled at him warmly, and he thought for the umpteenth time how lucky he was to have her. She hadn't been that old when he was born, and his father—well, the man had tried for a few years before bailing. Cy hadn't blamed him—he remembered the fights, and as much as he loved his mother, he knew she hadn't always been the easiest person to get along with. Single motherhood had suited her, though—she liked being self-sufficient, and he had always been proud that she'd taken "a way with hair" and turned it into a cottage business. He also liked that she helped him with *his* hair, because he'd never been a fan of the usual, and the *un*usual got spendy.

"I was talking to a friend," he said, twisting said hair up behind him and snagging a clip from her drawer. It was hot in the house—felt good to get it off his neck.

"A good friend?" she said gently. "What's she like?"

Cy just regarded her steadily, thinking she was stunningly pretty, with strong cheekbones, full lips, and a round chin, one of those women who wouldn't show her age until she was eighty, and then she'd still put on a wig, do her makeup, and dress up right just to go out to brunch. Right now she was wearing a striking pantsuit in sapphire blue, trimmed with fake fur at the wrist and collar, with earrings to match. She even had sapphire pretties sprinkled around her updo and delicate little spring curls pulled coquettishly around her oval of a face. Cy had gotten his love of bold colors and bright fabrics honestly, and Helene seemed to appreciate how similar their tastes were.

And now she appreciated *him*. "*Not* a girl," she said in understanding. "Which is why you didn't bring your friend to see Nana."

He smiled, just a twist of the lips. "Yeah," he said. And then, because he and Helene had always been truthful with each other: "It sort of sucks. His family isn't… isn't down with the gay thing. I want to be with him tonight."

"And you're not because of…." His mom pulled her lips to the side. "That's sad. I'm sorry, son. I'll back you, you know. If you ever decide to bring him home for a holiday, it's my goddamned house, so you bring who you please."

Cy's smile was real this time. "Thanks, Mama. I'll be honest. We're a little new, or I would have done it this time. I hate leaving him alone."

"So he's a nice boy?" she asked, sitting down on the bed, ready to stop her life just for him.

"The best," Cy told her. "He's kind, Mama. And funny." His smile grew until it stretched his cheeks. "And he can *dance*."

"Oh, you're gone, then," she said. "A boy who can dance and who treats you right? How can you turn that down?"

"I can't," Cy said humbly. "I… I'm sort of scared. Mama, what if this doesn't work? It's the first time I've *ever* wanted someone enough to not give a damn what's around the corner. What if there *is* something better around the corner?"

"There's not," his mother said certainly.

"You have one of those mirror things?" He arched his eyebrow.

"No—it's just, once you're in this place, you start looking just at your person. If you're not *looking* around the corner, there's nothing waiting for you there." She grimaced. "Believe me, I have learned that the hard way."

Cy had always had that feeling, that maybe his parents' breakup hadn't been all his dad. And twenty years ago, it hadn't been particularly fashionable for a man to stay involved. "Well," he said, refusing to hold any grudges against either of them, "thanks for just giving me that advice for free."

Helene smiled, grabbed his hand, and pulled it to her lips to kiss like he was still a child. "Cy, can I tell you something?"

"Yeah, sure."

"It's something that may hurt you," she said hesitantly. "But… I think you need to know."

Uh-oh. "Hit me!"

"Your dad—when he left, he was pretty mad at me. But he still wanted to be your dad, you know?"

Cy nodded. He remembered awkward visits to McDonald's and the zoo. He'd always been a happy kid—hadn't really let the reality of his father's gradual absorption into the void outside his life bother him.

"And I was okay with that. But… God, you were around eight, right? And you came back from something—I think it was one of those things at Arco, right? The light show, the drama, those things. Anyway, you came in talking about how the girl in the show was awesome and kickass, and your dad said, 'So you're going to marry a girl spy?' and you said, 'Or a boy spy, because they were pretty awesome too!' And I knew right then—I knew who you'd be dating."

"*Everybody*," Cy laughed, because, well, yeah!

"And your dad opened his mouth to say... well, I'm sure it was something to tell you that you couldn't. I told you to go wash up, and we had our last fight."

Cy opened his eyes wide. His dad *had* done the Disneyland dad thing—and he couldn't remember this moment. Apparently it had changed his life.

"Why was this one the last one?" He tried to keep his voice light, but he was still too weighted from missing Robbie, and he heard the quaver.

"Because he wanted to come down like the hammer of God, honey. He wanted to tell you that you couldn't be like that. And you know me." She gave a crooked smile. "I've always been all for letting you be you. So this thing with being afraid if someone's going to let you down? *I* told your father he couldn't visit anymore if he was going to try to 'make a man out of you' or some such bullshit. *I* told him he had to let you be you or walk away. And it was hard for him to visit anyway. He loved you. He still does—"

"How do you—?"

"I send him pictures once a year. A letter at Christmas, one at your birthday. I tell him. I told him about the dancing and the makeup and the boys and the girls. He...." Her smile was so damned crooked. "His last letter back, he said, 'You've done a good job with him, Helene. But I don't know if I'd be good as his dad.'"

Cy took a deep breath, and another one, trying to wrap his mind around this. "That's... I mean...."

Helene wiped under her eyes with the back of her hand, and Cy reached to her dresser for a tissue, which she took. "See, I still don't know which one would have hurt you the most. The dad who would have tried to make you ashamed of who you are, or the dad who wasn't there. So... if *that's* why you keep looking, if *that's* why nobody's been good enough until now, you maybe need to know that. Your dad didn't stop loving you—not ever. *I* just didn't want you to ever think love could hurt."

Cy was wearing eyeliner and green sparkly eye shadow, mostly to make his older cousins think he was cool, but partly because it was

Christmas. He grabbed a tissue too and dabbed carefully around his makeup.

"Mama," he said after a moment, "I have *no* idea what to do with this."

"I told you," she said after a deep, quaking breath, "so you could maybe trust your instincts a little. So maybe you wouldn't be so scared. If it's real, it won't go away. That doesn't mean it can't hurt you—and I'd really like it not to—"

Cy shook his head, thinking of that terrible week when he didn't know if Robbie was going to call back or not. Thought of that moment, seeing Robbie shaking and pale in Adam and Finn's bedroom, absolutely certain that nobody could love him, or even like him, ever again because of the thing he'd done out of fear.

Seeing him bruised in the hospital, so *very* happy to see Cy and wanting so badly not to intrude on Cy's happy, free, solipsistic little life.

Thought of what would have happened, how he would have felt, if he had walked away from Robbie at any one of those times because he'd decided he just couldn't do relationships, nope, not Cyril McVeigh.

"Love hurts," he said, because it was a revelation. He hadn't thought of it that way, but he'd been living it since Robbie had first stepped up on the boardwalk and danced with him. "I… I guess I knew that."

"I'm sorry," she whispered, and he wondered if maybe later, he'd be mad at her. He couldn't right now. Right now, she'd given him the tools to look inside himself and see that he could do this thing.

"Love hurts," he repeated, touching her face gently. "But maybe I can survive."

She nodded, her chin trembling and her lips thinning as she threatened to fall apart for good. "You're so strong, son." He reached around her slender shoulders and let her rest her head on his much broader chest. "If anyone can survive love, you can."

They sat quietly, and he let her pull herself together while he thought of all the things he wanted to text Robbie *now*.

Robbie, I know why you were afraid of being rejected for who you are. I get that hurt now. But I'm not afraid of it anymore. It doesn't worry me to trust in love, or in you, because love hurts, and it can be weak, and it can even be deceitful, but if you love back, you can survive. I know that now. I'll love you back. I'm not even worried. We're going to be okay.

The door creaked, and Helene sat up quickly, checking her makeup and her hair on automatic.

"What are you doing in here?" Cy's nana said, leaning hard on her cane. She wasn't a big woman, but her hips and knees had been giving out one by one, until the cane had become her only means of mobility. Cy's mother had said frequently that she could probably use a walker, but Nana was afraid it would be too easy and sweeten her temper.

"Having a big meaningful talk, Mom," Helene said, managing to sound like a bored teenager at the tender age of forty-seven. "Do you mind?"

"We're all waiting for roast turkey and mashed potatoes. Of course I mind. Get out here and celebrate Christmas."

Helene stood up and turned to give Cy a hand up. He took it and bowed to her, just like they were on the dance floor. This was an old game from his first year in dance, and she curtseyed back and laughed.

"Merry Christmas, Mama."

"Merry Christmas, Cyril. Let's go eat."

Family, Family, and Family

ROBBIE ENJOYED his time at Micah and Teddy's grandparents' house. He met an *amazing* assortment of relatives, some related by blood, some related by friendship, and some just sort of related. (He still couldn't follow the convoluted series of marriage and family history that made Truman and Conway Micah's cousins. He just let it go.) He got to meet the infamous Aunt Stacy, who was little and plump and who dyed her hair platinum blonde and wore dramatically bold jewel-toned kaftans that flattered her not at all. She had six children, a family of blond, blue-eyed clones—or they would have been, if not for the varying degrees of mod, anime, and Goth hairstyles, piercings, and tattoos that decorated the older kids. Hair color from blue to green to magenta—he almost made them stop for a picture.

Micah had been right: the sturdy nine-year-old with the waist-length yellow hair and wearing the mismatched *everything* had been the fiercest proponent of women's rights Robbie had ever met. He found himself spending a lot of time with her, because she was a little diva and made him her personal valet for the evening. He fetched her everything from cookies to presents, for once giving her a leg up on the tumbling puppy shelter that was apparently her everyday life.

"It's okay to be chivalrous," she said when he first offered to hang her coat. "It doesn't undermine my power as a woman if you give me basic courtesy."

"Of course not," he said, bowing slightly, and that was it. He was hers for the rest of the night. Together they came up with the feminist equivalent of "testicles, spectacles, wallet, and watch"—although Robbie couldn't promise to make "ovaries, umbrella, backpack, and sweater" catch on before they next saw each other.

Robbie promised Micah's grandmother, a tidy midsize woman with deep laugh lines and Micah's gray eyes, that he would come during Easter and he'd bring his young man with him.

For a moment he almost didn't. Such a big, tumbling, happy family! They reminded him an awful lot of his own parents, actually. What if they *were* like his own parents, but only okay with the gay. Would he subject Cy to that, when Cy expected things to be safe?

Then he remembered that Cy was brave. Robbie could be too.

"Yeah," he said after a swallow. "I'd love to come back."

"You have to," Kisha, his small blonde shadow, said seriously. "Someone has to hold my Easter basket and help me find eggs."

"You can't find your own?" Aunt Stacy asked caustically.

Her youngest simply raised her eyebrows. "Yes, but I can find so many I will need help." She flashed a winning smile at Robbie. "You will be my help."

"Oh thank God," Micah muttered under his breath. "I'm off the hook for this year."

His mother, Karen, who was also small and plump, but with gray eyes much like her son's, smacked him in the arm. "Don't be lazy!"

"Mom, she's gotten all the candy since she was born!"

"I can tell that's been a hardship," she drawled. "You look like you've suffered candy deficiency for every day of your young life. I can't apologize enough."

"Oh my God!" Micah looked at Robbie in exasperation. "Do you see? Do you *see* what I have to put up with?"

Robbie held up a finger to put him on pause, then turned to the giant table full of sweets and cookies made by the entire family, and turned back with an enormous iced brownie topped with peppermint sprinkles. He offered it to Micah, who took it with a raised eyebrow.

"Yes," Robbie said dryly. "I see. But the deficiency appears to be cured now, so I think you'll be okay by Easter."

There was general laughter, and Robbie winked smugly. And decided that he liked this place, and he could take a risk. After the white elephant gift exchange (Robbie, upon urging from Micah and Teddy, had brought a two-pound candy bar and wrapped it in an oversized box), he drove home from the foothills happy, and careful of the ice on the road.

His apartment was cold when he got in, but one of his purchases when he and Cy had gone shopping was one of those wax warmers that was essentially a pretty ceramic thing on top of a light bulb and some low-temp wax to put into the tiny basin. He had some that smelled like cinnamon and vanilla, and he turned the warmer on as soon as he got into the room. The lighted felt Christmas tree, *A Christmas Story* on television, and the nice smell coming from the light that looked like a 49ers' helmet—it wasn't Cy, and it wasn't his folks' house, but it was a better place of his own making.

It was like a Christmas present to himself.

At ten thirty, he got two texts—one from Cy and one from his mother.

Cy: *Are you home yet?*

Robbie: *Yeah—are you?*

Cy: *Not yet. Brb*

Huh. But they would talk later, and that was encouraging.

Mom: *Robbie, we missed you tonight. If you promise to take it all back, we can have breakfast tomorrow.*

Oh *hell* no.

Robbie: *I missed you too. But coming out was still better than lying to the rest of the world. Merry Christmas.*

He scowled at the phone and tried to capture some more of his goodwill. Dammit—he'd had *such* a good self-actualizing moment going there too! Well, fucking hell.

Determinedly he tried to immerse himself back into silly Christmas movies, and did such a good job of it that the knock on the door made him jump.

Cy was there in a sapphire velveteen shirt and black jazz-flared pants and that gorgeous, gorgeous purple puffy coat.

Robbie threw open the door and pulled him in, kissing him hot and welcoming while he slid the coat off and covered Cy's body with his own. Cy burrowed into him for a moment, complaining, "God, it's cold out there!"

"Dangerous to drive up in the foothills," Robbie mumbled. "Come sit down—do you want some coffee or chocolate?" He hadn't made chocolate for himself, but suddenly that seemed like an awesome idea.

"Chocolate?" Cy perked up. "Oh my God, I love this movie. It just started too! Here." And suddenly he was completely in charge. "Let me go steal some of your clothes and a blanket, and then you put your jammies on too, and we'll sit down and have chocolate and veg. You think?"

Robbie nodded. "I think," he said, a stupid smile on his face. "I think I love you like *super* huge right now, and seeing you is the best present ever."

Cy was already heading back to Robbie's room, and he paused and turned with a small smile on his face. "Soldier, you have not stopped saying the good shit."

He had bourbon and marshmallows, both of which made hot chocolate better. Together they snuggled up in their sweats and watched *A Christmas Story* and, when that was over, *Love Actually*. They didn't talk—not about their evenings, not about family—both of them just content to hold each other and smell the vanilla cinnamon and drink spiked hot chocolate. Toward the end of *Love Actually*, Cy turned around and kissed Robbie, and for a moment he thought it would turn sexual.

And it *was* sexual, and sexy and slow, but it didn't lead to sex. It wasn't until the movie was over and they'd both brushed their teeth and crawled into bed that it hit Robbie that they really *had* done things ass-backward. Making out—and *just* making out—was sort of an amazing thing. He was a fan.

"But tomorrow," he said, "we can have sex." He was spooning Cy, and he pulled Cy's ponytail aside so he could nuzzle his ear.

"You know," Cy said sleepily, "I'm just sort of glowy that we *didn't* tonight. God, I'm tired."

"I know." Robbie turned his head and yawned. "And God, so much I wanted to tell you but…." Ugh.

"Talked and talked," Cy agreed. "Yeah. And more talking tomorrow night." He yawned. "But see, best thing about the I love you?"

"Hit me."

"I love you even when we're not doing the thing."

Robbie laughed softly. "Merry Christmas, Cy. I love you even when we're not doing the thing."

"Merry Christmas, soldier. We'll do the thing tomorrow."

Of course they would.

IN FACT they woke up that way, Robbie hard and thrusting against Cy's backside through their clothes. Cy groaned, and they kicked their sweats off, and then Cy kept his back to Robbie's front, even as he reached for the condoms and lube and handed it back.

"How long?" he demanded tersely.

Robbie's brain struggled to wake up. "About seven inches, but I never measured?"

Cy turned his head and torso around just to pinch Robbie's cheek. "You're *adorable*. How long before your window clears and we can fuck each other bare?"

Oh! That made so much more sense. "Two months," Robbie muttered. He sheathed himself in record time and squirted lube on his fingers. "Two months and then...."

"Ah...," Cy breathed as Robbie breached him with his fingers. "Yeah. Then that. Then your come inside me. I sort of love that—it's sexy-dirty as hell."

With that he rocked backward, taking Robbie's fingers deeper and moaning breathily.

"So're you," Robbie growled. He spread his fingers, delighting in Cy's sex noises.

"I'm gonna grab myself," Cy said. "You'd better be inside me before I come."

So it was like that, was it? Robbie grabbed Cy's thigh and pulled until his leg was closer to his chest. His ass was spread like this, exposed and ready, and Robbie adjusted his angle and thrust in. Ahh.... Cy's body was heaven, and Robbie could live there. The hot friction of his ass felt dynamically sensual, but it was more than that.

It was that the two of them merged felt right, like their natural state. Like every night should be spent in front of the television, making out in their sweats, and every morning should be spent deep inside each other, pulsing with need.

Cy grunted and started meeting Robbie thrust for thrust. He was getting close, and Robbie felt the swelling under his cockhead, the one that said Cy's sweet spot was *right there*. He changed his angle one more time and Cy cried out, and again, and again, and—"I'm coming, dammit!"

He did, clenching *so hard* Robbie's vision went black. He stopped thrusting and started rutting, shifting until he was on top and Cy was spread below him, clutching the sheet.

"Faster?" Robbie begged.

"Yes, please!"

"Harder!"

"Please!"

"*Fucking now!*"

Augh! Yes! Robbie clenched and came, his entire body washing with the boiling cold of climax. For a few moments he quivered, stuck inside Cy, suspended by the force of his ejaculation, and then his limbs went slack. He collapsed on Cy's back, happy and boneless and willing to give sleep another try for a few minutes.

"Robbie?" Cy mumbled, still mashed against the pillow.

"Yeah?"

"Haven't stopped loving you."

"Me neither."

Not moving proved to be a really viable action for a long time.

THEY EVENTUALLY moved and showered. Then Robbie made oatmeal, and they talked quietly while they ate. They exchanged Christmas stories, as it were, and Robbie listened respectfully while Cy unburdened himself about his father.

"That's...." Robbie didn't even know how he felt about it. "I want to say messed up, but I...." He grimaced.

"What?" Cy regarded him steadily over his bright blue bowl of plain brown oatmeal. "I'm... I'm sort of dying to hear your take on it."

Robbie set his bowl down and decided that honesty hadn't failed them yet. "My mom told me that if I took it all back, I could go home this morning."

"Oh *fuck* no!" Cy's expression was validating.

"Yeah. I told her that. But you know, no swearing."

"Because Mama," Cy said seriously.

"Exactly. But... but she still loves me. I don't know if my...." His throat thickened. "I don't know if my dad will. I know that thing I did to Adam—that was 70 percent fear of what my father would do, hands down. And that was a fear you didn't have to have. I mean, I love you, so I'm biased, and I think maybe you being you, your dad would have just learned how not to be an asshole and loved you anyway. But what if he hadn't? I mean...." Robbie wasn't sure how to say this. "The guy I fell in love with—he was happy and free. I *needed* to see someone happy and free. You taught me how I was *supposed* to be. And... I mean, your mom sounds terrific, so maybe you would have been that way regardless, but...." Oh, how to say this?

"But what if I had grown up different, if I was afraid all the time?" Cy asked, saving him a little.

Robbie shrugged. "You might have grown up to be me," he said simply.

Cy got up from the table and wrapped his arms around Robbie's neck, close and warm and kind. "Nothing wrong with that, soldier," he said gently, kissing Robbie's temple. "But then, I'm not sure if I'm as strong as you are, so maybe this way is best."

Robbie turned his head and kissed the corner of Cy's mouth. He tasted like butter and sugar and cinnamon, and when he opened his mouth and furthered the kiss, for a moment Robbie thought the conversation was over.

But he found he had something to say, so he pulled back.

"I think you can handle anything," he said, knowing he sounded besotted and not caring.

Cy gazed at him steadily. "Not anymore," he said soberly. "I don't know if I can handle heartbreak. Not from you. I mean, maybe in a couple of years when I know all your faults—" He laughed a little. "—but not now. Not when I think we've got the world at our feet. I think it would destroy me."

Robbie nodded, knowing exactly what he was saying. "Then I'll take real good care of your heart," he said soberly.

It was a promise. They both knew it. On Christmas Day, no less.

Robbie's vows of being brave were going to have to be for real and true, because he had a whole lot to lose.

CY LOVED his scarf—wore it that night, in fact, tied around his ponytail, because, as he said, house parties got hot, even in the winter. Before they went to the party, they stopped by his house so he could dress and give Robbie *his* present of a hand-knitted scarf and gloves in a handsome brown and blue.

"Is this, like, a hint?" Robbie asked, grinning. He'd forgotten hat and gloves a few times, yes.

"Well, yeah," Cy said, winking. He sobered then. "That and, see, I was going to be all cool—no gifts, it hasn't been that long, blah blah blah. But there was this woman with a little semilegal cart outside of the K Street Mall, close to where all the construction is—you know?"

Robbie nodded. Yeah, he'd seen them building the big arena right off K Street, and he'd wondered how the locals liked all of the road construction to go with it. It was nice that they were thinking ahead and fixing the roads for the hordes to come, but it *sucked* if you drove by at the wrong time of day. "Yeah, I know the place."

"Well, I was walking down there and... well, she was selling handmade knitted stuff. And I *like* those colors on you!"

Robbie looked at them ruefully. "I like them too," he said, "but they're sort of plain."

Cy tugged the ends of the brilliant length of silk in his hair. "Yeah— but see? You get me and I get you. That's really all we need."

He'd put on makeup and his lipstick was still not dry, but Robbie wanted to kiss him in the worst of ways.

"Not yet," Cy said, putting a finger on Robbie's lips while he smacked his own. "And if we kiss, we'll never make it to the party, and I *want* to go to that party!" He started out of the apartment, and Robbie followed him downstairs.

"Why?" Robbie asked, although he wanted to go too.

Cy turned and pinned him with a gaze. "Because these people can be our friends," he said levelly. "But we need to go there like friends."

"You got the cookies and wine?" Robbie asked. It was important to bring something to a house party, right?

"Right here!" Cy held the expensive gift bag up as his feet hit the bottom landing. "Now can we... oh!"

Ravi and Anish were down at the bottom of the stairs, looking woefully up.

"Hi, guys!" Robbie put his hands on Cy's shoulder to steady them both from the abrupt stop. "What's up?"

Anish looked sheepish. "Our car broke down," he said, shaking his head. "We couldn't call someone to come pick us up, because—"

"Party?" Robbie asked, winking.

"Yes!" Ravi flailed his hands. "They got the downstairs neighbor to participate, and the old lady across the hall is *on a cruise*. It's the entire house! *Everybody!* And we may have to walk, because I don't think the busses run this late!"

"Or you could just ask us for a ride," Cy said dryly.

Ravi winked. "Well, since we knew you were going anyway and we saw the truck...." They both grinned, showing all their teeth, and Robbie had to laugh. Yeah, he and Cy had been planning to bail early, but why not? This was apparently an event for friends, and he was starting to learn you couldn't have too many.

"It's going to be a tight squeeze in the jump seats," he warned.

"Not for me," Anish said brightly. "I'm short!"

"Crap," Cy muttered, because good sport that he was, Ravi was nearly Robbie's height.

When Robbie and Ravi were settled in the front, Ravi said they'd try to find a different ride home, but Robbie was thinking it might not matter. They had assumed—right off the bat—that Cy and Robbie would be going. That they were welcome. That Robbie would have a good time. No whispering, no looking at each other warily. Maybe all it really took was the word of the man he'd once wronged.

They had to park down the block because the street was full on both sides. As they chattered their way through the darkness, careful of the patches of ice, it became apparent that *everybody* knew about the party.

Finn and Ezra stood outside the house, greeting people and taking coats and gifts. Finn took Cy's offering of wine and cookies and balanced them on his arm cast, smiled at both Cy and Robbie without batting an eye, and said, "Okay, so the food is going here on the bottom floor—Mr. Kazim." Finn looked around like he was telling a deep secret. "See, we asked him if it was okay if we could hold the party, and he got mad and asked why he wasn't invited. And the thing was, we kept thinking he was the mean guy downstairs, 'cause, you know, he just yells at us a lot, but it turns out? He was *lonely*. And I felt so bad! Adam and I have lived here for a *year* and he was mostly just the old guy who fought with the lady who lives across from us. But he was *so happy* to be invited. He's sort of in charge of drinks and snacks, so make sure you talk to him for a few minutes, okay? We're going to be inviting him to more stuff 'cause he's been, like, *so awesome* about this, right?"

Robbie found himself nodding enthusiastically, and when he looked around, he saw that everybody else was too. Apparently first impressions and Adam's instincts were right—there really *was* something magic about this kid. Robbie approved.

"We'll be sure to say thank you," Cy said earnestly, and Ravi and Anish echoed the thought.

"Here." Ezra took the bag from Finn before he dropped it, and gave it back to Cy. "If you go do that *now*, you can mingle. And give *me* the coats, because *he's* still hobbling around on a brace."

Finn paused for a moment and then grinned. "Wow. Yeah. Logic—usually I'm a fan, but dude. Planning for this thing...."

Robbie surveyed the brightly lit house and the people moving up and down the stairs, drinks in hand. "It looks huge," he said and then shivered completely without an agenda.

"And I'm keeping you out in the cold!" Finn laughed. "Go say hi to Mr. Kazim and then hang everywhere else."

"Hey," Robbie said, thinking about that quiet interlude in the bedroom, with the dog snoring at his feet and Jake the cat a deadweight in his arms. "What did you do with the animals?"

"Well, Clopper's at Rico's," Finn said, "because... *dogs*. But mine and Adam's room is off-limits—it's for anyone who needs a quiet place. So we set Jake up in there—mini cat box, food, water. He's pretty low-key anyway, but this way, he'll probably just hang."

"Good," Robbie said.

"You bonded too, right?" Ezra asked, and Robbie nodded. "Yeah, 'cause that cat—he's like a magic cat. He's important."

"Powerful," Robbie agreed with no irony whatsoever.

"Powerful cat," Cy muttered, shaking his head. "Whatever. C'mon—I need a beer and a canapé, and I need them stat!"

Robbie had been to a few big parties—before he'd enlisted, that had been about all his graduating class *did*. After he enlisted, there had been parties off base that had turned into big bacchanals with lots of sex, lots of drinking, and lots of assholes hoping to get blown in the closet.

He had never been to a big party quite this nice.

Mr. Kazim was every bit as sweet as Finn said he was. A compact man, about five six, he had silvering black hair and a handsome—almost impossibly handsome—middle-aged face. He walked them through the several ice chests full of soda and beer, the wine on the counter, and the table laden with... well, everything.

"Oh, look!" Ravi said excitedly. "Our curry dish is all gone!"

"That's because we brought it yesterday," Anish said dryly. "With as many people as Finn's parents had over, we're lucky the dish made it to the table."

"They did this *yesterday*?" Damn, Robbie was impressed.

"Well, sort of," Anish corrected. "Yesterday was family—so, well, friends and family and boyfriends—"

"Yeah, I get the idea," Robbie said dryly. Apparently Micah and Finn needed to meet.

"This is bigger," Ravi said simply, explaining nothing at all.

"So, yeah," Cy filled in. "They did this yesterday, except Finn's parents did it then, and Finn and his friends are doing it now."

"I'm surprised Adam isn't hiding in the closet with the cat," Robbie said soberly.

"I think he goes in there for minutes at a time to recharge."

Robbie turned around at the new voice and found Miguel there, with Ezra at his elbow. "Hey, Miguel. You all moved in?"

Miguel nodded, rolling his eyes. "Easy when you don't got so much to move, but simple, right?"

"Damned easy to clean," Ezra said, nodding. "Hey—you guys wouldn't want to take over meet-and-greet duty? We promise it won't be for more than twenty minutes, but Finn's getting tired, and we were going to carry him upstairs and ensconce him in his fucking throne. Remember—"

"Say hi to Mr. Kazim, one of us takes the coats and puts them...?"

"Oh—we set a coatrack upstairs, opposite of Adam's door, in front of Ms. Z's door. It's one of the big ones, but we got extra hangers, so you can just put them on the railing of the stairs going up to our place too."

"The good news is, there's so many people that the rooms are staying warm even with all the people in and out. The bad news is, we gotta be careful nobody's best winter coat gets knocked on the ground."

"We will take first shift!" Ravi said, and although Anish smacked him on the arm, they still left to do just that, bickering companionably.

"We'll take over after that," Robbie offered, grateful when Cy didn't smack him. He liked this whole idea—he wanted to help.

And help they did. They caught the tail end of the rush in, and Robbie welcomed a family with a tiny woman who looked a lot like Miguel, whose buff football player of a husband was holding a teeny baby in a carrier. Miguel came out to greet them and asked where the other children were, and the woman laughed and said something about giving them to Berto for "dog whispering." Robbie didn't understand any of it, but he did get that some of Miguel's family had come and that they were nice people too.

There were others—a middle-aged man with curly graying hair, blue eyes, and a sweet moue of a smile that seemed awfully familiar, and his stunningly beautiful wife, who came perfectly coiffed in a white wool suit that Robbie thought probably repelled dirt because no dirt would dare. It did not surprise him in the least when the man introduced himself as George Stewart and asked where his lazy son was.

Two girls came after that, obviously a couple, one of them stocky with a buzz cut and what seemed to be a natural scowl, and the other a tiny confection of blue hair and diamond-studded piercings *everywhere*. When the tiny blue-haired one helped buzz cut take off her coat with the grace and elegance of a chevalier, the scowl melted, became somewhat besotted and warm, and the waifish girl's serene smile said it all.

There were others, but Robbie felt like part of the big group when his shift was over. He and Cy got separated when Robbie went up to organize the coats. He ended up in Ezra and Miguel's apartment with a beer and a big plate of cookies, while one of the girls he'd seen on moving day—Mari, Finn's sister—tried to tell him about how dramatic Adam's cousin's family had been. It was a good story—because hey, girls in jail for a day was hard to top—but it was made better by Adam's cousin. Rico looked like a shorter, softer, gentler version of Adam, complete with big limpid brown eyes, and he stood across from her with his hand over his face like he couldn't be more embarrassed. His boyfriend, Derek, cute as apple pie but with more freckles, added little details, like Adam stalking the front of the jail, waiting for the women to come out, and how Finn's family was terrifying, like cute little fairy pixy people, and Mari just laughed and kept telling the story.

When she was done, Rico said something about how it took a trip to San Francisco to get over the trauma, and Derek said, "Yeah, and then we got back from *that* and Ezra was on the front lawn."

"Ezra?" Robbie asked, not sure of the relationship.

"My ex, and the very nice guy who lives here," Rico said dryly. "Derek has, like, one thing to bitch about, and it's Ezra, but fact is, he *likes* Ezra, so it sort of lacks oomph."

"It's hard not to like Ezra," Robbie said, remembering his empathy when Robbie had first stumbled into Candy Heaven.

"Yeah," Rico said, "except he's getting a little spooky, you know, like that Darrin guy?"

"Right?" Derek said, leaning in with big eyes. "Like, Darrin just shook my hand and said, 'They just met.' Out of the blue—no context."

"Who just met?" Robbie was lost.

"'Your baby's parents.' *That's* what he said to me. I *swear*. And Rico and I, we'd just said the night before that maybe two, three years down the road—"

Robbie got a chill. "And they just met?" And then he and Mari said "*Damn!*" in stereo.

"Oh thank God." Darrin's face intruded on their little huddle. "*Finally* an end to the saga of dumb yuppies. You cannot *imagine* my joy."

Rico's smile was a teeny bit strained. "Well, you know when we're parents, we're probably going to be total health-food fiends, so you may see a bit less of us."

Darrin laughed so hard he almost spilled his beer. Robbie rescued it from him while he whooped, smacking his knees and choking on guffaws. When he came up for air, he gasped, "Said every parent of every screaming toddler who dragged them into my store *ever*. Oh my *God*, parenthood cannot come soon enough for the two of you. I cannot *wait*! Your kid alone will pay off my car!"

He straightened and retrieved his beer, then put his hand on Robbie's shoulder. "C'mere, junior," he said brusquely. "I want a word with you, and I don't care enough about what they think to come up with a good excuse." He cast an arch smile over his shoulder at a relieved Rico and Derek and waved flirtily at Mari, who waved back.

Robbie found himself at the end of the hall by what looked to be the bathroom, wishing there was more beer in his beer and having a quiet conversation with Darrin.

"You're going to be fine," Darrin said when it was all quiet.

Robbie looked back at him blankly. "Yeah, I was sort of getting that idea."

"No, it's just…." Darrin pursed his mouth thoughtfully. "You have the daddy thing—I don't have to be psychic, you may as well have it tattooed on your forehead."

"Which I won't," Robbie said seriously, because he'd had two beers and was feeling a little bit precious.

"It's a free world. But… but every moment of falling has a moment of redemption. This is your sign from the universe that you're going to be just fine."

Suddenly those beers weren't sitting too well. "I... redemption? Doesn't, you know, this whole month of falling in love and recovery count?"

"Do you have a boyfriend you love after an appallingly short courtship?" Darrin asked smartly.

"Uh... yeah."

"Do you have family and friends where you did not before?"

"Uh... yeah."

"So, no. Sure, it was painful, but there has been no defining act yet. All of *your* defining has gone into defining *yourself*. And you clean up well." Darrin made a sort of vague gesture with his hand. "Hair shirt removed, no more self-flagellation with a licorice whip—you're looking a lot more blue-gray and a lot less puke orange. It's an improvement."

Robbie's eyes widened at the thought of ever being puke orange. "God, I hope so. So... there's more... uh... defining coming up?"

Darrin patted his cheek. "Oh, sweet boy. There is *always* defining coming up. If you're lucky, that is. How boring would it be to wake up tomorrow the same person you were yesterday?"

How long ago had it been? Right after Thanksgiving? Robbie had woken up next to a girl he couldn't stand, and tonight he'd go to sleep next to a boy he loved.

"That would be *awful*," he said with feeling. "I hope you're right—I hope I *never* stop changing."

Darrin's hand went to his shoulder and squeezed. Robbie closed his eyes, because for a moment, that felt like his father's hand, like when he'd been a little kid and the old family cat had died. For a moment there was comfort, and everything was going to be all right.

"It *will* be all right," Darrin said softly. "And junior, I think you need to get a new cat."

Robbie blinked. "I'm sorry?"

"Everyone needs one. Hie thee to a shelter. Ezra is picking one out next week—in fact, here, get out your phone."

Robbie complied, bemused, and Darrin pinged in Ezra's number and sent him a text.

"Oh my God! Give that back—what the—"

This is Robbie and Darrin said I need to get a cat with you and no Darrin has not had too much beer.

The hallway darkened and Ezra ambled down, holding up his phone.

"Robbie, this is Ezra, and I'd be happy to go get a cat with you, and Darrin, you'd better have somebody drive you home!"

Darrin smiled coquettishly and batted his eyes. "Why do that, dear boy, when you and Miguel have the most comfortable couch in the world! Daddy needs a new beer."

He toddled away, leaving Robbie and Ezra shaking their heads and laughing.

"Joke's on him," Ezra said. "I slept on that couch when Miguel and I were dating, and it's gonna fuck up his back like *whoa*!"

"I heard that!" Darrin called. "I'll take Finn and Adam's, then! They know how to treat people right!"

Ezra winked and held up a finger, counting. Five, four, three, two, one…. When he was sure Darrin was gone, he said lowly, "He's going to end up at Rico and Derek's, on *their* couch."

"Oh my God," Robbie said, because *that* really would be hilarious.

"Right?" Ezra had his own beer, and he tipped it back and swallowed. "They deserve each other, all of them. Anyway, you want to get a cat?"

Why not? New beginnings? A new lease on life? Robbie had always thought of himself as a dog person, but Cy… Cy was a cat. Cy was sinuous and graceful and gentle when you needed it. Robbie could deal with a cat.

"Yeah," he said, not ruffled by absurdity any longer. "That sounds like a great idea."

Of course parties progress, and Robbie eventually found himself in need of a quiet rest. Cy could be seen in various groups, thrilling everybody with the story of the icy mats at Cal Expo, and if Robbie hadn't been just done on crowds, he could have watched him do that story again and again.

But he was happy to make his way down Finn and Adam's hallway and to cautiously open the door, being very careful not to let Jake out.

He needn't have worried. Adam was seated in the corner of the room on the floor, head tilted back against the wall, Jake purring in his lap.

"Oh!" Robbie murmured. "So sorry—"

Adam opened his eyes. "No. Don't go. Come sit."

Robbie did, perching on the bed, allowing his shoulders to relax in the quiet room. "Good party," he said awkwardly.

"It's great," Adam agreed. "But… you know."

"Loud."

"Yeah. When Finn asked if we could do this, having a quiet room was his idea. A place for the cat, a place to chill. I was a fan."

"Me too. Finn's pretty awesome."

Adam's laugh was soft and throaty, and Robbie appreciated it, but his stomach didn't clench and neither did his heart. A friend. An *attractive* friend, but that was all.

"It was his idea to invite Cy," he confided. "And to tell him to invite you. You're right. Awesome doesn't cover it."

Robbie nodded. "Well, good. *Great*. You deserve awesome, Adam."

Adam's smile was uninhibited—sweet. "I do, don't I," he conceded.

"Always have."

Adam nodded and closed his eyes. "You too. Do you believe that yet?"

"I'm starting to." A cat. That sudden, he *really* wanted a cat.

"Good. So what now?"

Robbie thought about it seriously. "I don't know. How's school treating you?"

"Like *ass*," Adam said irritably, leaning forward again and opening his eyes. "I mean... *Jesus*. I know we survived basic and shit, but I am *tired*. It's like hey! Sixty-hour workweek? Not a problem! Just don't make me go to class in the middle!"

Robbie laughed. "But you're going to stick with it, right?" This felt really important to him.

"Yeah." Adam nodded. "Course. I mean, Finn's almost done with his degree. End of next semester. He's going to move on to architecture school, and what? I'm gonna be a moo who works in a candy store? No. Finn needs someone with a real job. Like a grown-up. We'll grow together."

Robbie swallowed the lump in his throat. Apparently adulthood really didn't come with your enlistment papers and the M-16. Apparently it came after.

"I make a good living," he admitted. "I mean, I keep getting certified in stuff. I could live the rest of my life working for the warehouse and have benefits and buy a house and shit."

Adam nodded, pursing his lips. "Good deal. You gonna do that?"

Shrug. "Well, maybe. But I've been looking into junior college. I could do that. Take some classes. See if maybe there's something else out there."

Another nod. "Also good. Education, it's sort of like travel—99 percent of the time, there's no bad way to do it."

"Truth," Robbie agreed, knocking back the last two inches of domestic. "But mostly, for me? I think it's… it's a way of looking outside myself. I… when I was in the service, you and me, my world was so little. I didn't even know what kind of box I'd built for myself until I got home and crawled back in. I want to see what's outside the box."

"God, listen to you, all wise and shit. Sayin'. What about Cy?"

Just his name made Robbie smile. "Cy lives there. I think we can live there together."

"Good," Adam said. He leaned back again, and that cat upped its psychotic purring on his chest. Robbie leaned sideways and put his bottle on the end table, stretching out with his head on the pillow and figuring he'd wait until Adam dozed off again before he left the room.

That was how Finn and Cy found them an hour later, when Cy and Ravi and Anish were ready to go home. They were asleep and peaceful, with the cat on Adam's chest. Like Cy told him on the way home, it was like brothers or cousins or something.

As innocent as children. Like they should have been all along.

TWO DAYS after New Year's, Robbie got his first text from his parents since Christmas Eve.

We missed you over the holidays, son. I'd like to see you for lunch.

"Who's that?" Micah asked as they were sitting in the break room. "Cy?" Micah and Teddy had gone out with Robbie and Cy for the New Year's pub crawl in downtown Sac. The boys had ended up crashing on Cy's couch and floor, and Robbie (and their father) had been giving them shit about sleeping in their own damned beds. But it had been a fun night—and Cy adored Micah and his brother as much as Robbie did, which was awesome. Robbie felt like he had something to contribute in the friend spectrum: *See? I as an individual can attract friends of my own!* Something the military didn't really train you to do, actually. But it had also cemented the fact that Micah got to be up in Robbie's business as a friend.

Robbie looked up from his sandwich now, frowning. "Folks. Want to get back together and… I dunno. Bond."

Micah cocked his head. "Well, you sort of gotta go, don't you?" He looked like a puzzled puppy, so wholesome and without hurt that Robbie felt that to be a pressure all in itself. Micah believed in happy endings with family. Even though his own love life had proved to be a disaster, he knew a family was out there, waiting for him somewhere.

Robbie felt like he should believe in that too.

His phone buzzed again.

Lunch on Saturday? Your father wants to try River Burger.

Finn's family's place?

The one in Old Sac?

Yes. Can we meet at one?

Well, damn. Robbie and Cy were supposed to meet Ezra when he got off his shift at three. They were going to find cats. More friends, more family, and a cat for Robbie's apartment.

I'll be in the area, but I'm meeting friends at three.

Good. That way his folks would know that their time was limited, and if things got ugly, he could fake a text that said he had to leave early. It was almost serendipitous.

I'll be glad to see you. I hope you had a nice Christmas.

I did. I spent it with friends.

Micah snagged his phone. "Promising," he said speculatively. "But…."

"But what?"

"She said 'I'll.'"

Robbie swallowed. Yeah, he'd noticed that too. Until now, it had always been "we." "Well, Mom still loves me," he said brightly.

"My dad loves you!" Teddy said, nodding. "Especially after you gave him the premium alcohol."

Micah nodded seriously. "He, like, wants to take you to a Kings game after that. Better you than me, brother—they stink on ice since Karcek left."

"Was *fired*," Teddy said in deep disgust, and they started talking basketball after that, and Robbie thought his family thing might have been forgotten.

Until he was about to leave that night and his boss stopped him with a hand on his shoulder. "Robbie?"

"Yessir?"

"That was great to see you at Christmas. I'll be sure the boys send you invites to the other stuff, okay?"

Robbie smiled, flattered. Of course their grandma had already issued the invite, but this felt special. "Thank you," he said, humbled.

"And I'd *totally* take you to a basketball game," he said—but he said it over his shoulder, so obviously he was talking to Micah.

"Please?" Micah begged. "*Please?*"

Oh yeah—the kids had brought Robbie home like a puppy and initiated adoption proceedings. Robbie practically panted at Matt's feet. "That would be great, sir."

"Matt."

"Matt, sir."

Matt batted the top of his head. "They're moving into the new arena soon." He glared at his son. "Just remember that when I'm taking Robbie instead of you."

"Yes, Dad, I'll remember that while the other basketball teams laugh at us. You loved Robbie more, but *I* didn't have to suffer through the agony of defeat. It's a fair trade!"

General laugher then, and Robbie kept that moment in mind as the week slogged on—because.

Because he'd been so afraid he'd lose his family, his little corner of the world, when he'd turned his back on Adam. And here he was, back in the same little corner of the world—and he saw that he had options. The minute he'd decided that the world was a bigger place than his parents saw, it had opened up at his feet.

And something as small as his boss wanting to take him to watch the Kings lose or his friends from work sleeping on his boyfriend's couch or another new friend taking him to pick out a rescue kitten could be huge. In fact, *any* of the things that had happened to him between Thanksgiving and New Year's, both good and bad—added up to a vast, beautiful landscape of verdant pastures and sunny skies.

And even if it opened up to storm clouds and rough waters, at least there was a journey ahead, right? Someplace far away from the frightened kid who had betrayed his lover and punished himself for…

God.

Two years?

He'd grown—his *world* had grown. Adam may have moved on, but so had he.

Even if it was down to the new arena to watch a basketball game.

HOW'S IT going?

Robbie glanced at Cy's text and then looked back at his mom and smiled weakly. They were at one of the few inside tables at River Burger. Finn had greeted them cheerfully, asked him if he was going with Ezra that day, talked about Christmas—and Robbie had responded happily. His mom watched the exchange while Robbie ordered three of their specialty burgers with garlic fries—at her request.

He honestly wasn't sure who the third burger was for, since the chair next to his mother was decidedly empty.

Dad's not here yet. He shook his head and tried to catch his mother's eyes. She was proving adept at gazing out the window behind him.

"Seriously, Mom, it's okay if he's not coming," Robbie said at last, picking up his burger and charging ahead. Food was fuel, and bleu cheese, mushrooms, and bordeaux sauce was not to be wasted.

"He said he'd come," she told him with simple, defeated dignity. "He promised me he just needed a few minutes to wrap his head around it—that's all."

Chew, chew, swallow. "Well, he didn't," Robbie said wiping his mouth and determining to continue on. "So tell me, how was Christmas?"

His mother very carefully wiped under her eyeliner with the tip of her third finger. "It was… quiet," she said. "Your father and I didn't do presents this year. We watched some nice movies on television and woke up and went to brunch. I… I remember when you were little and I used to try to buy out Toys 'R' Us. Grandma and Grandpa were alive then, and, you know—"

"You were still speaking to Aunt Pam," he said, remembering a falling-out of some sort and how he'd missed his cousins for a while. "Yeah. Christmas used to be a big deal."

"So," she said, her voice watery, "you said you didn't spend it alone?"

Robbie smiled, because it was a good memory. "No. Actually, no part of it. Christmas Eve I spent at my coworker's grandmother's house. She had about a thousand people—I mean, maybe forty, but potluck and everybody brought a white elephant gift. There was like… candy for *miles*, and younger cousins, and…." His smile stretched, became a grin. "A nine-year-old named Kisha who made me promise to come for Easter so she can cheat against her brothers and sisters to find more eggs."

His mom laughed, surprised. "Wow. That's—like forty people? Really?"

"Oh yeah. Micah's grandma, she doesn't leave anybody out. They've got this big stretch of property out in Gold Hill—they worked their asses off, I think, but it looks great. Horse property next to it—good place. Easter-egg hunting is going to be a blast, you know?"

"That's nice," his mom said, and for a moment it was a regular conversation. Then her face fell. "Uh, Micah, is he your…?"

"Boyfriend?" Robbie filled in with a twitch of his lips. "No. He's just a friend. He and his brother came with me and my"—he smiled grimly—"*boyfriend* on New Year's Eve, so a good one. But I saw my boyfriend on Christmas Eve—he came over that night after his own family thing, and we…." He looked at his mother, feeling a poignant connection in a simple common activity. "We watched movies together. The next night we went to Finn's house party—he's the guy behind the counter. He and his… *boyfriend* had, like, a blowout. They live in one of those converted Victorians, and their friends live on the top floor, and they apparently *created* a friend on the bottom floor, and the lady across the hall was on a cruise. It was great! I mean, nobody got wasted and puked, and everybody talked to everyone and…." His smile turned soft. "And I talked to an ex, and everything was all right at the end. The best Christmas I can remember since before Aunt Pam stopped coming."

His mom nodded, her lower lip wobbling out of control, and it hit Robbie—his father hadn't shown.

"So, uh…." God. Small talk. "Aunt Pam. Why *did* she stop coming?"

Oh shit. The wobble got worse. "Because your father said something horrible," she whispered. "I don't want to talk about it."

Wonderful. "Okay. So, uh, what did you want to talk about?"

His mom closed and opened eyes that were moistening like big gray bloodshot morning glories. "I… uhm… so, what are you doing at three?" she asked desperately.

"Going to get a cat," he said, still excited. "See, I figure my hours are pretty even, and I live close enough to work so I can check in on it at lunch until we get a routine down. Also, Cy teaches at a branch in Roseville, so he can come check in on it when he doesn't have a bussing shift. We figure that between us and Micah and Teddy, I can actually be a successful pet owner." He beamed. "It's just Finn and Adam, they've got this cat, and it's like a super magical awesome cat. I… I mean, I know every cat can't possibly be like Jake, but it's unconditional love, right? Can't beat it with a stick, and who'd want to!"

His mother burst into tears.

Robbie stood up, horrified. "Mom? Mom? Here, let me get you some napkins. And some soda. And… oh, hell—" He looked up over the counter in a panic, and Finn stared back at him.

"Cheesecake!" Finn said, looking to his dad for confirmation. "Dad! Robbie needs cheesecake!"

"Of course he does," Finn's father said, not even blinking. He handed a slice from the refrigerator to Finn, and Finn handed it over the counter before Robbie could protest or even look to his mom to see if her outburst had been caused by a sudden cheesecake depletion in her bloodstream.

Robbie slid the slice of cheesecake in front of his mother and sat down next to her, rubbing her back with one hand. "Mom," he said gently. "It'll be all—"

"No, it won't," she said on a sob. "Because. Because you've got a life, and you've moved on, and I can't get your father to come to lunch, and you were all I had left…." She ended on a particularly high-note wail, and Robbie grimaced even as he patted her back and tried to calm her down.

"Mom, it's fine. I'm here. Next year you just let me invite Cy and we'll all be happy fine, right?"

"But—" She hiccupped. "But—" She hiccupped again. "But your father won't let you back in the hooooouuuuuuuse!" She burst into loud, noisy sobs then, and Robbie just kept hugging her and patting her on the back and looking at Finn in horror. Oh hell. So much for a neutral location. The entire world was staring at them and Robbie wanted to *die*, but she was his mother and he loved her.

"Mom," he said gently. "Look, you don't have to do everything he says. You're a person. You drive. You and me, we can have a relationship without him." Robbie heard what he just said and his chest ached with it. This was it—he'd lost his father. But his mother—*she* wanted him. Just like Cy's mom.

The thought of Cy gave him strength.

"Robbie!" his mother protested, and he pulled her in and kissed her temple.

"Don't worry," he told her, voice soft and a warm arm around her shoulders. "You and me, we can be a family. I'll have you over to dinner. You can meet Cy. And the cat. And my friends. It'll be good."

"But your father," she asked, staring at her knotted fingers. "How can I just… he'll be so mad!"

"Well then he shouldn't have been so excited about kicking me to the curb," Robbie snapped, upset again. "Mom, if you want a relationship with me, this is your time to step up!"

His mom nodded and sniffled and finally looked on the verge of calming down when two things happened.

One was that Cy appeared in the doorway, looking anxiously their way. Robbie smiled, relieved, because… because *Cyril*, who was charming and bright and bouncy. God, if his mom couldn't be charmed by the guy walking through the doorway right now, then she obviously had no soul and he'd been birthed from pod people.

But Cy never got a chance to walk through the doorway, because Don Chambers came barreling through. He didn't shove Cy, he just didn't *see* him as he strode through the little eatery, snapping, "Get your hands off of her!" at the top of his lungs.

Robbie recoiled. "Jesus, Dad, she's my *mother* and she was crying!"

"If she is, it's all your fault," his father snarled. "God, I know you're an only child, but how fucking selfish can you *be*?"

Robbie's heart froze, brittle in his chest. Selfish? He was selfish?

"Selfish?" he asked through numb lips. "Because I'm not the son you want?"

"Selfish?" Cy echoed, weaving gracefully around Robbie's barrel-chested father. "That's bullshit and we all know it!" His hand on Robbie's shoulder was nothing but compassion, and the warmth started to seep through the ice in his blood.

"Robbie? Who in the fuck is *this*?"

And now all of Robbie froze. His father snarling at him, frightening and unforgiving. His mother in tears, afraid of his father's wrath.

And Cy wanting nothing more than to help.

He looked up into Cy's face, those warm brown eyes concerned and upset, and for a heartbeat, Robbie relived that other moment from his past, the harsh word and Adam recoiling, wounded possibly for life.

"Robbie?" his father demanded.

Robbie stood then, time feeling oddly out of joint, and all he could do was protect Cy. Protect him from the bad words, protect him from the recoil of Robbie's cowardice. Robbie had seen the fallout of that—it had nearly ruined two people.

It needed to never happen again.

"This is my boyfriend," Robbie said softly. "Cyril. He's…." Reality caught up to him. "What are you doing here?" he asked Cy, but kindly. "I… I mean, we were going to meet at three."

Cy grimaced, and the sweep of his eyes took in the public disaster of Robbie's private life. "Yeah, but I had the feeling this was going tits up. What did you do?" He laughed as he said it, and Robbie's stomach thawed infinitesimally.

"I don't know," Robbie told him, feeling helpless. "But whatever it was, cheesecake was *not* the answer."

Cy waved his hand and took Robbie's seat. "Bullshit. Finn's dad's cheesecake? That is *always* the answer." He reached out to the plate and took a bite, oohed appreciatively, and smiled at Robbie's mother like he wasn't the nightmare apparition of diversity that had been haunting her for her entire life.

And she just nodded and took the bite he offered without question, apparently so bemused not even her prejudices were functioning.

The same could not be said for Robbie's father.

"Don't let him—*Robbie*! *This*—this is your… your… your—"

"Boyfriend!" Finn hollered over the counter. "Jesus, Robbie— you seem normal, but why do your parents have such a problem with that word?"

Finn's father was grimacing and rubbing his temples. "Okay, people," he said commandingly. "We're going to do this again. River Burger is a socially and ethnically diverse establishment. The following family drama will have *no* racial epithets, *no* homophobic slurs, and the first person to say something even *moderately* offensive will get escorted out by my son's big scary boyfriend. Mari, go get Adam. Finn, go talk to your people. Everybody else, have your order ready, sodas are on me."

Robbie suddenly loved Adam's *boyfriend* with a terrible fierceness, and Finn's father placed a close second.

"Dad," he said calmly, "let's start agay—I mean again." Cy choked-snorted next to him, and he continued with a certain grim tenacity. "I am gay. This is my *boyfriend*, Cy. I'll state the obvious. He's African-American."

"You can say black," Cy said helpfully.

"Or black." Robbie took a deep breath into his father's disapproving silence. "For the record, I have come out to my boss, who invited me to a Kings game, and his sons, who invited me to Christmas. I have come out to my doctor, who was concerned about my health. And to a nurse, who was glad I had someone in my life. I came out to an entire room full of people—"

"That was my fault," Finn said, appearing at his elbow and wiping his hands on his apron. "Sorry."

"No worries," Robbie murmured before turning back to his dad. "And my neighbors. And an insurance guy. And people I can't even *remember* at this point. And everybody was kind and accepting and generous. Except you. Now if you and Mom turn your backs on me, it's going to hurt. I can't lie. But I was *so afraid* of that hurt, I hurt other people. I hurt a guy I cared a lot about. I hurt Ashley when I tried to lock this shit away inside me. I hurt myself because I didn't think I deserved anything better. So I have to say, all of that was worse. It was worse than the way you're looking at me right now, and worse than Mom crying. Because I could *do* something about that—and I have. I've set about trying to live a life that doesn't hurt people anymore. But I can't *do* anything about your prejudices. You're going to have to live with them—or get rid of them—all by yourself. So if you can't love me for me? If you can't be civil to someone important to me? Then maybe just turn around and walk away."

Cy's hand fumbled for his, and he clasped it and held on tight—but he kept his eyes on his father.

Who was staring back, jaw locked, eyes little and sunken as though he had not slept.

"I…." Don Chambers swallowed hard. "Robert—you… you can't mean that."

Robbie held so tight to Cy's hand that he was afraid of hurting him, but he couldn't loosen that grip to save his life. "I can," he said. "I do.

Don looked around then, lost. Realized that people were staring at them—Robbie saw the moment, because his father's face waxed red, then waned to an ashen gray. Looked back, focusing on Cy's fingers twined with his own.

"I...." He swallowed again. "Uhm—"

Cy broke the silence. "Would you like some cheesecake?" he asked out of the blue. "It's good stuff—chocolate and raspberry. I don't think Robbie's mom is going to do it justice."

It's stunning what problems basic human courtesy can fix. Robbie's father walked to the table, and the silence of the room eased back. People breathed, swallowed their food, took another bite, and exchanged glances.

Finn's father said, "Oh thank God. Finn, get your ass back here and help."

Finn cast Robbie a quick are-you-okay look, and Robbie nodded and ruffled his hair. Twenty-five years old Robbie's *ass*—this kid was ageless, like a sci-fi character.

Awkwardly, Don turned to an empty chair and dragged it around to sit on, since Cy had apparently usurped his seat. Robbie took a deep breath and took his own seat, letting go of Cy's hand so he didn't snap his forearm with the change of angle. As soon as he sat down, Cy's fingers, damp and cold, fumbled for his again, and he found them and squeezed.

"Dad, Mom, this is Cyril. He goes by Cy. He teaches dance." Something in Robbie's chest loosened, and he smiled, feeling soft and radiant all over. "He's a *beautiful* dancer."

"I know," his mother said, her voice hitching and wrecked. "We saw him right after Thanksgiving, remember."

Robbie grinned and nodded. "Yeah, Mom—I do."

Don's eyes went wide and his mouth gaped like he had just then put it together. He glared at Cy, like he was somehow to blame, and then back at Robbie, and then at his wife.

Who glared defiantly back. "A dance teacher, Don," she said, her voice bright and brittle. "He's not a girl, but, you know, that's nice."

Robbie's mouth fell open, and he exchanged an uncomfortable look with Cy. "Seat belts fastened?" he asked.

Cy smiled gamely. "Tray tables in the locked and upright position."

They both turned toward Robbie's parents.

"So," Don asked, wrinkling his forehead, "speaking of girl... how do you know which one of you fellas is gonna...?"

They swallowed in tandem. Cy said, "Turbulence ahead," in a voice so soft only Robbie could hear him.

At that moment there was a pounding on the floorboards and Adam burst in. "You needed me?" he asked, disgustingly enough not even out of breath.

"No," Finn said perkily. "Robbie's dad decided not to be a douche canoe after all. But since you're here, take your break." Finn leaned over the counter and pursed his lips, and Adam didn't leave him hanging. They met in a brief kiss, and Robbie's dad sucked air in through his teeth.

Commence lunch.

"HE DID not!" Ezra exclaimed when Cy and Robbie gave him the breakdown later.

"Swear to God he did," Robbie said, shuddering with the horror.

Ezra gaped at Cy. "He asked you if you wore lingerie?"

"He called it 'ladies' silk things.'" Cy rolled his expressive eyes. "But yeah."

"So what did you say?" Ezra moved to the next cage in the shelter, where a tiny fluffy mama cat curled in a ball, ignoring three rambunctious adolescents. "Yes," he said out of nowhere. "That one. The Siamese one with the blue eyes. She's good."

Cy and Robbie gaped. The Siamese one with the blue eyes was so far back in the cage that they almost hadn't spotted her.

"How did you do that?" Cy asked.

Ezra smiled at him with eyes the same color as the Siamese cat's. "I just know." Carefully he unhooked the cage and stuck his fingers in, making catcalling hisses with tongue against his palate. "Puss puss puss?"

The Siamese cat padded across the cage, rubbed its delicate little nose against Ezra's finger, and allowed itself to be unresistingly removed from the cage.

"How do you like that," Robbie said. "He—"

"She," Ezra told him, double-checking under the tail.

"She didn't even say good-bye." Cy looked back into the cage where the other kittens lounged about indolently, a fluffy black one and a fluffy tortoiseshell. The mother cat opened one eye and gave a plaintive "Meow."

"Maybe she said everything she needed to," Ezra said mildly. "Except…." He frowned and looked at the shelter volunteer, a teenaged boy with unruly brown hair, flaming spots of acne, and a tremendous

Adam's apple and ears, who had followed them down the corridors of displaced animals. He had listened to Robbie and Cy's recounting of their lunch meeting with wide eyes—but had reached into the occasional cage for them with infinite compassion.

"She'll mourn," the boy said suddenly.

"She will," Ezra replied, frowning in an absent way, like someone talking and texting at the same time. "Mom likes the fluffy black one best." He looked at Cy and Robbie expectantly.

"Uh, I'll hold the fluffy black one," Cy said, giving a flash of teeth and shaking out his hair.

"I'll take Mom," Robbie said with a sigh. Apparently their cat family had been waiting for them. "They can keep each other company."

Ezra stuck his finger in the cage and "puss-pussed" some more, and the torti came as obediently as a dog.

"That is just freaky," Cy muttered.

"Shut up and grab our cats."

"Yeah, but tell us what you said first!" Ezra held both of his new adoptees, placid and purring, one in each hand, chests resting on his palms, legs dangling good-naturedly below them.

"About the lingerie?" The kid gave Robbie the delicate, small-boned mama cat, who peered at him uncertainly, her muscles going taut in an exploratory way. He rubbed the sweet spot between her eyes with a respectful finger and she relaxed. "Yeah. I told Dad that unless he wanted me in Mom's underwear drawer, he didn't get to ask that question."

"*Gross!*" Ezra burst out, laughing.

Robbie shook himself again, trying to get that whole moment out of his chromatic makeup. "I'm saying. But you know, after that lunch, things can't possibly get more awkward."

"Shut your mouth," Cy muttered, just as the fluffy black cat sank its teeth into the ball of his thumb. "You'll be lucky if your mom doesn't ask me to cook when they have us over for dinner. And by lucky I mean I hate cooking, and I'm dreading the fuck out of dinner. And cat, *you* are lucky I'm still trying to impress him!"

The cat hissed at him, and Cy grabbed it by the scruff of its neck to keep it under control. "Junior, can we have a cat carrier or something? My friend here needs some 'me' time."

"Be right back," the kid said, trotting off. He turned around midway down the corridor and grinned, the expression giving the hint of some future beauty to his bony teenaged visage. "And thanks, guys—I really like those cats. It's good to know they won't be lonely."

The three of them watched him go.

"Yeah," Ezra murmured, rubbing his nose against one cat and then the other. *His* cats purred and snuggled and pretty much made out with him on the spot.

"Sluts," Cy said, his voice dripping with judgment. "We're going to have to woo this asshole with canned food and one of those cat toys on the little fishing pole, aren't we?"

"Nope," Robbie said complacently, the mama cat giving in and snuggling into the crook of his arm with boneless joy. "Just you."

Cy regarded him with unfriendly eyes. "Why me?"

"Because," Robbie told him smugly. "He'll keep you coming back to the apartment. You charm everybody—you won't be able to resist a challenge."

"The cat," Cy stated. "The *cat* is why I'll be coming back to the apartment."

Robbie winked. "Well, it might be *all* the company in there. You never know."

"The cat."

"It's what I said."

"Soldier boy, it's a good thing I love you, 'cause you are just—"

Robbie never found out what he was "just," because he leaned over their respective cats and kissed him.

He wished he could draw like Adam in that moment. He wanted that picture, Cy's surprised pleasure, Ezra's laughter, even the cats and their suspicious acceptance of love, etched in pen and ink and posted on his wall. A simple time but a good one—one of those small good moments that a lifetime of good moments is built upon.

He and Cy, they had a lifetime of good moments to discover. This was only the beginning.

THEY SPENT that night at Robbie's apartment, watching the cats for the first hour because playing with them and seeing the mama cat curl up and be safe while her hellion of a son tried to destroy Robbie's icicle plant was almost better than television.

"The cat box in the bathroom is gonna be a *joy*," Cy cautioned, and Robbie grimaced.

"Yeah, well, what's a little bit of doo-doo when I have someone to keep me company when you're not here."

Cy exploded into giggles. "Doo-doo? *Doo-doo?*" And then Robbie had to attack him on the couch, tickling him to see if he giggled more, and then fending him off when he tickled back. Cy was wily, finding that spot behind Robbie's armpit unerringly, and the whole tickle fight ended up with Robbie facedown, pounding the couch, crying "Uncle! Uncle!" his voice hoarse from laughing too much.

Cy whispered in his ear, "Loser bottoms," and then *that* was fun too.

At the end of the evening, Robbie sprawled on his bed feeling stretched and sexed and used. Cy lay with his head on Robbie's chest, playing with the hair that Robbie grew unapologetically and occasionally taking a lazy swipe of Robbie's nipple with his tongue.

"Robbie?"

"Yeah?"

"That thing you did today—when your dad burst into the store?"

"Yeah?"

"That thing was pretty brave."

Robbie blinked slowly. "What else was I supposed to do?"

Cy pushed himself up on his elbow, and suddenly they were face-to-face. "You could have chosen your family. You did it once, with Adam."

Oh. *Oh.* Suddenly Robbie remembered what Darrin had said about defining moments. "Yeah," Robbie admitted. "But I'm working at being a better person than that, remember?"

Cy's smile always hit him right in the gut. "Mission accomplished."

Robbie reached up and touched his temple with delicate fingers. "Cy?"

"Yeah?"

"I want you to start thinking about how you and me can make this permanent. I mean, you've got the sweet setup in the city and I've got my shitty place here. But I want...."

Cy nodded soberly. "Yeah. We'll get there." He lowered himself back to Robbie's chest again. "Right now, I'm like, it's all got to happen for us, you know?"

Robbie smiled, so content he was almost limp with it. "Yeah," he sighed. "I know."

At that moment the black kitten, who had no name as of yet, leaped onto the bed and bit Cy's toe through the sheet. In the laughing chaos that followed, Robbie never lost that feeling of contentment. When he and Cy finally settled down—after naming the cat Satan and making sure it stayed at the foot of the bed, where it regarded them with hate-filled green eyes—it hit him.

He was going to have to work on being brave, being truthful and true, and he was going to have to do that every day.

But if he *could* do that—this feeling here, it was his reward.

He wrapped his arm tighter around Cy and closed his eyes and prayed. Please God, oh please. Let him be the kind of person who could deserve this every day.

Even the cat biting their toes. That part was good too.

Epilogue: Down a Lazy River

DARRIN SAT behind the smaller candy counter and pretended to read a travel brochure, but the truth was, he would have *slapped* anyone who walked in right then during the "dead hour" of three o'clock on a weekday afternoon.

"Davis?" Adam said incredulously, looking at the acceptance letter and course catalog Finn had brought in on a cold blast of March wind. "I didn't know they had an architecture program."

Finn smiled faintly and looked at him sideways over the larger counter. "They have an environmental design program—you know, how to build things that are eco-friendly and sustainable. It's a good program."

"But…." Adam sounded suspicious, and Darrin didn't blame him. He heard the word too.

"Adam, I don't know if I want to go for my master's," Finn said, voice sober. "I'm thinking… you know. I've had some offers from some of the firms around town. I could, you know, start working in the real world, and you wouldn't have to work so hard while you finish up your BA."

Darrin's heart almost stopped. Oh no. Not yet. He wasn't ready for Adam and Finn to graduate—not now. Yes, all of his adult "children" tended to move on to other things, but it had barely been a year! God, Darrin wasn't ready to let go yet!

"No," Adam said, and Darrin's chest stopped squeezing him so hard. "No—you and me, we're stronger than that. I mean, this year was tough, sure. But I cut back on my units some, and that helped. You can get some student loans and maybe not work so much for your dad. You're *so close*, baby. I want you to make it all the way to your dream."

Finn bit his lip and smiled shyly at the love of his life. "We can do it, right? I mean, a year to get my master's and…."

Adam's smile was warm and open, all of the things that he *hadn't* been a little more than a year before, when he'd walked into Darrin's store, hungry and angry and looking for a job. "Yeah. C'mon, Finn.

Have a little faith. You're going to *graduate* in a few months. You can do *anything*."

Finn nodded like he hadn't had any doubts at all. "I can, can't I."

"Course," Adam said, tapping him on the cheek. "I have no doubts."

"Eavesdropping, boss?"

Darrin startled and turned toward Ezra, who had walked in the far door—or just appeared by magic. "Yes," he said shortly. "And if you have to ask that, you haven't been paying attention."

Ezra laughed softly and moved to the office so he could hang his peacoat up. Or, rather, Miguel's peacoat. Darrin noticed that the two of them swapped clothes a lot, which he found endearing. He missed Miguel now that he worked mostly for Derek's firm, but Ezra and Miguel's energy was so tightly intertwined that Darrin often felt like he was there in the store when Ezra was.

When Ezra returned, Finn and Adam were still immersed in making their plans, but Cy had wandered in. He heard them talking about schools, rolled his eyes, and wandered over to Darrin and Ezra.

"Yeah," he said with a hint of pride. "Robbie's all excited. He's starting junior college in the fall. Humanities classes, at least, because that's the fun stuff."

"You gonna take some with him?" Ezra asked. Darrin listened curiously for the answer. He'd been so relieved when the sad-eyed soldier of his dreams had found happiness—he wanted to make sure the man who made him happy was doing fine as well.

Cy shrugged. "Maybe. Anna moved me to take over her Roseville branch. Makes a little more money, more of a responsibility. I love teaching, but I swear, as these kids get older, it's harder to help them with their homework so they can stay in dance. I wouldn't mind a math or an English refresher just so I can keep the high school kids in school, you know?"

Ezra nodded. "Sure. Set a good example. That sort of thing."

Cy's bright smile cut through the almost melancholy air that had permeated Darrin's little store. "Exactly. Anyway, I'll be able to quit bussing at Gatsby's Nick—"

"But we'll still go dancing, right?" Ezra asked anxiously. Darrin knew that for Ezra, that had been one of the best things about Cy hooking up with Robbie—he and Miguel had a *couple* to go out dancing with.

Yes, Darrin wasn't the only one who was reluctant to see friendships end and people drift apart.

"You know it!" Cy nodded. "Although I'll probably be moving into Robbie's crappy apartment in April."

"You're moving in with him?" Because from what Ravi and Anish said, Cy's setup was pretty sweet.

"Yeah." Cy shrugged nonchalantly, but Darrin could see that he'd only *just* made the decision. "See, we're talking about saving up for a house—Robbie makes pretty good money, but I can't pitch in if we're living in separate places. That, and it's a lot closer to Anna's dance studio branch in Roseville." Darrin could hear the regret in losing his apartment and having to start over, but it wasn't too heavy. "I mean, a *house*, right? I could deal with a place with an extra bedroom and a yard. I mean, the cats are going to stay indoors, but a *dog*—wouldn't that be awesome?"

Ezra nodded. "Sounds permanent—you scared?"

Again, that brilliant smile. Darrin liked this kid, he really did.

"Of course!" Cy said, nodding animatedly. "But I'm not bored!"

Ezra laughed, and Cy asked for some help at the chocolate counter. A gift for Robbie, apparently, who didn't know what Cy had decided yet. Darrin watched them go and thought fondly that all of his boys were growing up—and it was going to be okay. For one thing, Ezra was turning into a fine heir for the parts of running Candy Heaven that *didn't* come with the business degree.

He examined the brochure in his hand with a little more determination. A cruise. He and Ro would take a cruise, and for two weeks there would be nothing but a stack of paperback books, baking in the sun, meals he didn't have to cook, and Ro, who waited patiently for him every night when he was done with his beloved little shop.

It was time to give some back to the man who worked so hard to keep him happy.

"Finn?"

The smugness in the voice made Darrin look up.

"Perry?" Finn's little bee-stung mouth was pulled up in an expression of distaste. "What are *you* doing here?"

The man wearing the stylish trench coat was Adam's age, maybe, sporting a slick beige wool suit and three-hundred-dollar oxfords under the coat. His dark hair was thinning just a tad already, and unremarkable eyes looked out through wire-framed glasses.

"Well, I finish my master's at the end of this year," said Perry-the-rat (as the store called him). "I… you know. I was in town. I thought I'd check your old haunts…." He trailed off meaningfully while giving a smug little arch of his eyebrows.

Finn looked back, unimpressed. "My boyfriend is standing right here," he said, sounding bored. "Adam, baby, stand up straight, okay?"

Adam pursed his lips drolly and pulled himself up to his full height. All six feet four inches of him. He regarded Perry-the-rat with a flat, unfriendly look and crossed his arms. "This good?" he asked Finn.

Finn smiled at him besottedly. "That's great. Can you tilt your head a little? The neck tats add to the image."

Adam winked at him. "Yeah, yeah—I'm your hired muscle. I get it."

"No," Finn said, suddenly not playing anymore. "You're my *everything*. That's what I want *him* to get."

Perry was looking incredulously from Adam to Finn and back again. "Really?" he asked—himself, apparently. Adam and Finn were once again wrapped up in each other's eyes. "Seriously? That's your—"

"They're getting married next Christmas," Darrin said, giving up on trying to read the travel brochure without his bifocals. He pulled them out and looked carefully at the price tag on a midpriced suite for two. Yes. Yes, he *could* do that, and he should. "They don't know it yet—give them a minute."

Perry stared at him, wandering over when it became apparent that Adam and Finn had forgotten he existed. "Wait—Finn's going to *marry* that guy?"

Darrin glanced up from his brochure. "Yes. I haven't dreamed about you."

"So what?" Perry had tiny eyes, really, and a sort of permanent curl to his lip. Darrin hadn't liked him much when he and Finn had been dating, but now, after the last year of hard-luck hearts and second chances, Darrin liked him even less.

"So you really have no business in my store. Leave. Begone. Fly away. Finn outgrew you, and if you get weird about it, Adam will eat your spleen."

Perry swallowed suddenly and cast a nervous glance at Adam, like he really believed that tripe. Prick.

"Yeah, fine," he muttered, slinking out of Darrin's store. Darrin didn't care enough to watch him go. He was just so *relieved*.

Adam noticed, though. "So, boss, you're not going to try to set that guy up?"

Darrin glared at him. "I'm exhausted," he said grandly. "I'm not wasting my Pixy Stix mojo on that asshole—he'd whine that it hurt his teeth. You people stay and mind the fort while I go on a cruise."

"A cruise? When?" Ezra returned to the register to ring Cy up for a box of truffles.

"May," Darrin decided. "Before the schools get out. You people are finally grown, I don't have to worry about anyone for a while. Even the dumb yuppies are done angsting. For fuck's sake, I need a vacation."

Adam shrugged. "A cruise. Go figure. We'll keep the place running. No worries, boss."

Darrin smiled slightly and stepped aside so Ezra could ring up Cy's "Surprise, I *will* move in with you!" gift. Darrin happened to know that it wasn't the chocolates that would make Robbie achingly happy, but who could turn down chocolates?

"I have no worries at all," Darrin said truthfully. "Not just now. That's why I'm going on the cruise. For once—for a brief, short time—all is right with my little corner of the world. I'm going to get gone before all that changes."

Ezra nodded and touched him on the shoulder, reassuring him, and Darrin resumed his perusal of the travel brochure.

Yup. The Sacramento River still ran lazily in front of his store, but all was peaceful here. Darrin could go on his own adventures with his *own* lover and see what was out there in the great wide world, where Candy Heaven was *not* the center of the universe.

Then he'd come back and fall in love with his store and his friends all over again.

Choose your Lane to love!

Yellow

Amy Lane Lite
Contemporary Romance

Available at
www.dreamspinnerpress.com

A Candy Man Book

Adam Macias has been thrown a few curve balls in his life, but losing his VA grant because his car broke down and he missed a class was the one that struck him out. One relative away from homelessness, he's taking the bus to Sacramento, where his cousin has offered a house-sitting job and a new start. He has one goal, and that's to get his life back on track. Friends, pets, lovers? Need not apply.

Finn Stewart takes one look at Adam as he's applying to Candy Heaven and decides he's much too fascinating to leave alone. Finn is bright and shiny—and has never been hurt. Adam is wary of his attention from the very beginning—Finn is dangerous to every sort of peace Adam is forging, and Adam may just be too damaged to let him in at all.

But Finn is tenacious, and Adam's new boss, Darrin, doesn't take bullshit for an answer. Adam is going to have to ask himself which is harder—letting Finn in or living without him? With the holidays approaching it seems like an easy question, but Adam knows from experience that life is seldom simple, and the world seldom cooperates with hope, faith, or the plans of cats and men.

www.dreamspinnerpress.com

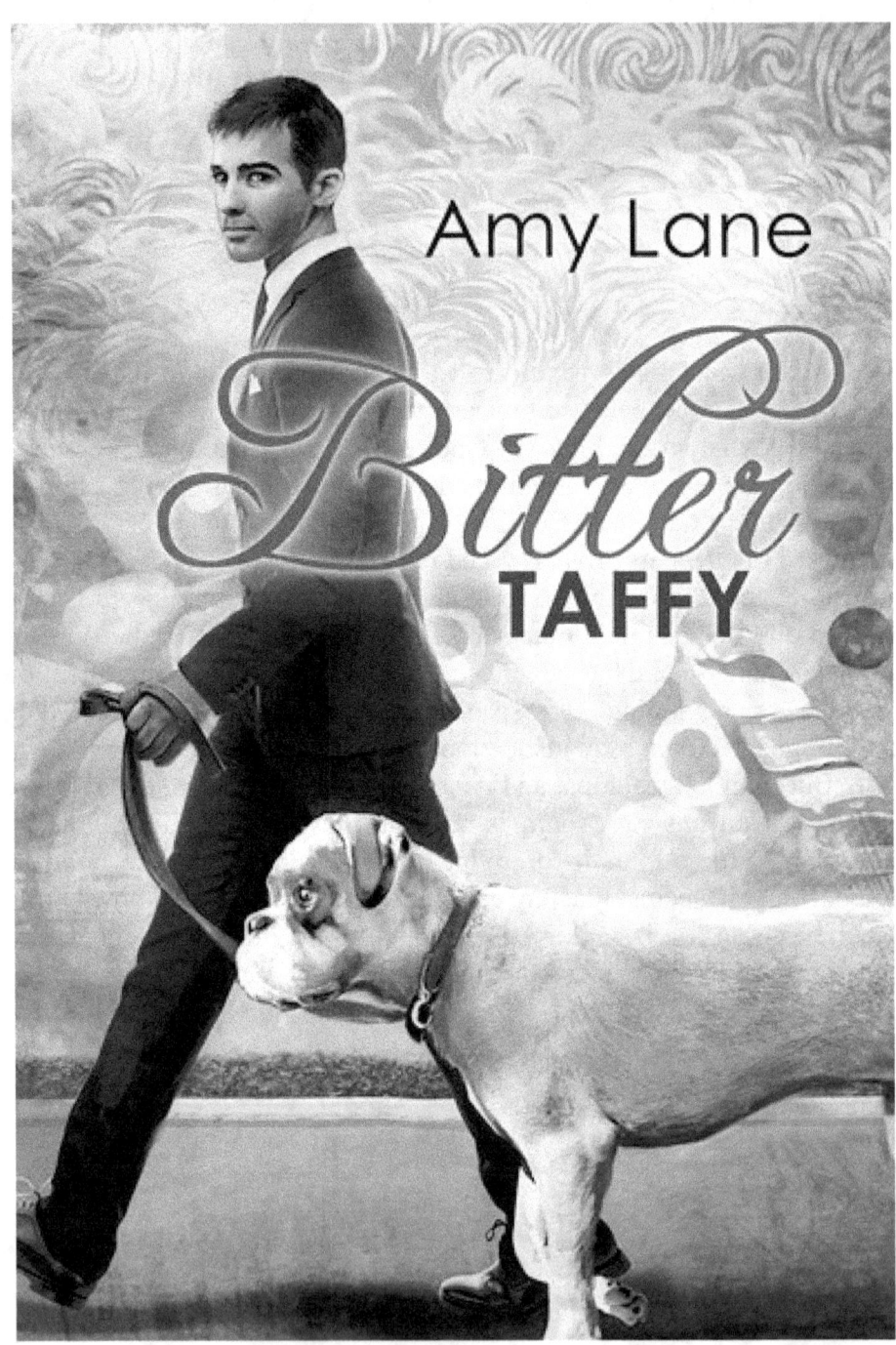

Amy Lane

Bitter TAFFY

A Candy Man Book

Rico Gonzalves-Macias didn't expect to fall in love during his internship in New York—and he didn't expect the boss's son to out them both and get him fired either. When he returns to Sacramento stunned and heartbroken, he finds his cousin, Adam, and Adam's boyfriend, Finn, haven't just been house-sitting—they've made his once sterile apartment into a home.

When Adam gets him a job interview with the adorable, magnetic, practically perfect Derek Huston, Rico feels especially out of his depth. Derek makes it no secret that he wants Rico, but Rico is just starting to figure out that he's a beginner at the really important stuff and doesn't want to jump into anything with both feet.

Derek is a both-feet kind of guy. But he's also made mistakes of his own and doesn't want to pressure Rico into anything. Together they work to find a compromise between instant attraction and long-lasting love, and while they're working, Rico gets a primer in why family isn't always a bad idea. He needs to believe Derek can be his family before Derek's formidable patience runs out—because even a practically perfect boyfriend is capable of being hurt.

www.dreamspinnerpress.com

Lollipop

Amy Lane

A Candy Man Book

Ezra Kellerman flew across country to see if he had another chance with the man he let slip through his fingers. He didn't. Rico has moved on, but he doesn't just leave his ex high and dry. Instead, Rico entrusts his family and friends with Ezra's care. Ezra, confused, hurt, and lost, clings to Rico's cousin and his boyfriend as the lifelines they are—but their friend Miguel is another story.

Miguel Rodriguez had great plans and ambition—but a hearty dose of real life crushed those flat. When Miguel finds himself partially in charge of the befuddled, dreamy, healing Ezra, he's pretty resentful at first. But Ezra's placid nature and sincere wonder at the simple life Miguel has taken for granted begin to soften Miguel's hardened shell. Miguel starts to notice that Ezra isn't just amazingly sweet—he's achingly beautiful as well. Suddenly Miguel is fending off every currently single man on the planet to give Ezra room to get over Rico—while fighting a burning suspicion that the best thing to help Ezra get over his broken heart is Miguel.

www.dreamspinnerpress.com

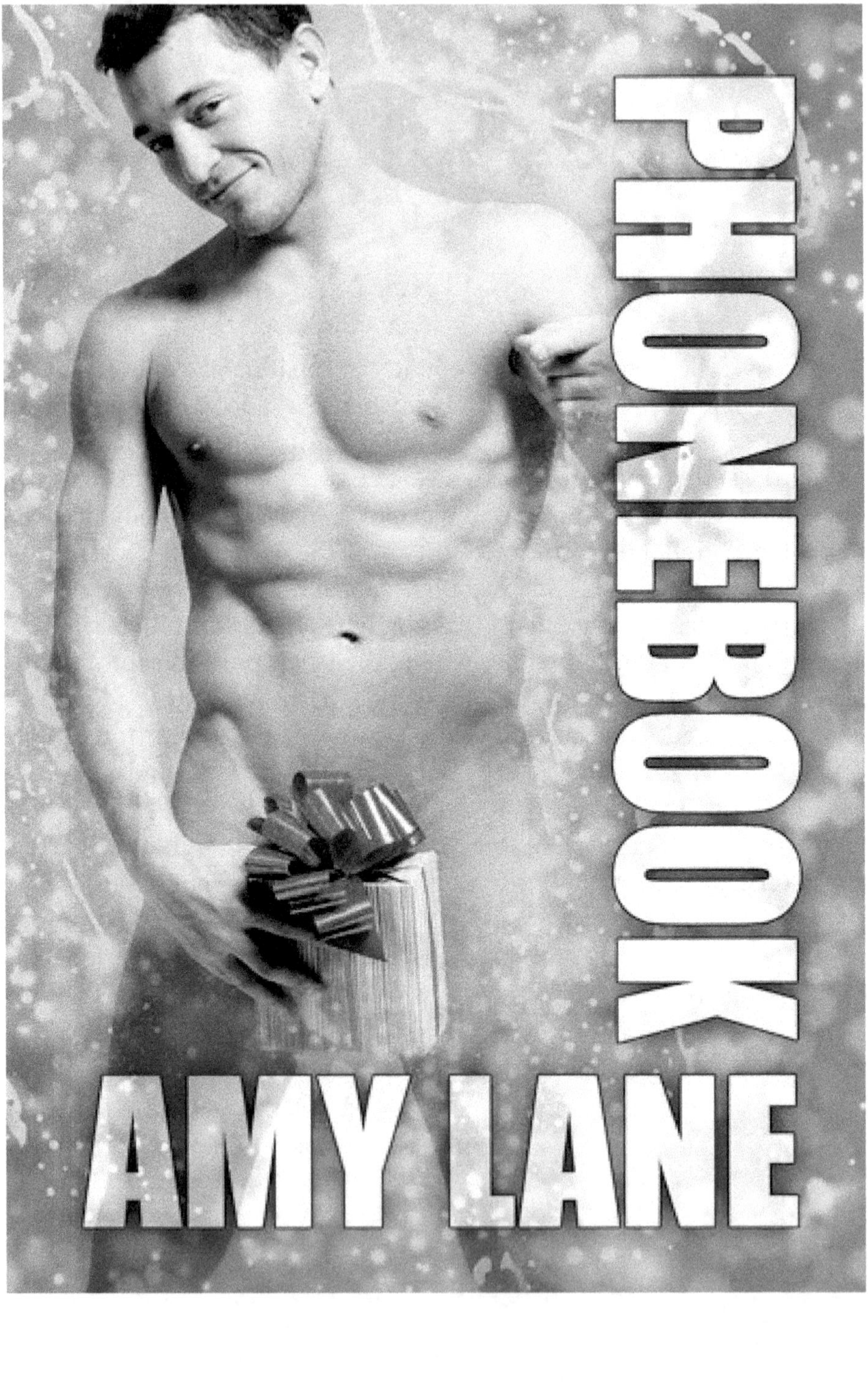
PHONEBOOK
AMY LANE

Stuck away from home on business, all Ryan can do is talk with his lover, Scott, on the phone. But the conservative Ryan finds no comfort in phone sex—he's far too embarrassed. Fortunately, his playful lover has not only planned ahead, but he can think on his back as well. It turns out that the heart really is where good sex starts!

www.dreamspinnerpress.com

After a meet-cute in a bathroom and a whirlwind courtship, Ryan is ready to introduce Scotty to his parents. But a misunderstanding and some stubborn cuff buttons tangle Ryan up in an oxford shirt at a *really* inopportune time. Can Scotty take this opportunity to teach Ryan one or two more lessons about falling in love?

www.dreamspinnerpress.com

AMY LANE is a mother of two college students, two grade-schoolers, and two small dogs. She is also a compulsive knitter who writes because she can't silence the voices in her head. She adores fur-babies, knitting socks, and hawt menz, and she dislikes moths, cat boxes, and knuckle-headed macspazzmatrons. She is rarely found cooking, cleaning, or doing domestic chores, but she has been known to knit up an emergency hat/blanket/pair of socks for any occasion whatsoever, or sometimes for no reason at all. Her award-winning writing has three flavors: twisty-purple alternative universe, angsty-orange contemporary, and sunshine-yellow happy. By necessity, she has learned to type like the wind. She's been married for twenty-plus years to her beloved Mate and still believes in Twu Wuv, with a capital Twu and a capital Wuv, and she doesn't see any reason at all for that to change.

Website: www.greenshill.com
Blog: www.writerslane.blogspot.com
E-mail: amylane@greenshill.com
Facebook: www.facebook.com/amy.lane.167
Twitter: @amymaclane

www.ingramcontent.com/pod-product-compliance
Lightning Source LLC
Chambersburg PA
CBHW070115260626
47160CB00004B/1472